Revival of the Court

The Other Realm Series, Book 7

Heather G. Harris

Dedication

Huge thanks to all of my Other Realmers in my Facebook Group who brighten my day every single Monday without fail. Thanks, as always, to my Patrons, my advance reader team and my beta reader team. I am so grateful to have such an amazing support network around me.

Finally, special mention to Mel, Beba, Kass and Amanda Peterman. Thank you for believing in me.

Chapter 1

Sweat was pouring off Emory as he continued doing one-handed push-ups. 'I think we should get married,' I blurted out.

He froze mid push-up and looked at me. 'We *are* already engaged, right? I distinctly remember proposing.'

I rolled my eyes at him. 'I didn't say we should get *engaged*. I said we should get *married*. Let's just do it,' I urged, feeling excited now that the idea was taking root in my brain.

Emory finished his last push-up and sat up. 'Vegas or Gretna Green?' he asked evenly.

That's one of the things that I love most about him: he never hesitates to dive right in with me. We're a team – sometimes a team that makes bad decisions – but a team nonetheless. It makes my heart happy.

'Neither. We've got this massive wedding planned in a few weeks. Let's just take the bits we like, slim it down and do it.' I grinned. 'Like, tomorrow.'

He blinked. 'Tomorrow?'

'Why not?'

'I'm not sure we can do flowers and cake on such short notice,' he admitted. Trust Emory to be the voice of reason.

I snorted. 'I don't give a fuck about flowers and cake. Let's get married and go on our honeymoon.' Our honeymoon was supposed to be a month-long trip to Thailand, and we were both looking forward to leaving the shackles of responsibility far behind us.

Besides, Emory needed to do something. Why not me? Not like that – well, okay, like *that* – but also he just needed *something*. He'd spent the two weeks since losing his Primeship buying things, mostly companies. When he wasn't buying things, he was working out. He was going through some sort of identity crisis. I couldn't blame him but I wanted to give him something else to hold on to. Let it be me.

'What are we going to be?' Emory queried.

I wondered if that was a trick question. 'Erm ... happily married?'

'Mr and Mrs Sharp, or Mr and Mrs Elite?' he asked in all seriousness.

'We can be Mr and Mrs Flammkuchen for all I care,' I said, exasperated.

He grinned, emerald eyes flashing with warmth and humour. 'You've been spending too long with Mrs Jones.'

'She makes the best flammkuchen,' I confirmed. 'Flatbread, crème fraiche and bacon. What's not to love?'

'It's the bacon that wins your seal of approval, isn't it?' He smirked at me.

He wasn't wrong. 'Smart-ass. You're avoiding the question.'

'I think it's you that's avoiding the question,' he replied. 'What will we be, Jess?' His question was serious and I didn't want to give the wrong answer.

I pulled him up to me, sweaty skin and all, to give myself a moment to think. 'We'll be married, love. Everything else is window dressing. We can be Mr and Mrs Elite. You don't have to lose your name as well as your Primeship. The dragons have taken enough from you.' I worked hard to keep the bitterness out of my voice. 'Besides, all the other creatures have expressed their undying loyalty to you. The dryads still want you, the centaurs still want you, the merfolk still want you. You're their Elite,' I said firmly.

'For now. But when reality hits and I haven't got the money or clout of the dragon nation behind me, they'll kneel to the new Prime. Whoever that may be.' He shrugged; he was trying to be philosophical about it, but I could feel the kernel of dread inside him.

'You said it yourself, it will take months to name the new Prime,' I pointed out.

'It's been known to take years,' he admitted. 'That's the biggest problem with not having a line of succession. I expect the other creatures think that I'm better than having no one right now.'

'You'd think the dragons would agree,' I muttered mutinously under my breath. He shot me a look. Dragon hearing is excellent; muttering under my breath means nothing, especially when we're tucked up close and personal. I flashed him a too-big smile that made him laugh and shake his head. I amused him. Thank goodness.

'I don't blame them for their decision,' Emory said firmly. It rang as *true*, but although I knew he meant it, sometimes I couldn't understand how he could be so forgiving. Was it any wonder I loved this man?

'That's okay. I blame them enough for both of us,' I confessed. Especially Geneve. Emory and Geneve had once had a thing, and when he turned down her offer to rekindle it she'd helped kick him out of office.

It was outrageous that she'd been allowed to have a voice in his future. She should have recused herself, but I guess the dragons didn't care about due process. The whole dragon system needed an overhaul; having ancient dragons who were teetering on the edge of madness deciding the fate of all of dragonkind in the UK seemed to be asking for trouble. Oh, and asking a funky jewel to be a part of the decision process – whose idea was that? Sure, I have a sentient dagger, but I don't let it dictate my life choices.

My phone buzzed with a text from Mo, my tech guy. He's as Common realm as they come but I still use him for any non-magical work that I can throw his way. I use Fritz for the magical stuff – he may be a teenager but he's a prodigy, and there's nothing that kid can't find, given enough time. I'd hired Mo for my latest case because it was in the Common realm – drugs and espionage. I wanted a licence to kill and my own 00 number.

Your man has had a text from a burner phone bought by Luke Fazel from Tantis. They're meeting at the Adelphi Hotel in half an hour – Mo.

Shit. Half an hour didn't give me much time.

Emory gave me a wry glance. 'Go. Sort your case. I'll sort us a wedding.'

'Really?' I asked. 'We're really going to do it?' It was hard to contain the happiness bubbling through me. Emory's smile widened and I knew he could feel my exuberant joy, just as I could feel his.

'Yes. Let's do it. Tomorrow, right?'

I beamed at him. 'You bet your soon-to-be-married ass.'

He gave me a quick kiss. 'Go catch some bad guys up to no good. It's the perfect hen night for you.' I laughed at that: he wasn't wrong. I'm not a normal girl; skulking around suits me to a T. He kissed me more slowly. 'I'll see you later,' he promised.

'You absolutely will not!' I protested. 'You can't see me the night before our wedding. It's bad luck!' Inspiration struck. 'I'll stay at the Adelphi.'

Emory grimaced. 'It's not a five-star hotel any more. Let me book you somewhere else. Besides, it doesn't seem right to kick you out of your house.'

'Are you kidding? The Adelphi is steeped in history. Who cares how many stars it's got now? Winston Churchill stayed there! Honestly, it's fine, I get to stay in a hotel and you get to stay in Bromborough.' I smirked. 'Why don't you have Tom, Fritz and Mike come over? Have an impromptu stag do.'

It was easy for me to say that because there was no chance Emory would turn up drunk or hungover to our wedding. Dragons pretty much can't get drunk or high, no matter what. Emory could down a bottle of tequila and still be as sober as a judge while I would be drunk as a lord. I frowned a little at the thought. 'Hey, why are judges sober and lords drunk?' I asked, voicing my thoughts aloud.

'It's one of those "as it says on the tin" type of thing. Lords used to get shitfaced, and judges had to show sobriety. No one wanted a drunk judge presiding over their case.'

'I guess that makes sense,' I agreed. 'But honestly, it's kind of disappointing. I want to hear elaborate tales of inebriated lords who crossed a sobriety-focused judge, guns and pistols at dawn.'

'Next time I'll make up some elaborate BS for you,' Emory promised.

I grinned. 'You do that. Listen, I've got to split. I'm going to grab my go-bag and skedaddle. I'm already going to be late. Can you look after Gato and Indy tonight?' I asked hopefully. 'I don't know what the Adelphi's policy is on pets.'

'Of course. It's only right that Gato and your dad be with the lads tonight.' He pulled me in for one long goodbye kiss. 'Next time I see you, it'll be at the end of the aisle,' he murmured, his eyes darkening with promise.

The image gave me a visceral thrill. I couldn't have stopped the mile-wide smile that spread across my face even if I'd tried. 'Damn right.'

'I'll see you tomorrow, *Miss* Sharp,' Emory purred.

'I love you, Mr Elite. Sleep well. Tomorrow is going to be awesome,' I promised.

'Damn right.'

Chapter 2

It was hard to keep my brain focused on my current case when all I wanted to do was walk on cloud nine. Tomorrow, I was going to marry Emory! I just had this teensy case to wrap up first, otherwise I'd have to leave it with Hes while I was on my honeymoon and I wasn't sure she was ready for fieldwork just yet.

I drove to Liverpool faster than I should have, only slowing through the tunnel that takes you under the River Mersey. On a good day it takes twenty-five minutes to get to Liverpool and I'd done it in twenty: speeding laws *may* have been broken.

Luckily the Adelphi had its own car park so at least I didn't have to faff around when I arrived. I grabbed my duffel bag – I'd check in later – and made my way inside. I borrowed a newspaper from the reception desk and went directly to the bar.

It was midday and quiet, with only a chap in the far corner drinking a cappuccino. My target was alone at a table in the middle of the room, clutching a leather man-bag on his lap. Even from a distance I could see his leg jiggling up and down with nerves. Emmet Travers was shit at covert stuff, which was probably why he'd been spotted as a spy almost right away,

I had been hired to follow Mr Travers, who worked for a pharmaceutical company called Sanisar Pharma. On a number of occasions a rival company, Tantis Pharmaceuticals, had made leaps in drug development just after Sanisar had made the same advances, so Sanisar suspected they had a mole: Emmet Travers.

Travers was one of the few personnel with access to all the projects that appeared to have been compromised. I had followed him dutifully for five boring days before I'd caved and brought in Mo. He could do things I couldn't, like hack into Tantis Pharmaceuticals' emails. With Mo on the case, it became clear almost immediately that Emmet was being a naughty boy. Mo's text had told me that today Emmet was supposed to be meeting Luke Fazel, the PA to the managing director of Tantis.

Since Luke hadn't shown up yet, I ordered a chai latte from the bar and settled at a table behind Emmet where I'd get an excellent view of any handover. I spread out the newspaper and set up a little tripod on my table for my phone, then I took a bunch of makeup out of my duffle bag. Ostensibly I was using my phone selfie set-up to do my face, but the camera lens was pointing at Emmet. I took my time doing my makeup so I would still be doing it when Luke showed up.

He arrived moments later, frowned at Emmet and gestured at the table. 'It's not exactly discreet,' he huffed. 'Come on, over here.' They moved to a booth at the side of the room.

Damn. I couldn't move tables without drawing attention to myself, but I couldn't get any good photos from where I was sitting. I hastily finished my makeup and waited until Emmet reached for his bag. As he slipped out an envelope, I started my 'vain selfie-taker' disguise instead.

I took my phone off the tripod, stood up and started making pouty faces at my screen. I fluffed out my hair and changed the angle of the phone a few times to make it look good – and I got plenty of shots of Emmet and Luke.

Luke opened the envelope and looked at the documents inside. I used my camera's maximum zoom to try and get sight of them. They meant nothing to me, but hopefully they would mean something to my employer at Sanisar Pharma. Gotcha, Emmet.

The two men talked for ten or fifteen minutes, then Luke put the documents back in the envelope and slunk away. You'd think that in this day and age they could have emailed them or at least used a USB pen drive, but maybe Emmet was old-fashioned. He was also soon going to be unemployed and almost certainly prosecuted.

Bearing that in mind, I pulled out my laptop from my duffel bag and started typing up a contemporaneous witness statement while it was fresh in my mind. I e-signed it with an affidavit of truth and hit send. Off it flew to my client, along with a Dropbox link to two dozen photos.

Emmet nursed a beer, looking calmer than he had before. *You shouldn't be,* I thought. *Shit is about to hit the fan.*

I didn't feel guilty about my part in the coming shitstorm. If he hadn't been selling trade secrets, he wouldn't have had anything to fear. As it was, he had Damocles' sword hanging over his head and he didn't know it. I have my own moral code – and sometimes it doesn't quite match up to the law – but this time we were in sync. You don't break a promise or, in this case, a contract of employment. That's why I'm always super-careful about the contracts I sign because once I'm in, I'm all in.

I texted Mo to tell him his information was gold, as always, and to drop me an invoice for his time. I would include it with my fee note to Sanisar Pharma and be reimbursed. I also texted Emory to let him know that my case was finished and I was officially off the clock. Let the wedding festivities begin!

I put away my laptop in the duffel. Emmet left just after I'd fired off my report to his employer, so I was completely relaxed. The case was wrapped up with a bow and soon I would be wrapped up for Emory – in a wedding dress rather than a bow, though I was game for that too.

I shouldered my bag and headed to reception to check in. 'Hi!' I smiled at the receptionist. 'I'd like to book a room for tonight?'

She smiled back warmly. 'Of course, ma'am. Can I take your name?'

'Jessica Sharp.'

'Ah, Miss Sharp. Your fiancé has called ahead and booked you a suite. He faxed you a private note. His team of private cleaners have already been up there.' Private cleaners? What the heck?

I kept my smile fixed in place. The receptionist probably thought I had severe dust allergies or something, but she was totally professional. I guess you see a lot of weird shit in a big hotel. She passed me an electronic key card and a small envelope with my name scrawled on it in an unfamiliar hand. 'You're on the third floor, ma'am. Room thirteen.' She pointed to the lifts and stairs on the right-hand side of the lobby.

Room thirteen: unlucky for some but lucky for me! I was getting to marry Emory tomorrow! I fought to keep the manic grin off my face.

'Thanks.' I pocketed the key card and the envelope. I made my way to the third floor, climbing the staircase rather than taking the lift, I hadn't walked too much today so I needed the added step-count.

The Adelphi wasn't the fanciest hotel in town anymore, not by a long shot, but back in the day it had been *the* place to stay for the wealthy and the elite. It was the hotel of choice for the rich and famous, including guests embarking on the *Titanic*. Winston Churchill had enjoyed staying there so much that he returned a handful of times and even hosted strategy meetings there during his time as Prime Minister.

The Adelphi had gained fame in the nineteenth century by offering its guests turtle soup; it had even had a tank in the cellars for the live turtles. Luckily the turtle soup had long since been discontinued, though the restaurant still offered 'faux' turtle soup on the menu. Despite its flaws, it was still an iconic and much-loved hotel. If I'd been going for fancy I would have headed to the Radisson Red or the Staybridge Suites on the docks, but I wasn't going for fancy, I was going for *memorable*. I could now officially say I'd stayed at the Adelphi, and that was still cool.

I tapped my card against the security swipe lock. It flashed green and I turned the handle. Wow. The room was lined with olde-worlde dark-wood panelling. There was a leather sofa and a huge TV, but the focal point was the four-poster bed and the bright red curtains that hung across the windows like those in a theatre. There was a table to sit at – and, most importantly, a kettle and individual packs of biscuits on a cabinet at the side of the room.

Humming happily, I dumped my duffel bag on the bed and went to have a snoop in the bathroom. It had been brought up to modern standards with sumptuous white-marbled walls and floors, a new double shower and a claw-footed bath. Nice. I could absolutely while away an hour or two in here.

I moseyed back to the main suite and opened the envelope from Emory.

I can't wait to marry you tomorrow, Jessica. I have arranged for the ceremony to take place at a secret venue at 2pm. I have also arranged for the witches to rune your hotel room for you. Have a good night's sleep, and I'll see you tomorrow. I'll arrange a car to pick you up. I love you so much. Emory x

So thoughtful. I hadn't even considered that I would be vulnerable spending the night in a hotel room, but of course it was open to the public. Without any extra runes in place a vampyr could phase in, and I didn't have Gato guarding me. I was under Clan Volderiss's protection, but that didn't mean that a rival vampyr clan wouldn't see an opportunity to take me out. Emory had taken care of even that vague possibility. I looked around the walls but I couldn't see any runes so he'd obviously paid for the pricey, invisible ones.

I ordered a sandwich from room service and settled down with a book. I rarely get time to read these days, but I enjoy a good bit of escapism as much as the next girl. I thoroughly enjoy urban fantasy novels, if only so I can snort at how wrong the authors get the descriptions of the magical creatures.

I was having a lovely afternoon to myself, although I was missing Gato and Indy's solid presence. I was used to having *someone* with me, and it felt a little weird being alone. I wished Lucy was here but she was hip-deep in pack politics and I didn't want to distract her. I'd call her later and see if she could make it for the wedding tomorrow.

I'd just started reading on my phone but I couldn't focus. I found myself reading the same page, again, when my phone rang. I checked the caller ID and smiled. *Lucy Bestie calling.*

Chapter 3

I swiped to answer the call, hoping for good news. 'Hey Lucy!' I said brightly. Sometimes she rang me to talk about the dead bodies that she'd found; sometimes she rang to say hey. Since it was kind of my hen night, I was hoping for the latter. Dead bodies are more of a week-night thing.

'Hey, Jess,' she replied cheerfully. Phew. Cheerful meant that dead bodies were less likely. 'I'm in reception. Can I come up to your room?'

I blinked. 'You're in Liverpool?'

'I'm not going to miss my best-friend's wedding day, am I?' she half-laughed, half-huffed. 'I'm downstairs. What number are you?'

'Thirteen.' A broad grin stretched across my face. I was betting this was another gift from Emory. He'd told my bestie to come and play.

'Brilliant, see you in a minute, love!'

I hung up, brushed off the biscuit crumbs and tidied up the few bits I'd flung around. I'd just finished returning the room to perfection when there was a knock at the door. Grinning, I heaved it open ready to accept an armful of Lucy barrelling into me.

'You're getting married tomorrow!' she squealed. We hugged and jumped up and down then fell apart, laughing.

'I'm so glad you're here. Emory called?' I surmised.

She beamed. 'You bet your ass he did. He's so sweet. Greg dropped me off – he's on his way to Emory's stag do.'

'Awesome. I'm glad they're doing something for him.'

'Greg and Tom have been texting all morning. I think they're planning all sorts of activities.' Lucy waggled her eyebrows.

Oh, great. 'Strippers? Shooting? Shots?' I guessed. The shots would be for the brethren because they'd do nothing for Emory. Dragon metabolism is a powerful thing.

Lucy laughed. 'Nope, wait until you hear this. They're going to take him ... curling!'

I burst out laughing.

'No,' Lucy muttered to her wolf, Esme. 'It's nothing to do with hair. It's a sport on ice. You use brooms to make a massive stone slide around.' She paused. 'Well, of course it's weird.'

'It *is* weird,' I agreed with Esme. 'I can't believe they're taking him curling. That's hilarious.'

'If it's good enough for the Olympics, it's good enough for Mr Elite. Oh man, I can't believe you're going to become Mrs Elite tomorrow.' She gave a happy squeal.

We had another moment of jumping up and down. I hope that, no matter how old I get, I'll always have a moment to jump up and down from sheer happiness with my best friend. 'Me neither. I can't wait! In fact, waiting is going to be actual torture. What shall we do tonight? I need to keep busy. I was reading a book before you came, but I must have read the same page sixteen times.'

'Shall we go out for dinner?' Lucy suggested. 'Then we could have a little dance and an early night? You need your beauty sleep.'

'I really do. Emory always looks so effortlessly handsome but I need at least seven hours sleep or I have bags under my eyes and look like a troll. Well, not a real one, but you know what I mean.' Real trolls are hulking creatures with pointy, shrew-like noses.

'I do, and you definitely don't.' She snorted. 'You never look like a troll. You're beautiful.'

I rolled my eyes. Yeah, right.

Lucy sighed. 'One day you're going to believe me.'

'When I'm eighty and I look back on pictures of me in my twenties, then I'll appreciate the youthful vigour of my cheeks,' I promised.

'You're going to live a lot more than eighty years, love. Tapping an immortal dragon is good for your life expectancy. I wished I'd known that before falling in love with Greg – I could have fallen in love with another dragon so we could be immortal together.' She huffed. 'That was a poorly thought-out plan.'

'You could always marry Leonard,' I suggested with a straight face. 'He's still single.' At least I assumed he was; who'd have him?

'If he's as gorgeous as Emory, I'll absolutely consider it.' *Lie.* 'Is there something wrong with him?' Lucy asked curiously.

'Too much to document,' I admitted.

'See?' she complained. 'You snagged the only eligible bachelor. I'll have to settle for Greg.'

'There's nothing settling about Greg!'

A goofy smile appeared on her face. 'No, there isn't.'

Lucy chucked her pink duffel on the bed next to mine and started rifling through it. She pulled out a dress and some heels and chucked them at me. We both winced when one of the shoes went a little wide and the heel smashed the small mirror on the desk.

'Shit,' Lucy swore loudly. 'It's probably not bad luck if it's not *your* mirror. It's a hotel mirror – it totally doesn't count as seven years bad luck.'

'It's okay, I don't believe in stuff like that anyway. It's just a silly superstition.' *Lie.* Stupid truth detector.

'Uh-huh,' she agreed, eyes wide. 'Me neither.' *Lie.*

I picked up the errant heel then carefully piled the shards of glass on the desk. I shook the shoe to make sure it was empty.

'I'll sort the mess.' Lucy made shooing motions with her hands. 'Go on, get in the dress, ready for a lovely meal out.' She frowned. 'Hey, you're already wearing make-up. What gives?'

'It was part of my disguise earlier today,' I explained.

She laughed. 'Of course you'd only wear it for a disguise. Well, it looks great. Just give me a minute to pile some on and I'll be ready, too.'

I shimmied into the dress that Lucy had brought for me, a beautiful dark-blue, one-shouldered number with ruching across the body. It was also incredibly short. If I bent over, people were in danger of seeing my full moon. The heels looked high but actually had a secret platform sole built in so that I could walk quite comfortably in them. My bestie had thought of everything.

It didn't take us long to get ready. Lucy had booked a table at a restaurant just around the corner from the Cavern Quarter, but she refused to tell me where we were going because she wanted it to be a surprise.

Tiger Rock was a Thai restaurant that Emory and I had been meaning to try out. 'You can get a little taste of your honeymoon!' Lucy grinned at me.

'Perfect, Luce. Thanks!' I enthused. I was excited. She was right: it was the perfect way to start the night. I couldn't wait to spend a month in Thailand – yum-yum, here I come.

We were pretty early, so the restaurant wasn't too busy. We slid into a booth and stared at the menu, mouths watering. 'I only had a sandwich on room service for lunch,' I admitted. 'I'm starving.'

'Go nuts. I'm paying.'

'You don't need to—' I started to protest.

'Shush. Let me spoil my bestie on the night before her wedding. You can return the favour when it's my turn.' She winked.

I gave in gracefully, though I promised myself that I'd sneak some cash into her bag later when she wasn't looking. 'Sure, that's a deal.' *Lie.* Oops. 'Have you and Greg talked about marriage?' I asked curiously.

'Not really. We've been pretty busy with the "Queen" situation,' she said drily.

'And how's that going?'

Lucy glared. 'Like it's work. No work talk!'

I held my hands up in surrender.

'I saw Greg's mum, Elizabeth, that day in the dragon court but she didn't say anything to me. What do you think of her?' Lucy asked.

My lips flattened into a hard line. 'No work talk,' I said firmly. I didn't want to bitch about her vile mother-in-law-to-be. I didn't have anything nice to say about her, so it was best to say nothing at all. Let Lucy form her own opinion.

'That good, huh?' She sighed; she knows me too well. 'It's fine. I can take her.' She squared her shoulders.

'You absolutely can,' I agreed and was surprised when the radar pinged *true*. My subconscious believed that Lucy was tougher than Elizabeth. Interesting.

We devoured several dishes of Thai food, paired with a couple of Singha beers – I didn't want to drink too much – then Lucy settled our bill and we headed into the Cavern Quarter. The night was still young; it was barely 7pm so the streets were quiet.

'The Cavern Club?' Lucy suggested.

'Sure.'

The Cavern is where The Beatles used to play back in the day. It is full of Beatles' memorabilia, including signed guitars and old autographed photos. We went down into the dark pub – it really was underground, hence its name. Brick archways swept across the low roof, making the place feel warm and friendly. It felt like the dragon's catacombs in Caernarfon in model form.

A band was on the stage, setting up and tuning their instruments. 'Cool. Live music is starting soon,' Lucy said happily.

It was just like the old days. I was half-tempted to buy a pint of snakebite – half beer and half cider – just for old times' sake, but my tastebuds wouldn't let me. Despite my best intentions, they'd refined a little. I grabbed a bottle of Corona instead while Lucy opted for Prosecco. It wasn't really a Prosecco sort of place but that had never stopped her.

We tucked ourselves in a booth and waited for the band to get started. Soon the bar was heaving as more and more people packed in and we gave up our cubby so we could get closer to the band. The singer was crooning away; it was exactly my type of music – loud, lyrical and acoustic.

We were having a great time dancing and shouting at each other between sets, but after a while I noticed a guy glaring at us – and not just any guy. This dude was a far-too-handsome vampyr. Model-like beauty is a sure-fire giveaway; something happens when they turn that burns away their imperfections.

This vampyr may have been beautiful but he sure had a chip on his shoulder. 'Do you know that guy over there?' I shouted into Lucy's ear.

She shook her head, her eyes cool and assessing. Neither of us had our usual posse of guards, but he was only one vampyr and I wasn't going to let him intimidate us. Even so, I snapped a couple of pictures of him. We went on dancing, but we kept him in our sights. The easy relaxation of the previous hour was gone.

Lucy tensed as he started to move towards us. Vampyrs and werewolves have a hate-hate relationship, as do vampyrs and dragons. The common denominator is the vampyrs. However, I am bonded to Nate and I know there is far more to their species than most people are aware of.

I gathered the Intention and Release within me, the IR, ready to act if I needed to. The capacity for violence rang tense and heavy in the air.

The vampyr pulled back his lips and flashed his fangs at us derisively, threateningly. 'Dragon whore,' he spat at me. 'You're an abomination. Fucking that *thing*.'

Wonderful. He wasn't just a vampyr; he was an Anti-Crea vampyr.

Chapter 4

'That *thing* is a better man than you'll ever be!' I bitched back, holding the IR steady inside me, ready to lash out at him. I'd use air to push him back because I didn't want to start a magical fight in a Common bar. That was one sure way to end up on the Connection's shit list.

'I should show you what a real man can do,' the vampyr sneered suggestively, grabbing his crotch. Eww. Did he fancy me or hate me? Both? I checked his hands for the telltale sign of daemon influence but they were steady. He was just a regular Anti-Crea asshole. No one was responsible for his shitty behaviour but him.

'Try and touch her and I'll rip your head off,' Lucy snarled.

'You're a disgrace.' The vampyr's voice dripped with disdain as he snarled at me. 'A wizard fucking an *animal*. You're a bestiality-loving bitch. You're vile.'

Lucy growled, her lips curled back to show her bared teeth and then her eyes flashed gold. Whoops. I needed to intervene before Esme came out to play.

I let the IR recede because a little shove with some air wasn't going to de-escalate the situation. Vampyrs respect strength, so I'd show him strength. I called fire to my fingertips, little enough for a Common realmer to mistake it for a lighter, but he saw it for what it was. A threat: a threat to flambé him.

The vampyr looked at us both and I could see him warring with his instincts. He wanted to attack us but we were surrounded by Common folk. An attack in this place would bring the full wrath of the Connection down on *all* of our heads. I saw the moment he decided to let it go.

He sneered. 'You'll get yours, you pathetic slut. I'll dance on your grave. We're coming for you.' With that final threat, he melted into the shadows and away.

'We'd better go,' I shouted into Lucy's ear. 'Just in case he returns with back-up.'

She grimaced but nodded and we pushed through the heavy crowd into the relative cool of the April evening. Night had fallen, and we were both on the lookout, staring into the shadows a little too hard. I kept the fire ready within me, a crackling readiness that was hard to hold.

'Sorry,' I said in a normal tone as we wove through the Liverpool streets back to the hotel. 'I really wasn't expecting the Anti-Crea.'

'"Nobody expects the Anti-Crea! Their chief weapon is fear and surprise ... and ruthless efficiency..." ' she quoted with a grin, making light of the whole episode.

I burst out laughing. That was one of my favourite Monty Python sketches about the Spanish Inquisition.

'"Our three main weapons are fear, surprise, ruthless efficiency and an almost fanatical devotion to Elliot Randall",' I finished the scene wryly.

'Who is Elliot Randall?' Lucy quirked an elegant eyebrow.

'The dude that heads up the Anti-Crea. I had the misfortune to meet his son, Jonathan.'

'Was he short on brain cells?'

'He was short on manners,' I huffed. 'And probably brain cells, too. He's a jumped-up little shit, very impressed with his own importance.'

'And is he?' Lucy asked.

'Is he what?'

'Important?'

I laughed. 'Not in the slightest. He's working as a detective for the Connection. He's working *under* Elvira.'

'Lucky her,' Lucy said sarcastically. 'I bet that grinds his gears.'

I frowned, thinking of Elvira. We'd gotten to a place where a tentative friendship was forming, then I'd withheld some information from her. I'd felt bad about it – but she'd felt worse. I couldn't regret the decision because more than my morals had been at stake. The Other Circus's secrets hadn't been mine to divulge. We hadn't spoken since Elvira had stormed out of my hen do. I had left her a couple of voicemails but she hadn't replied.

'Sorry,' Lucy mumbled, as she caught sight of my frown. 'I didn't mean to bring her up.'

I smoothed the lines on my forehead. 'You didn't, I did. It's fine.'

'Come on. Let's get back to our room and have another drink.' She looped an arm through mine. 'We can get shit-faced.' There was a pause and then she muttered to Esme, 'Of course you don't smear excrement on your face! What is *wrong* with you? That's gross.'

I snickered. 'Translating "shitfaced" for Esme?'

'Some things just don't translate,' she grumbled.

'I dare you to explain rat-arsed.'

'Why are all the terms for being drunk so silly?'

I thought about it. 'Half-cut isn't too bad.'

'Except that it makes no sense?'

'Sure it does. It stands for "half cut in the leg". It means you're staggering around like you've got a leg injury,' I explained.

Lucy blinked. 'I had no idea that's where it came from. You know such weird stuff.'

My brain is quite encyclopaedic but I couldn't claim any credit for that one. 'Back in Emory's day, everyone used the full saying. He explained it to me once.'

'That's one of the advantages of having an ancient boyfriend, I guess,' she teased me.

'Hey! He's not *ancient*. He's just a little ... long lived.'

'If you say so.' She thought for a moment. 'What about "four sheets to the wind"? A bunch of laundry flying around?'

I laughed. 'No. That one is nautical. It comes from sailors. A loose sheet makes the boat unsteady and difficult to control. Four loose sheets... '

'...you're shitfaced.'

'Yup,' I agreed.

She looked down at my legs. 'How are you managing in my heels. Are your feet okay?'

'They're fine,' I said, surprised. 'They're actually really comfortable.'

'I wore them in for you. That's what best friends are for.'

'Only best friends with the same shoe size,' I pointed out.

'True. My best-friend capabilities are endless for you. Same shoe size, same outfit size. I'm very handy.' She brushed invisible lint off her shoulders with a faux superior expression painted on her face.

'The same can't be said of me,' I said drily. 'Well, obviously I'm the same shoe size and the same outfit size, and you're always welcome to borrow anything you like, but realistically you're never going to borrow anything from my wardrobe.'

'Too much black,' she agreed. She was kind enough not to criticise my fashion sense, which was non-existent. Emory was far more knowledgeable than me in that department.

Lucy and I both have our own strengths. Mine are being nosy and discreet. I love finding out people's secrets; it makes me a great PI.

There was a noise from what looked like an empty side street. I tensed, resisting drawing fire into my hands with all of my might. I was on edge, and I wanted to chuck a fireball down there. The night was dark and there were a lot of shadows for vampyrs to phase out of. I felt vulnerable, not a sensation I enjoyed.

A cat stepped out from behind a bin and I exhaled sharply. I'd nearly barbecued a feline.

'Come on.' Lucy tugged on my arm. Both of us were uneasy, our eyes darting this way and that; we needed to get back to the safety of the hotel. We fell silent; holding a conversation was too much effort while we were both on high alert.

We hustled through the Liverpool streets. I felt something inside me ease when I saw the Adelphi hotel. Just a few more steps...

We walked into the hotel with its blazing lights burning away all the shadows, and the tension dropped from my shoulders as we reached the relative safety of the lobby. Even so, we hurried into the lift. We hit the floor number and started upwards. It pinged at our floor and we almost ran to Room 13. We pressed the key card to the security pad and dashed inside.

As the door closed, I let the intention go and felt it fizzle out. I gave an explosive breath that I couldn't hold back and Lucy did the same as she flopped onto the sofa. 'Well,' she sighed, 'that was a total bust. I'm so sorry. Stupid Anti-Crea knobhead.'

I smiled, at ease now that we were safely ensconced in our room. I kicked off the high heels; no matter how comfy they were, nothing is better than bare feet. 'I had a lovely dinner and the music at the Cavern was awesome. Honestly, it was a wonderful evening.' *True.*

'It's 9.30pm,' she said flatly.

'Perfect. We have time for a movie. Let's get comfy and snuggle up with a tear-jerker,' I suggested. 'My eyes always look good the day after a crying jag.'

'Great idea. Let's get into jammies and then we can watch *The Notebook*.'

'Now *there's* a tear-jerker!' I'd be bawling in minutes.

'But it's romantic too, so it's perfect for tonight. A movie about long lasting love.' Lucy clasped her hands to her chest and fluttered her eyelashes theatrically.

I snorted at her antics. 'Sounds like a plan. Let me just clean this makeup off. My face feels stiff with it on.'

'Yeah, me too.'

At my insistence, Lucy went into the bathroom first. I used her absence to give Nate a quick call. 'Hey!' he answered warmly.

'Hey, Nate. What's up?'

'Nothing. Are you okay? I've been invited to a certain wedding tomorrow. Do you need rescuing? Have you got cold feet?' he teased.

'My feet are toasty warm! I can't wait to marry Emory.'

'Are you sure? He *is* a dragon.'

'I thought you were over that.' I sighed.

'Relax, I'm just teasing. Mostly. But you know I'm here for you whenever you need me, right?' His voice was suddenly serious.

'Yes. And on that note, Lucy and I were accosted by a vampyr this evening.'

'In Liverpool?' he asked sharply. 'You're under Clan Volderiss's protection. That's a violation of Clan law. What was his name?'

'We didn't exchange pleasantries,' I said drily. 'He snarled insults and left. He was Anti-Crea. I got a picture of him, though. If I send it to you, can you find out who he is?'

'I'll find out who he is and I'll make him perma-dead,' Nate threatened.

'You say the nicest things.'

He laughed. 'I'm a nice guy.'

'You are. Send my love to Hes.'

'I will. Send me the photo.' He rang off.

I sent him it quickly before Lucy returned. I didn't want her worrying.

'All done,' she called moments later. 'Your turn!'

I grabbed my jammies and headed into the bathroom. While I was in there, Lucy called down for a bottle of Prosecco and some popcorn. Room service didn't keep us waiting long and soon we were popping the cork and pouring a glass of fizz each.

'Cheers,' Lucy toasted me. 'To your beautiful wedding day tomorrow. May it be everything you've ever dreamed of.'

'Cheers!' I clinked my glass to hers, but suddenly I couldn't quite manage a full smile. I was super-excited about my wedding and I couldn't wait to be married to Emory – but it could never be the wedding day that I had dreamed of. In my dreams, my mum and dad were there with me, my dad walking me down the aisle while my mum bawled discreetly into a handkerchief.

My heart ached. I tried to put my sadness aside; my mum wouldn't want to be the cause of upset on my wedding day. She'd want it to be perfect – but it could never be anything but flawed without her there.

'Hey,' Lucy said softly, reading my thoughts, 'Mary would have given anything to be there with you.'

'I know. I know.' My eyes filled with hot tears. 'Hey, look! We didn't even need *The Notebook* for our crying jag,' I joked weakly.

She cuddled me into her. 'Cry for her tonight, because she would absolutely kick your ass if you cried tomorrow on her account.'

I nodded against her shoulder because she was completely right. So, for this one time, I let go.

Chapter 5

'You're getting married today!' Lucy screeched as she bounced up and down on the bed like a toddler on Christmas morning.

I beamed back. 'I am!'

We shared a moment of excited squealing. Lucy put on 'We Go Together' from Grease and we danced around our room like we used to do when we were teenagers. It was a moment of pure joy and nostalgia, the perfect way to start off my wedding day with Emory.

I'd expected to wake up feeling nervous and maybe still a little sad about Mum, but instead I was filled with excitement. Lucy was right: Mum wouldn't want me to be sad. Grief hadn't scored an invitation to my wedding.

I couldn't stop grinning and I couldn't wait to see my fiancé waiting for me at the end of the aisle.

'I'll order us some breakfast,' Lucy said bossily. 'What do you fancy? Cereals, toast?'

I snorted. 'It's going to be a long day. Better get me a full English.'

'I like your style!'

'I'll hop in the shower first, if that's okay?' I asked. No bridezillas in sight.

'No problem. Take your time – but *don't* wash your hair,' Lucy instructed.

'Eww. Why not?'

'Every hair stylist I know prefers to work with dirty hair. Hair with a little grease holds better, apparently.'

'That's gross!' She knows more about these things than I do.

Lucy chucked me a shower cap and I stuffed my hair inside it. She took a photo. 'For your wedding album.'

'Thanks,' I said flatly, making her laugh even more.

I wondered if Emory had remembered to line up a wedding photographer, but then I decided it really didn't matter. Some of our guests could snap a few candid shots, if necessary.

I turned the water on to hot, showered and took my time to shave everything that needed shaving; a girl needs to look her best on her wedding night. After I'd dried off, I dabbed myself in some high-end moisturiser that Emory had given to me. It was the only luxury item that I was genuinely attached to; it smelled great, and if I was going to live for a really long time then I guessed it was time to start taking extra care of my skin. Lucy had been harping on about a good skincare regime for the last seven years; finally I was willing to slather on some moisturiser now and again.

Emory and I had exchanged mushy texts last night, leaving me feeling warm and loved, and despite Lucy snoring like a freight train I'd managed to get a good night's sleep. He'd told me he had booked a siren stylist for 11am. The car would pick us up at 1pm and take us across the water to the venue that Emory had lined up.

Apparently Reynard had got himself ordained so he could perform the ceremony but Emory had lined up the High Seer Priestess instead, so the gargoyle was sulking. Emory tried to play it off by saying that he didn't want Reynard working at our wedding, just relaxing as a valued guest.

Finding the gargoyles – sorry, dark seraph – something to do had been hard for Emory. They all wanted to serve him, so he'd deployed most of them to his training camp. Tom Smith was giving them a crash course in how to be brethren.

I checked the time – it was already 10.30am! I needed to get my skates on. Luckily breakfast had arrived while I showered and slathered. Lucy had set it out on our table:

croissants and Danishes, as well as enough sausage, eggs and bacon to feed a small army. My stomach growled.

'I may have over-ordered,' she admitted. 'I'm used to catering for shifters.'

'Tell me about it. Between you and Emory ordering food for me, I'll start piling on the pounds.'

'You run, so you'll be fine.' Lucy poured us both a brew made exactly how I liked it.

'Thanks.' I took a happy sip of the scorching cup of goodness.

'You're welcome. After the tea, we'll start on the Prosecco. We've still got a good half a bottle to drink left over from last night. I put a teaspoon in the bottle to keep it fresh.'

'Does that really work?' I asked dubiously. 'I mean, what's the science behind it?'

'Metal spoons encourage bubbles?' She shrugged.

'So instead of bubble bath, I can just chuck in some silverware?' I suggested sarcastically. 'And who was the first to come up with that? Like who half-finished a bottle of fizz and thought, "I know what I'll do, I'll dangle my silverware into my bottle and see if it keeps it fresh"?'

Lucy burst out laughing, 'It sounds ludicrous when you put it like that.'

We tucked into our food with relish. I was starving. We'd almost finished when there was a knock at the door. 'I'll get it!' Lucy hopped up and opened it to reveal the siren stylist. She was blonde, pregnant and beaming.

'Hi! I'm Alyse, I'm here to style you both.' She was carrying five dress carriers in her arms.

'Let me help with those,' Lucy offered hastily, eyeing her bump and taking the heavy bags from her.

'Thanks. Can you hang them up, maybe on the curtain rail?' the siren suggested. 'Can you reach?'

'No problem.' Lucy carefully hooked the dress bags and turned to me. 'It looks like Emory has sent you some choices for your wedding dress!'

'I've already picked mine,' I told her. 'These are for you.' At least I hoped they were.

Lucy squealed and clapped her hands, then froze mid-clap. 'I hope he's not made them ugly.' She grimaced. Some brides like to dress their bridesmaids in ugly clothes, all the better to let their own wedding dress shine. That concept was beyond me; true beauty is happiness radiating out, not the dress you're wearing or the shape of your body.

'No,' Alyse reassured her. 'They're all really beautiful.' She unzipped a couple so Lucy could ogle. 'You try these on while I start Jinx's hair and makeup.'

'I'll take a quick shower first.' Lucy marched off to the bathroom with her arms full of product.

Alyse sat me down and started putting my hair in hot rollers. 'We want a pretty updo, right? With natural looking makeup? That was my brief from the – from Mr Elite.' She coughed to cover her mis-step.

I politely ignored it. 'That would be perfect.' I gestured at her massive bump. 'When are you due?' She definitely couldn't get much bigger.

'In three weeks' time.'

'Congratulations! Your first?' I asked, even though I could tell it was. She looked well-rested, she was glowing and she was humming with energy. She didn't know what was coming, but she was excited about it. I wondered if I'd hum with the same energy one day.

'Yes,' Alyse confirmed serenely. 'I can't wait to find out what it is.' For a moment I wondered uncharitably if she was talking about what species the baby was – a siren or a witch or wizard. But of course she was talking about whether it was a boy or a girl.

'I'd have to find out,' I confessed. 'I'm a total control freak. I think I'd need to know to help get my head round it.'

'I'm excited for the surprise.' She beamed some more. 'It'll help me push harder at the end.'

I wanted to say that she'd probably be pushing as hard as she could regardless, but there was no need to burst her bubble so I smiled instead.

Once my hair was in the rollers, she opened the fridge and poured me a glass of the Prosecco. It was still fizzy, so maybe the spoon thing does work. Stranger things have happened – like having a siren do my makeup before I marry a dragon.

Lucy came out from the bathroom wrapped in a towel. She tugged it off so she was buck-naked, unzipped one of the dress bags, pulled down a dress and shimmied into it. 'She's a werewolf,' I explained half-apologetically to the siren. 'Nudity isn't a thing to them.'

'Oh, sorry!' Lucy said. 'I've gotten so used to being in my birthday suit.'

'I'd prance around naked all day if I looked like you,' Alyse reassured her. 'But at the moment I'm a whale.'

'You look great. You've got that glowing thing going on,' Lucy assured her.

Alyse grinned. 'That's mostly good makeup. I use air-spray makeup like they do for the movie stars. Is that okay?'

'Sure! Who doesn't want to be movie-star beautiful on their wedding day?' I asked rhetorically.

'You're going to look a million pounds when I'm done with you.' Alyse promised confidently. She ran some air through the machine before dropping in some makeup and testing it against the back of her hand.

Lucy carried on trying the dresses. 'This one!' She was dressed in a dark-green sheath dress that made her look even more tall and willowy than usual. It had a sweetheart neckline and a silk sash that tied around the waist.

'Beautiful,' Alyse agreed. 'But we need to warm your skin tone up a little. Do you have any bronzing moisturiser with you? If not, I have some.'

'I have some.' Lucy dug it out of her bag. She shimmied back out of the dress and sat down, still naked, moisturising herself head to toe until she had a soft golden glow.

'Perfect,' Alyse commented as she sprayed my face with all sorts of crap. She applied fake eyelashes but they were relatively short and they merely accentuated what I already had rather than making me look like a drag queen on a raucous night out. She gave me soft pink lips, then started removing the curlers.

'Before you get much further,' Lucy interrupted, 'I have something for Jess – if she wants to wear it. You can say no.' Lucy held out a small black box and opened the lid. Inside was a small pearl tiara.

I gasped. 'Lucy, it's beautiful.'

'Well, I just wanted to say—' she cleared her throat '—Queen of the dragons or not, you're still a queen in my eyes. You deserve a crown.'

'Thanks, love. It's really beautiful.'

'And classy, like you.' Like Emory, I thought. Maybe some of his class was rubbing off on me.

Lucy cleared her throat, 'I had another gift planned but it's not finished yet. I'm so sorry.' She looked dejected.

'Don't be silly! This gorgeous tiara is more than gift enough. It's stunning!'

'It's perfect,' Alyse agreed. 'I can pop it on now and weave the hair around it to keep it in place.' She cleared her throat and lowered her voice. 'If you want, I can use a little of my siren magic to make you look even more amazing. Nothing ... illegal, just a little enhancer.'

'I appreciate the offer,' I said, trying not to insult her, 'but I really just want to look like *me*. You know?'

She smiled. 'Of course. No to the magic.'

'No to the magic,' I agreed.

Before long my hair was in a beautiful updo, complete with my very own tiara. 'I'll just have a little look in the mirror.' I stood up.

'Don't you dare!' Lucy exclaimed. 'Wait until you've got the dress on and then do a big reveal.'

I rolled my eyes but indulged her. 'Fine.' I avoided looking at the remaining mirror in the room and went to the window to unhook the one dress that Lucy hadn't tried on. I had chosen it when I'd gone shopping with Audrey. My own mum wasn't there to go with me, but Audrey had stepped into the breach without being asked. She was the best mother-in-law I could have asked for.

As if I had summoned her with my thoughts, there was a knock at the door and I opened the door to find Audrey standing there. She was wearing a green-and-white dress and an emerald-coloured fascinator.

'Hi! Come on in,' I stepped back. 'We're just doing final touches.' Well, Lucy was still naked, but *I* was doing final touches.

'Emory sent me,' Audrey offered quietly. 'I hope I'm not intruding.'

'Not at all! Thank you so much for coming.'

'We're going to need more Prosecco,' Lucy said, passing Audrey a glass.

'You're looking so beautiful, Jessica, but you still look like yourself.' Audrey observed.

'That was what I was aiming for.'

'Well, you hit the nail on the head. Stunning.'

'I'm about to get into my dress so I can see for myself.'

With Audrey's help, I removed my dressing gown and slipped into the dress. She zipped me up then started the arduous process of doing up the long row of small buttons that covered the zip.

'Oh!' Lucy said softly, tears welling in her eyes. 'Jess. Oh wow. Jess.'

'Do you like it?' I smiled.

'You look amazing. Absolutely amazing.' She was crying. She waved her hands at her eyes. '*You* stop our eyes leaking, then,' she muttered to Esme.

Audrey took some pictures, then I couldn't hold back anymore. I hustled to the full-length mirror. I looked – beautiful. More beautiful than I had ever looked. But Audrey was right – it was still me. Me on a good day. A really good day.

My dress was off-white, which complemented my pale skin. It was made of lace; it had a sheer back then the material plunged into a soft mermaid tail with a small train. It was simple and elegant.

Yes, I felt like a million pounds. Today was going to be the best day of my life.

Chapter 6

Emory hadn't skimped on anything, including the vintage Rolls-Royce that showed up to take me to the mysterious wedding venue. The car was being driven by Chris, who gave me two thumbs-up when he saw me. I grinned back. I'd once asked him to fly me in a helicopter on my wedding day, but maybe the new venue wasn't helicopter accessible. I didn't mind; a car was a lot easier in a fancy dress.

As I opened the rear door, a familiar scent wafted out. Eau de dog. Gato gave me a big woof and wagged madly as he saw me. 'Dad, Isaac.' I greeted them individually and felt my face split in two with my smile. 'I'm so glad you're both here.' Gato barked and tapped his tail; he was happy to be with me, too.

The car was huge and we easily fitted into it. Audrey, Lucy, Gato and I were in the back together, though Gato had to sit upright on a seat like a real boy. A bottle of champagne was cooling in an ice bucket in the centre console. 'Shall I?' Lucy asked, already knowing the answer.

'Go for it.' Suddenly I felt ebullient and I wanted to celebrate. I'd barely touched the Prosecco in the room, but at that moment another glass of bubbles seemed like a great idea. Lucy popped the cork and poured out three glasses. Gato gave an audible huff.

'Sorry, Mr Sharp,' Lucy apologised. 'Did you want some?' She poured the tiniest amount into a dog bowl and set it on the car floor. He gave her a flat look for the meagre quantity but lapped up the bubbles.

Lucy reached out and touched him. 'Is there anything you'd like to say to Jess?' she asked my dad. She listened intently before turning back to me. 'He wants you to know how proud he is of you. How proud your mum would be. His darling daughter has grown up to be a wonderful woman, and he is so excited to see what you're going to achieve in the rest of your long life with Emory. He wants you to know that he really likes Emory and he thinks you've been wise in your choice of life partner.'

Lucy cleared her throat and spoke Dad's words verbatim. 'I always knew you were special, and I'm glad Emory knows it too. I love you so much, Jessica, and I couldn't be prouder of the woman you've become. If you and Emory have half the happiness that your mother and I achieved, you'll be blessed indeed.'

I blinked rapidly to avoid letting tears fall. Lucy blew in my eyes. 'Don't cry!' she said on a sob of her own.

That made me laugh a little. 'So why do you get to cry?'

'Because it's not my wedding day!'

I hugged Gato. 'Thanks, Dad. I'm so happy you're here with me. I know Emory is the right choice. No doubt we'll have our ups and downs but there's nothing we can't achieve together.' I cuddled my dog for a long moment before I sat up straight and tried to pull myself together.

'Now, we need some songs!' Lucy wiped her eyes and pulled out her phone. She put on The Dixie Cups 'Chapel of Love' and we all sang along, laughing and drinking champagne. Everything was perfect. This was going to be the happiest day of my life.

I saw the sign for Ness Gardens and my smile widened. Emory and I had talked often about what we'd like for a wedding day, and I'd always voted for an outside venue. His secretary, Summer, had mostly overruled me, and before Emory was kicked out of office we'd been planning to get married at Caernarfon Castle because there really wasn't any choice. Now the castle wasn't an option, we could get married outside like I'd always wanted. Emory was giving me the wedding I'd dreamed of.

It was a beautiful day; everything was in bloom and the lilac sky looked warm and calming as the car rolled to a stop. Manners was waiting for us at the end of the path dressed in a suit, with his blond hair shorn. He was holding a teardrop bouquet of cream flowers and dark-green foliage. Even holding a bouquet, he still managed to look as manly as they come. He grinned. 'Looking good, Jinx.'

'Back at you, Manners. You scrub up well – and you look so pretty with your bouquet,' I teased.

'Catch.' He chucked it over and I caught it easily in one hand. I was surprised by its weight – it was heavier than I'd expected.

'We've done that the wrong way around,' I complained. 'I'm supposed to be the one throwing the bouquet, not you.'

He opened his mouth to say something witty but the words died as his eyes flicked to Lucy. His smile faded slightly and his jaw dropped. 'Wow,' he breathed. 'You look...' He trailed off.

Lucy, my headstrong, body-proud Lucy, blushed like a virgin. 'Thanks. You look yummy.' Her blush deepened. 'Sorry,' she muttered. 'Esme was making cracks about us eating you... I'll explain to her what a double entendre is later.'

Manners smirked. 'I think she's right. You should totally eat me later.' He winked salaciously and Lucy hit him lightly on his washboard abs, making him laugh. 'I'm kidding. Mostly.' He offered us each an arm. 'Come on; let me help you down the path. I know you're both kick-ass independent ladies, but you're probably wearing ridiculous stiletto heels and the path is steep.'

I picked up my dress, flashing the Converse I was wearing. 'I'm good.'

Lucy unhooked herself from his arm. 'And I need to look after the train.' She went behind me and picked it up.

Manners held out his arm to me. 'Shoes or not, I'd be honoured to escort you.' For once his tone wasn't jovial and teasing, and I suddenly had another lump in my throat. 'Thank you ... Greg.'

Audrey moved in front of us. 'I'll go first and make sure they're ready for you.' She stopped and turned back to kiss me on my cheek. 'Cuth and I are so grateful that you came into Emory's life – and that you came into ours, as well. We are blessed to have you as a daughter-in-law.'

'Oh.' I blinked rapidly to stem yet more tears. 'I feel the same.'

Lucy leaned around to blow into my eyes again. 'Don't you dare cry! You are *not* ruining this makeup.'

It was enough to make me laugh and stop the tears before they really started. 'I'm good,' I promised, my voice wobbling.

'You better be,' she threatened, but she was smiling too.

Audrey started briskly down the path as we slowly followed to give them time to prepare for us. Greg held my arm and Gato trotted beside me. Lucy was carrying the train of the dress to stop the dirt wrecking it.

Gato and I shared a look. We were both wishing it was Dad holding my arm. I gave a tight smile. *You're here. That's all that matters,* I thought.

Greg led us down a winding path that snaked back on itself as it curved down the hill. Ahead, I could make out a lake. The gazebo next to it had a thatched roof but was open to the elements, so I could see the guests milling around. Hes and Nate were standing next to each other. I raised an eyebrow at Nate and he gave a slight headshake – he hadn't identified our attacker yet. I shelved it; no work thoughts today.

Roscoe and Maxwell were wearing matching three-piece suits, complete with flames dancing on their heads. Two griffins were standing at either side of the gazebo. I couldn't tell if they were there for the ceremony or as security; either way, I had Shirdal and Bastion here for my big day. Amber was next to Cuthbert, and Audrey hastened to join them.

And there was Emory.

He was wearing a slate-grey suit with a green shirt that complemented his eyes and our colour scheme, and it was nice to see him in something other than black. I met his eyes across the garden and we both reached out with our bond. The feeling of love and happiness that rocketed down it was overwhelming in the best possible way. I was so excited to marry the man who had become my everything.

Beside Emory was a purple-skinned seer, her weathered skin lined with age and her grey hair loosely framing her face. She was dressed in a deep-blue smock. Deep laughter lines surrounded her eyes; she was obviously a woman who smiled and laughed often. That was definitely the vibe I wanted.

Emory's best man was Tom Smith. He had been Emory's right-hand man during every moment of Emory's tenure as Prime, but their relationship was more complicated than that. He smiled warmly at me as we made eye contact and I grinned back. When Emory was booted out, Tom had quit so he was Emory's best man in more ways than one.

Indy was wearing a smart forest-green collar and sitting nicely next to Tom, but she sprang up when she saw me, tail wagging enthusiastically. Tom did some sort of hand signal and she obediently sat back down. Huh. Tom was a dog whisperer.

As I walked towards them all, a harpist started playing music – Pachelbel's Canon to be precise. A photographer was snapping away discreetly, capturing this amazing moment. Emory *had* organised a photographer.

Moving closer, I saw more guests. Jack Fairglass, green hair tied neatly at the nape of his neck, was next to the love of his life, Catriona Barnes. Things must be moving along nicely if he was taking her out to public events.

There was a bunch of brethren, all suited and booted. I knew some of them well, like Mike, Chris and Mrs Jones, but others I could barely name. I didn't care; they were here for Emory, not for me. Summer and Mike were standing together, smiling into each other's eyes. She was batting her eyelashes, flirting for all she was worth, and I was very glad that she seemed to be over her infatuation with Emory. She deserved happiness, too, just not with *my* man.

Interestingly, the only ones who'd made the cut from the dragons were Veronica, Tobias and Elizabeth. The presence of the latter took me aback. Emory must have seen some hidden goodness in the woman that I had yet to witness. She had apologised to him after he was deposed. He'd been very calm and accepting about the whole thing, but calm was not how I felt. Anger threatened to bubble up but I shoved it firmly down. This was my wedding day and nothing was going to ruin it. Not even Elizabeth Manners.

Reynard stood to one side, a little away from Shirdal. Reynard was the only dark seraph representative. His clothes were toga-like; they wrapped around him yet allowed his black-feathered wings the freedom to stretch out around him.

Almost everyone that Emory and I loved was there. That Emory had managed to rustle up the perfect wedding in one day was mind-blowing. There was nothing he couldn't do – except cook.

Manners and I continued our slow pace with Gato by my side. I had my left arm looped through Manners' arm so I swapped the bouquet from my right hand to my left to free it up. Then I reached out my right hand and rested it on Gato's back. It was a little awkward because of his lack of height, but he clearly reached the same conclusion because a moment later he shifted into his battle cat form and became the size of a small horse.

He stopped walking and looked at me mischievously. I smirked back and gave Manners' arm one last squeeze. 'Give me a leg up,' I said to him.

Manners barked a laugh and obligingly cradled his hands so I could hoist up onto Gato's back. I had to lift a lot of my dress so I could sit comfortably. Riding side-saddle would have been classier, but I'd never tried that so instead I had my dress hiked up around my thighs. I may not have looked like the classiest bride as I rode into my wedding, but I was the happiest one.

Lucy let go of the train as it flowed down Gato's back and looped her arm through Manners'. It was probably the weirdest wedding party ever, but it was perfect for Emory and me.

Gato walked slowly into the gazebo, lifting each paw dramatically like a dressage pony. 'Are you prancing?' I teased him. He let out a happy bark and blithely ignored me.

Finally we reached the man of my dreams. Emory stepped forward, gently put his hands around my waist and lifted me down. My dress smoothed into place. There, classy bride again.

Then Emory bowed low to Gato. 'Thank you,' he murmured for our ears alone. 'Thank you for bringing her to me, for trusting her with me. I will not let you down. I will love her with all that I am for every day that I live.'

My eyes prickled with tears again. Damn. I was going to bawl so hard during the vows.

In response to Emory's oath, Gato barked once and licked Emory's face. 'Dad!' I complained. 'Now he's going to smell of dog breath.' Gato came towards me tongue lolling with intent. 'Don't you dare! Touch my makeup and Lucy *will* kill you!' He gave a huffing laugh and gently nuzzled my neck instead as I threw my arms around him. 'I love you.'

Gato hooked his head around mine and I didn't need Lucy to tell me that he was saying it back. He nudged me towards Emory and I took the hint. I stepped up and took his hands in mine, then we were under the gazebo in full view of our guests. Twinkling fairy lights cast a soft glow.

Emory and I faced each other and had a moment of our own. 'Hi,' he breathed, his green eyes sparkling with warmth and love.

'Hi,' I replied, beaming back.

'You're so beautiful,' he murmured.

'You look amazing, too. I love the green on you.'

'I thought you'd object to black.'

'I absolutely would. You only wear black to hide the bloodstains,' I admonished.

'Indeed. And no one is going to bleed on our wedding day.'

'Not at this one,' the seer muttered with a benevolent smile.

'I'm sorry, what?' I frowned at her.

'Don't worry. Just think of this as a dress rehearsal,' the seer offered sagely.

I slid a look at Emory. Was the seer crazy? Emory gave a helpless shrug.

'Erm, we'd actually quite like to get married today,' I stated, in case there was any confusion that this was some sort of rehearsal. Maybe she'd misunderstood Emory's communication? Or maybe at such short notice he'd only managed to hustle the craziest seer in existence? Lucky us. At that point, Reynard was looking like a better choice. 'Hence all the wedding attire,' I added.

'Yes, and it's nice you've got all the photos for posterity,' the seer replied, still smiling serenely.

Bastion and Shirdal were either side of the entrance to the gazebo, so it was noticeable when both their eagle heads snapped to the right. 'Prime. We've got company,' Bastion said grimly.

Chapter 7

Bastion's feathers looked wilted and his fur flaxen. The witch's curse was still on him but, curse or no curse, he was still one of the deadliest creatures around. His growled observation made me clench my teeth. 'What do you mean, we've got company?' I demanded.

'It looks like the Connection.' Shirdal's eagle-eyed gaze fixed on the distance.

I looked at the seer and her cryptic comments suddenly made sense. I desperately hoped I was wrong. 'We're not getting married today, are we?' I asked.

'No dear, not today.' She gave me a comforting smile. 'Today is going to be hard for you, but you'll get through it – and the days to come.'

Disappointment welled up in me, so bitter and sharp that it took my breath away. It wasn't just my own upset I could feel, but Emory's. He'd been through so much these last few weeks; didn't we deserve our happily ever after? His anguish was so acute that I shoved mine aside.

'It's okay,' I hastened to reassure him. 'We'll do it again another day. Another way. It will be just as perfect.'

'We could do it now, quickly,' he pleaded.

'I'm not marrying you with the Connection's forces literally running down the hill towards us.' And they were. There had to be thirty or forty of them dressed in black suits, hurtling towards us, ready to ruin our wedding day.

I reached up to kiss Emory. 'Another day,' I repeated. 'Another way.' I was trying – and no doubt failing – to hide my distress.

The Connection was closing in on us, and our guests started to stir and exclaim amongst themselves. The brethren went for their weapons; even at a wedding they'd brought guns on their ankles and knives on their hips.

'Stand down,' Emory called wearily. 'Let them come. The wedding is already ruined.'

As the Connection forces came closer, tension ramped up around us. What the hell were they doing here?

My stomach dropped. Heading the forces was Elvira with a lighter in her hand, ready to use to cast a bunch of flames. It was her equivalent to having a loaded gun. She held a fist up and her forces stopped. She stepped forward, eyes down, looking awkward.

'Elvira?' I said in confusion. 'What the hell?'

'I invited you to *join* my wedding. To be a part of it. Not to destroy it.' Emory said through clenched teeth.

'I'm so sorry,' Elvira murmured so softly that I could hardly hear her. 'Randall saw the invitation and I had no choice. The Connection was coming, one way or another. At least this way it's me.'

'What is you?' Emory demanded.

Elvira kept her face as blank as she could as she raised her voice. 'Jessica Sharp, also known as Jinx, you are under arrest for falsely impersonating a Connection officer.'

'What the fuck?' I shook my head. 'What the hell are you talking about?'

'Evidence has come to light that you impersonated a Connection Inspector,' she said tightly.

'What evidence?' Emory snarled.

'During her rescue of Hester, Jinx inferred that she was a member of the Connection.'

'That's ancient history,' I spluttered, my stomach hot and heavy. 'And I wasn't *inferring* that I was a member of the Connection; I *was* a member of the Connection. Stone deputised me. Temporarily.'

'Unfortunately that is not recorded in Stone's reports,' Elvira said.

'But it was! He said that it was,' I argued, confusion and panic warring within me. I knew it was a big deal to impersonate the Connection, but I hadn't impersonated anyone. Stone had deputised me so I could use my empathy skills without any blowback, and it had all been above board. I didn't buy for one second that Stone hadn't included it in his reports. He was a dotting I's crossing T's guy. Someone was framing me. And because Stone was dead and gone, I had no way to prove my innocence.

'If it was recorded in the reports back then, it isn't there now.' Elvira spoke softly again, for our ears only.

'Then someone has tampered with the files. You know that happens all the time,' I said accusingly.

She looked at me with pity. 'I have to arrest you, Jinx. Don't make this harder than it is already.'

'Good! I'm glad it's hard for you,' I spat out. 'This is supposed to be my *wedding day*.' My voice cracked and I fought to blink away the tears that wanted to stream down my face. 'You've ruined everything.'

Elvira licked her lips. 'I have to do this. If it's not me, it'll be Randall or someone else.' She was pleading for understanding and forgiveness, but Emory and I gave her neither.

As she unhooked magic-cancelling handcuffs from behind her back, Gato gave a threatening growl. 'Gato,' I said warningly. 'No.' I raised my voice. 'Everyone, please just relax. This will be sorted out in no time.' *Lie.* Fuck you, lie detector.

Elvira stepped forward, holding out the cuffs. 'You do not have to say anything, but it may harm your defence if you do not mention when questioned something which you later rely on in court. Anything you do say may be given in evidence. Do you understand the rights that have been recited to you?'

'I do.' This wasn't the 'I do' I'd expected to say today. Crushing disappointment roiled through me.

Emory let out a sound that was close to a rumbling roar. His fury was absolute and it was hard to think as his anger washed through me. I needed him to calm down and let me go. I tried to calm him. 'I'm innocent. We just need a good lawyer.'

Elvira snapped the cuffs around my wrist and my magic was ripped away from me, as was my bond with Emory.

He gasped as I was torn from him. He was visibly warring with himself. His instincts were to hold me tight and not let me go, to rain dragon fire down on the Connection interlopers, but his years as Prime had taught him to put others first. Killing the officers would have far-reaching repercussions.

'I'm okay.' I reiterated.

He nodded, jaw tight. He managed to put a lid on his rage and I relaxed as his face resumed its blank mask. No death and destruction today.

'I'll have the best lawyer waiting for you,' he promised, his nostrils flaring white. His hands were still clenched. I prayed the Connection fools standing in front of us knew that they were one hastily spoken word away from being roasted alive.

'I know you will. It'll be fine.' I didn't need my lie detector to tell me that I was lying.

With my hands cuffed behind my back, I left my fiancé at the altar.

Chapter 8

I was frogmarched through the crowd of Connection goons. It felt like a bad joke: how many Connection thugs does it take to arrest one little truth seeker? At least thirty – one to do the arrest, and the rest to posture and look tough.

My magic had been ripped from me and the magic-cancelling handcuffs left me feeling bare and raw. Vulnerable. My ever-present bonds with Nate and Emory had also been torn away. For the first time in months, I was wholly alone with my thoughts and my emotions and I didn't like it one bit.

I tried not to feel the trickle of fear. I couldn't let them win so I needed to focus on anger – and I had that in spades. I let it fuel my steps as I strode furiously through the bunch of cowards who needed such a ridiculous show of force to arrest a woman on her wedding day.

Okay, I could admit that the show of force was probably to stop Emory, Bastion, Shirdal and the brethren from fighting them, but they were idiots. Whether there were two or twenty of them, Emory respected the Connection's rule. Even with all his rage, he wouldn't incinerate them for following orders. But he would find who had given the order and he would make them pay for it.

Emory is slow to anger, but once you get him burning he holds a grudge. Those who say that vengeance is a dish best served cold have clearly not met my fiery dragon. His vengeance is so hot that it will burn the skin off you. I hoped to be in the vicinity when he let the hammer fall; I'm not often petty, but I would make an exception for this.

I got *arrested* on my fucking *wedding day.* Someone's head was going to roll.

Thinking of rolling heads made me think of Stone, who was partly the reason I was in this mess. If he hadn't deputised me, I wouldn't have been in cuffs. Stone had told me once that ghosts weren't real, so I guessed that eliminated a séance as a way to clear my name, but surely it was simply a matter of taking a truth potion or something, then all this nonsense could be cleared up? Surely a truth potion or truth rune would sort it out?

I was shoved none too gently into the back of a black Land Rover. 'Be careful, you idiot! Do you want to be in the Prime's crosshairs?' Elvira bit out to the man who'd shoved me.

'He isn't Prime anymore.' His tone was mocking.

'For now,' Elvira cautioned. 'He's not a man who stays down for long.'

'He's not a man at all,' the bastard quipped.

I glared at him but didn't reply. I don't engage with bullies, and that's what he was. One with handcuffs on me and power over me, but still a bully.

'Fuck off, Holt,' Elvira snarled.

Holt left me alone with Elvira. She carefully pulled the seatbelt around me and clicked it into place then slid in next to me. Her lighter was still primed – for me? Or for her co-workers? Suddenly I wasn't so sure.

'Is this because I didn't tell you who the bludgeoning killer was?' I asked while we were alone.

'No! Of course not.' Her tone was passionate, entreating me to believe her. 'This isn't my doing. I'm hoping that arresting you will give me a pass into the Anti-Crea so we can work to bring them down once and for all. I'll do everything I can to help you behind the scenes...'

She fell silent as the front doors of the car opened and we were joined by two other men from the Connection.

One was Randall Junior, the Anti-Crea cop who'd wanted to arrest me when my car was bombed courtesy of Farrier; the other officer was Holt. He slid behind the driver's seat. Yay, the idiot was driving us. I hoped we'd make it alive to our destination.

Randall twisted in the front passenger seat to look at me. 'How the mighty have fallen,' he taunted me.

'At least I was mighty to start with, *detective.*'

The barb hit home and his nostrils flared in anger. 'It's Inspector Randall now, *Miss* Sharp.'

I swallowed down the 'fuck you' that wanted to spew forth. I was still Miss, thanks to him. I should be Mrs; I should be eating cake and laughing with friends right now.

'You should have let me arrest her weeks ago,' Randall bitched at Elvira.

Elvira's lips tightened but she didn't say anything. Presumably Randall's daddy had pulled more strings and had him made an inspector. He was now Elvira's equal in rank, but they were both acting like he was her superior and he was obviously in charge. What a pain in the ass.

The engine started and we drew away. I assumed we were heading towards Liverpool, though I had no idea where the Connection jail cells were. That was something I hadn't thought to dig into; now it seemed like an oversight. I should have learnt more about the Connection, more about the way it worked. Was I being taken to A Hard Day's Night or St George's Hall?

Neither, it transpired. Instead I was taken to a disused building complex, nestled in a forest in the middle of nowhere. An old sign welcomed us to the Old Assembly Hotel. It looked decrepit and derelict; if this was an hotel, I'd give it a hard pass and a one-star review on Trip Advisor.

I saw Elvira's fists clench as we arrived and I gave her a little kick to make her relax her fingers. She was nearly as bad as poor Emmett Travers – if she was on my side, she couldn't give herself away so blatantly. And man, I really wanted her on my side. I couldn't feel my magic and I couldn't feel Emory, so having Elvira on my side made me feel a little less alone.

I'd been furious when she'd arrested me and the betrayal had rocketed through me – I'd thought that we were friends. But if she was secretly working with me, that made me feel a little bit better. It would prove that she wasn't a backstabbing bitch, and it gave me a glimmer of hope.

Elvira hastily got out of the car and came round to my side. She undid my seatbelt and helped me out of the vehicle so that neither of the two men could do so. The ground was squelchy with mud. My poor dress. I had to resist the urge to try and lift its train; it would be tricky with my hands behind my back and I refused to display such indignity.

'Come on,' Randall ordered, 'we don't have all day.'

Holt went first, then Elvira grabbed my right arm and tugged me towards the building. Despite its rundown look, there was nothing wrong with the technology securing it. Holt used a thumbprint scanner as well as a keycode combination to get us inside.

I was led down a corridor with dark, damp wallpaper peeling off the walls. Holt unlocked a door while Randall tightened the cuffs around my wrists even further until they were tight to the point of causing pain. Asshole. 'We don't want these coming off, do we?' he murmured in my ear. Then he shoved me unceremoniously into a small room. 'We won't be long, but go ahead and get yourself comfy,' he laughed, as he shut the door behind me, plunging me into darkness.

Now I was truly on my own, I refused to succumb to despair and instead checked out my surroundings. It took my eyes a few moments to adjust to the lack of lighting – I no longer had the IR to give me instant night vision and I missed it. The tiny bedroom had a small single bed with a mattress but no bedding. Cosy. The narrow window was covered with white bars. The view through it was of the solid brick wall of an adjacent building. Lovely. No wonder there was so little light coming in. There was nothing in the room save for the bed and I thought with longing of the Adelphi Hotel. Had it only been this morning that I was there?

There was another door that I hoped would lead to an ensuite bathroom. With my hands behind my back it was difficult, but not impossible, to push down on the handle and get inside. Calling it a bathroom was a bit of a stretch. The bath and shower had been ripped out, leaving only a toilet and a sink. My couple of glasses of champagne had run through me, so I did my best to gather up my full skirt and hitch it up to my waist so that I could pee. I fumbled with my knickers and managed to get the job done. There was no toilet paper so I did a little shake; if they thought that these little indignities would break me, they were dead wrong.

I went back into the bedroom and tried to wait patiently for whatever was coming next. After an hour, my ass was numb and my hands were really beginning to hurt; the cuffs were so tight that I was sure my hands must be swollen and discoloured by now. When I got out of here, I was going to kick Randall's ass.

I'd once managed to pick my way out of a pair of magic-cancelling handcuffs, but I hadn't taken my set of lock-picks to my wedding. I got down on my knees and had a look around the floor, checking for an overlooked bobby pin or something like that. Nothing.

Emory had said that he would have a lawyer waiting for me but my lawyer was probably in St George's Hall. They didn't send lawyers to places like this. This was an unofficial op site.

I needed to get out, or I was going to become part of a grim statistic.

Chapter 9

I had no idea what time it was, but as the dim room got even darker I deduced that it was night. I'd been there at least six hours, maybe more. My stomach definitely thought it was more and my mouth was dry. I was lying on the bed, dreaming of the champagne I'd drunk earlier. I would have appreciated it more if I'd known what was coming. Hindsight is a bitch.

The mattress was soft enough but, with my arms tied behind me, my shoulders were aching and I couldn't find a single position to get comfortable.

I heard a key turn in the door. That was all the warning that I had before light flooded in. I sat up as Holt moved in front of me. He was pale-skinned with a square jaw and dark hair; at first glance he was handsome but look more closely and you saw the twist of cruelty in his mouth and the madness in his eyes.

He didn't try to hide his joy at seeing me so vulnerable. 'Dragon whore,' he growled, his voice low and menacing. 'It's time to be questioned.'

I lifted my chin. 'I have nothing to hide.'

'Shut up!' he snarled.

'That will make the questioning a bit one-sided, won't it?' I quipped. He backhanded me and I went sprawling. My head struck the stone flooring and I saw stars. Fuck, that hurt. My cheek was already throbbing from the blow.

'Get up, you pathetic bitch.' As he grabbed me by my cuffed wrists and hauled me to my feet, I bit back a cry of pain. Holt didn't wait for me to find my feet before he started dragging me forward, making me stumble and fall again. He laughed as my face hit the floor.

Fear was crawling through me and I hated it, hated that they could make me feel like this. I was scared. Tears threatened and I fought them with everything I had. These bastards didn't get to see me cry.

Holt dragged me up again and walked me down the corridor. The peeling paper was now illuminated by an odiously bright light. Fluorescent lighting isn't my friend, I thought inanely. I must look so washed out. Not that I needed to worry about my skin tone because I definitely had a bruise forming on my left cheek from that last fall.

Holt pulled me into another room furnished with a table and some chairs. He undid the magic-cancelling cuffs for a second and I had a moment, the tiniest second, with Emory. I could feel his towering rage and he could feel my pain and fear. Then Holt pulled my hands in front of me, secured them with the cuffs again and Emory was gone. Fuck.

Poor Emory. If I'd known what he was doing, maybe I could have gathered the IR or summoned fire or ... something. But I was tired, in pain and scared, and I wasn't thinking on my feet. The moment with Emory was torture because now I was without him again and alone with these assholes who had an agenda that I didn't like.

Come on, Jinx. Sharpen up. You can do this.

When Randall came in, his gaze swept over me and his lips twisted with pleasure. He mock-glared at his colleague. 'Holt, did you beat an unarmed lady?'

'She fell,' Holt said flatly.

'Ahh.' Randall smirked – then reared back and smacked me across my face. 'Oh dear,' he said. 'She fell again.' His smile made my skin crawl. How someone like this could become an officer of the Connection, an organisation that was supposed to protect and serve, was beyond me.

Thank goodness rage started to curb my fear and I could think again. 'Fuck you,' I swore, spitting out the blood that was pooling in my mouth from his blow.

'Is that an invitation?' Randall asked, quirking an eyebrow. 'Because I know how you like to put out for creatures. But maybe men don't do it for you any more?'

What was the point engaging in this farce? There was no answer that I could give that wouldn't earn me another slap. I glared and remained silent.

Randall smiled. 'You can keep silent, if you like, but later on I'll be making you scream. I'm very good with fire. I love to burn things – especially *creature* things.'

My stomach lurched. I didn't want to be burnt. 'I'm not a creature,' I pointed out as evenly as I could.

'No, you're *worse*. You're a creature sympathiser. A filthy, cross-species-marrying whore. I'm going to love hearing you scream.' Randall looked genuinely delighted at the prospect. He was obviously a few sandwiches short of a picnic.

I swallowed bile and battled with terror. I did not want to be set on fire by this crazy bastard.

'Let's have a taster,' Holt suggested enthusiastically.

'What a good idea,' Randall breathed. He pulled a lighter from his pocket and flicked it.

My heart started to race; panic was almost swallowing me whole. Holt grabbed my left hand and dragged it to the edge of the table. I tried pulling back and was back-handed again for my trouble. My head swam as Randall brought the lighter to my left hand. Despite my best intentions, I started to scream as he let the fire lick at my skin.

It felt like an age but it couldn't have been more than thirty seconds or so before he flicked the lighter closed. 'That was fun,' he chirped happily. 'We'll do it again later. We're going to cover your body in burns, every inch of you. But first we'd better do the official interview.'

He sneered at me as he pocketed the lighter. 'Any mention of this little fire incident and I'll give you to Holt to play with. Are we clear? Camera on, Holt.'

After Holt started the recording equipment, he stated, 'Inspectors Randall and Holt questioning Jessica Sharp, who is arrested on suspicion of impersonating a Connection inspector. Do you understand the charges levelled against you?'

'Yes. I want a lawyer,' I spat out. I cradled my burnt hand in my lap. Fuck, it hurt. Where was my spike of adrenaline to see me through this?

'One is being sourced for you, but in the meantime we will conduct preliminary enquiries,' Randall said smoothly.

'I don't want a lawyer sourced by you, I want the lawyer my fiancé is sending.'

'How can he send a lawyer when he doesn't know where you are?' Randall asked in a mocking voice.

'He's going to kill you,' I snarled.

'Oh, threatening an officer of the Connection? Gosh, you're racking up the charges now.' He sat back in his chair, arms folded behind his head.

'I'm not threatening you. It's a statement of fact. Emory's not going to let this go. You're going to die and it's going to be horrible.' I grinned at him, suddenly delighted. Whatever happened to me, Randall and Holt would both die. They'd hurt me and Emory had felt it. Oh, yeah. They were going to get it, and I felt not one whit of sympathy or regret. They were foul humans who used their power over others for their own twisted pleasure. Karma was coming for them, and its name was Emory.

Feeling braver, I asked, 'Are you going to ask me any questions? You know, pretend that this is actually an interview rather than a mockery of the justice system?'

'You pretended to be an officer of the Connection, true?' Randall snapped out.

'No. I *was* an officer of the Connection. Temporarily. It will have been included in Inspector Zachary Stone's reports,' I confirmed for the record.

I thought back; I hadn't appreciated exactly what was going on at the time.

'I want to deputise you,' Stone had said.

'You want to what?'

'Make you part of the Connection. It will afford you some protection and I can introduce you as my partner, Detective Sharp. You'll be able to question others with legal authority. If you compel someone by accident, you won't get into trouble. Your role will be temporary, just for the duration of the case. Do you agree to those terms?'

I chewed on that for a moment. 'I occasionally have authority issues,' I admitted.

'No shit,' Stone smirked. 'Look, all joking aside, I won't give you an order unless it's life or death, okay? We're a team. I need you to trust me and have my back. Deal?'

'Deal,' I agreed. I hoped I wouldn't come to regret it.

I was regretting it, all right. But Stone had been a by-the-book bloke and there was no way he wouldn't have included something like that in his report.

'Unfortunately,' Randall said with false, saccharine-sweet sympathy, 'His reports don't mention any such thing.' I bet if my lie detector had been working, it would have been pinging.

'Then use a truth potion on me,' I suggested. I was innocent; I just needed to prove it.

'It has recently come to light that some unsavoury characters can build up their resistance to truth potions, so truth-potion evidence is not being accepted in a court of law at the moment,' he said smugly.

'Well then, it looks like you guys will actually have to do some detective work. What the hell will you do?' I snarked. *Ugh. Don't antagonise your jailors, Jinx.* It was not a smart move, but I wasn't feeling smart, I was feeling scared and bolshy. I hated the way Holt was looking at me, like he wanted to test out the nickname he'd given me: dragon whore. No thanks.

Then something clicked. 'It was you two,' I said slowly. 'It was you who broke into my office with Hugo Arnold.'

Randall smirked, leaned forward and clicked off the camera. 'We've had our eye on you for a while. You're a disgrace, a little whore, a discredit to the human side. *A traitor.* We wanted to send a message to you and your dragon boyfriend that no one is safe from us, not even the Prime – as he was then. But he's nothing now, is he?'

I ignored the taunt and focused on what I really wanted to know about the break-in. 'Why did you send Alfie's file to Bronx?'

Randall's lips curved in a smile that had nothing humorous about it. 'To make a father and son fight. What better way to destroy the creatures than by letting them do it to themselves?'

'You're sick.'

'They're *centaurs*. They are beasts – less than beasts. They should be enslaved and treated like the cattle that they are. I watched the battle, you know, and I saw the moment Bronx died. He was starting to be a pain in my ass.'

I suddenly remembered something else. 'He was taking money from the Connection. He was your informant.'

'And he kept demanding more and more for the shit that he told us. As if we cared about herd politics,' Randall sneered.

'Why were you paying him if you didn't want the information that he gave you?' I probed. I had to keep him talking – better talking than burning. I had faith that Emory would come but I needed to give him enough time to find me.

'It's always helpful to know how your enemies work. Now we know where the herd lives and their seasonal patterns. If he hadn't upped his price, Bronx would still be alive, still betraying his people to their deaths.' He clapped his hands in delight and my stomach clenched. I didn't know what Randall was planning, but the centaurs were in his crosshairs.

'And Stone's prints? Why bother with those?' I asked the one thing that had been bothering me.

Randall looked at me blankly. 'What?'

'You put Stone's fingerprints in my office. Why?'

Randall's phone buzzed. He looked at the screen then smirked at me. 'It's my father. He's going to love this.' He swiped to answer and put the phone on speaker. 'Hello, Father. I'm sitting here with Jessica Sharp. Say hello, Whore.'

Holt kicked me in the leg when I didn't say anything.

'Jonathan, you're creating a stir.' His father's tone was disapproving. 'I told you to *wait.*'

Looking sulky, Randall took the phone off speaker and brought it to his ear. He listened as his father chewed him out. 'Take her back to her cell,' he snarled at Holt.

I wanted to taunt him that his father wasn't as impressed as he'd hoped, but my aching cheekbone and jaw made me guard my words.

When Holt chucked me back in my cell, his eyes lingered on my body before he closed the door. I was trying to keep a level head but I wanted out, right now. I didn't like the way Holt leered at me like I was a convenient hole, and I didn't like the way Randall was looking at me as if I were a steak to be seared gently to perfection.

They had shoved me in here with my hands still locked in front of me. Cuffs or not, it was time to see what damage I could do.

Chapter 10

I went to the window and started pulling on the white bars. At first I used my right hand but, even though I tugged hard, nothing gave. In the end I curled my burnt left hand around the bars as well and almost sobbed with agony as I strained against them. I even placed my feet against the wall and pulled with all of my might, but nothing gave – except for the skin on my ruined left palm.

The window had a fixed pane of glass with a slim, hinged vent at the top. The key was still in the lock, so I opened it to let in some fresh air. There was no way I could climb out of the top window – even a skinny two year old wouldn't make it through that. I wondered if my captors had left the key in the small window as additional psychological torture. I was so close to freedom, but the tiny gap was too small.

Frustration burned through me. I wanted out. Now. I so did not want to give Randall more time to set me on fire.

With the top window open, I could just about see the next building. It was a little further away than it had looked through the glass, maybe a foot away. If I could get through the bars and the window, I could shimmy my way between the buildings. If, if, if. If wishes were griffins, I'd be able to fly. That would be so cool.

I only hoped that Elvira had somehow managed to send a message to Emory. She was clearly under scrutiny herself, but hopefully leading the arrest against me had given her some breathing room. I had to believe that help was coming or despair would crush me; at the same time, I wasn't a damsel who'd sit and wait for a rescue. If I could, I'd get out under my own steam.

I looked at my hands. If I got my magic back, all bets would be off. All I needed was to get out of these damned cuffs. Somehow, anyhow.

I'd scoured the bedroom for something to pick the lock, but I hadn't checked properly in what passed for the bathroom so I went back into it. Only the tiniest bit of light was coming in from the window in the other room, so I had to crawl around on my knees feeling every sticky – eww – inch of the floor. I tried not to worry about the burn on my left palm getting infected. I'd deal with that later. If there was a later.

Despair welled up; I'd crawled over every disgusting inch of the floor and there was plenty of yuck – they clearly didn't clean in here – but nothing I could use. As I stood up, I was brought face to face with the remnants of an old shower that had been ripped out. A piece of sharp metal wire was protruding from the wall.

Hope made me catch my breath. The wire would be perfect to pick the cuffs. I reached up on my tiptoes and tried to pull it out of the wall but it wouldn't budge. Shit.

I wasn't giving up. The dirty room was so small that if I stood on the toilet and reached forward, I might be able to use the stiff wire to open the cuffs even though it was fixed to the wall. I had to try *something*.

I licked my parched lips. Earlier I'd been desperate enough to try and drink the sink water, but when I had turned on the tap it had come out brown and smelly so I'd given it a hard pass. I wondered how long it would be before I gave into my thirst and drank the revolting stuff.

I pushed my thirst aside and focused on the task at hand. I climbed up and stood on the toilet; there was no lid, so my feet were balanced precariously on either side of the bowl. I leaned forward slowly and felt in the darkness for the wire, then swore as the sharpened end cut my thumb.

I wasn't deterred. Angling my cuffs, I spent a painful ten minutes desperately raking them again with the thin wire.

I wasn't giving up, no matter how long it took. Another five minutes passed. I nearly sobbed when the cuffs gave a soft snick and came free from my wrists.

My magic flooded back. My first thought was Emory and I reached out to him through our bond. He wasn't raging now; he was ice cold and determined. I sagged against the wall in relief that I could feel him again. I hadn't realised how reassuring his constant presence was until it was gone. Now that our bond was open again, he could follow it to my location.

I decided that he wasn't going to find me wallowing in self-pity when he arrived. I was getting the fuck out of there. I wondered if Elvira had given Emory my location. If she had, I hoped she was okay.

My magic was back but I still needed to be subtle and quiet; blasting my way out was asking for a world of trouble. I needed a plan.

I reached out to Nate and tried to get him to phase to me. As I tugged and tugged, I felt his mounting frustration. He could feel me but not reach me, not like he had done when he'd phased to my side when Darius attacked me. This old hotel was thoroughly runed against vampyrs.

I huffed. Okay, Plan B. I needed a weapon.

I concentrated on Glimmer and summoned it. It always came when I needed it – and I *really* needed it now. I held up my palms and called it with all my might. Usually it arrived instantly. I screwed up my eyes tight and called with everything I had. I was about to drop my hands in defeat – Plan C? – when abruptly a familiar weight settled into my hands.

I opened my eyes and nearly screeched. I had Glimmer all right, but today it had a ride-along – Sally, the salamander. At least, it looked like her. I examined her closely and saw the little scar on her back leg where her horrible handler had stabbed her. Yup, it was Sally all right.

I'd first met her during the dragons' challenges. Sally had been the size of a huge lizard and Elizabeth had challenged me to fit her into a tiny box. She'd been counting on me not knowing that salamanders could grow or shrink in size. The little critters often bonded with dragons who were immune to their fire. That reminded me how much my left hand was throbbing. Damn; I wanted to be immune to fire right now.

Glimmer was singing in my head. Normally he was delighted to see me, but today he was stormy and ready for violence. His discordant tones threatened harm to anyone who had kept us apart. 'I'm okay,' I offered weakly. *Lie.* Ah – how nice to have my lie detector back. I wasn't even mad that it was calling me on my self-deceiving bullshit.

Sally jumped down off the dagger, scuttled along the floor and up the walls, a salamander on a mission. She hopped up to the bars that covered the window and promptly burst into flames. At first the flames were red but after a moment they turned white. I had fire in my arsenal of weapons too, but I had nothing on this little creature: she burned *hot*. In a matter of minutes, the metal bars were literally melting down the walls.

I was just about to smash the glass – to hell with the noise – when Sally turned her attention to it. I watched her dubiously; glass melts at nearly 3,000 degrees Fahrenheit and that was a big ask, even for her.

She flicked on the flames again and pushed her little body against the window. This time her dancing flames were blue, the colour of the hottest flames possible. I watched as she grew in size until she filled the whole window. One moment she was there – and the next she had fallen through it when the glass pane melted away.

I hastily stuck my head through the hole. 'Sally?' I hissed. 'Are you okay?'

She was back to gecko size, happily running up and down the wall. I wasted no time in joining her outside. I climbed out of the window, swearing as the train of my muddy wedding dress caught on the stump of one of melted metal bars. I tugged, then winced as a good chunk of dress was ripped away. Ah well, it wasn't getting a second use again. This wedding dress was cursed. Sure, blame the poor innocent dress.

I eased myself to the ground between the buildings. There wasn't a foot of space between the walls as I'd thought, there was a little less, so it was a good job Mother Nature hadn't blessed me in the bust department. I wriggled my way down, feeling my heart hammer as I moved. I wasn't claustrophobic but there really wasn't much space and my captors would surely check on me soon.

God, I hoped they'd leave me to starve a while longer. I could do with a head start.

Chapter 11

Once we were at the edge of the building, I sheathed Glimmer into the lace of my wedding dress. I held a hand out to Sally and she hopped from the wall into my right hand. My left hand was still on fire – it *hurt*. Burns are such a bitch. I looked left then right; just like the green cross code they teach you as kids. I couldn't see anyone patrolling, so I took a deep breath, plunged forward and ran for the edge of the forest around the hotel.

I didn't hear any shouts. I hadn't been spotted, so I kept going deeper into the woods. Once I was in its depths, I summoned Nate to my current location.

Our master-slave bond activated immediately and he walked out of the shadows. 'Jinx!' He pulled me into his arms. 'Emory has been going apeshit.' He examined me, jaw clenching as he took in the marks on my face. I must have looked a state. 'You look awful,' Nate offered.

'Thanks,' I said drily. 'That's just what a girl wants to hear.' I leaned into his hug and had a moment when I just wanted to break down. But I wasn't safe yet, and now wasn't the time. 'Get me out of here, please.' I hated how pathetic my voice sounded. Normally I'm tough, but at that moment I felt anything but.

I didn't want to stand in the forest any more, I wanted to be home.

I tucked Sally into the bodice of my ruined dress so that my hands were free. Obligingly, Nate stepped closer, wrapped his arms around me and pulled me into the shadows. The freezing cold penetrated my bones but I didn't care. The cold meant I was on my way home.

Nate pulled me out of the shadows from the forest and into the shadows in my own house. I was home.

I looked around automatically for Emory. 'He's not here,' Nate admitted. 'Sorry. Emory and Lucy are at the Connection headquarters making a very loud and visible spectacle while the dark seraph, brethren and Bastion and Shirdal attack the hotel at the co-ordinates Elvira gave him.'

'You should call off the attack,' I said wearily. The co-ordinates would give away Elvira, or at least reveal that we had *some* sort of mole. She had to be top of the list.

'I'm not sure Emory will want to do that,' Nate said. 'He's furious. He wants blood.'

'Attacking the hotel will put Elvira in a worse position. For now, it looks like I've escaped by myself. Let them keep thinking that,' I said firmly. 'Call them, please.'

He pulled out his phone and rang someone. 'I have her and she's safe. She wants to stop the attack on the hotel. Stand by for further orders.' Then he rolled his eyes and passed me the phone. 'Shirdal wants to speak to you.'

I put it to my ear. 'Hi, Shirdal.'

'Sweetheart. Are you okay?' He sounded sincere and concerned, which was not like him at all. He'd been worried. So had I.

'I've been better,' I admitted, hating how small my voice was.

'If they hurt you...' he growled.

'Not much. We need to refocus. They were talking about attacking the centaurs – the herd. We need to warn them and stop whatever's being planned. Come home.'

'I don't want to let the bastards live,' Shirdal snarled.

'Nor do I.' I was unsurprised when it pinged *true*. 'But leaving them alive for now gives us targets to follow. Kill Randall and Holt and we have two less people to spy on.'

'All right, I'll stand down,' Shirdal agreed grudgingly. In the background I heard Reynard saying, 'Give me the fucking phone, you flying lion.'

'You realise calling me a flying lion isn't an insult so much as an accurate description?' Shirdal replied drily.

The phone was passed to Reynard and his French accent filled my ears. 'My *petite pois*, are you all right? I wish to rain hell down upon these fucktards, *non*?'

'*Non*.' I sighed. 'Not yet. We bide our time. Get everyone to stand down,' I repeated.

Reynard huffed and the line went dead. I didn't pass the phone back to Nate; instead I dialled Emory.

'You have an update?' he barked, thinking it was Nate.

'It's me. I'm home safe.'

'I'm not free to talk,' Emory said tightly, but through our bond I felt relief crash through him. 'I will be back as soon as I can.'

'Okay. I love you.' I hung up quickly so that I didn't have to listen to the silence of him not saying it back. He was in the hornets' nest so he couldn't make kissy sounds at me.

I needed him home. I needed a shower and I needed some food and drink. 'I need a drink,' I said to Nate.

'Water or vodka?' he offered.

'Those are my only choices?' I asked.

'I guess I can make you a cup of tea.'

'Water and tea.' My stomach growled. 'And something to eat. Please.'

'I'll make some dinner for you. Do you want to grab a shower?' he asked delicately as he looked at the state of me.

'Yeah, but I'll get that water first.'

He passed me a pint of water and went into the kitchen to start cooking. I sipped carefully, struggling not to guzzle it all at once. I'd barely been eight hours without a drink, so I shuddered to think of children the world over who didn't have running water. My parched lips and sore throat had given me a keen insight into what they suffered, and I had a sudden urge to donate a wedge of my earnings to philanthropic causes. Money doesn't matter, people do.

I needed my people. I didn't have Emory or Gato or Lucy and I really wanted a hug. 'Nate? Can I have another hug?' I asked in a small voice.

He ran from the kitchen to my side in a vampyric instant, pulled me into his arms again and held me there until I took a long shuddering breath. 'Okay. I'm okay now. Thanks.' I pushed away from him and he gave me a little kiss on my uninjured cheek.

'My magic spit works on burns, cuts and scrapes but it doesn't deal with bruises and broken bones. We'll have to get you healed by a witch or wizard,' he said apologetically.

'Could you heal this?' I asked pathetically, holding out my left hand.

He swore at the blistered and broken skin but wasted no time spitting into it. 'There's blood,' he murmured, 'so I'd best not lick it, just in case. Sorry.'

'No, that's fine. Thanks.' I was already feeling much better, and in moments my palm was healed.

Nate checked the rest of my hands and found the cut on my thumb from the metal wire. He healed that, too. 'Anything else I can help with?' he asked solicitously.

'No, all that's left are just bruises. I'm going to shower now. I feel filthy.'

'I'll have dinner waiting for you when you come down.'

I headed up to my bathroom. Glimmer was still tucked into the lace of my dress – and I'd forgotten Sally! I reached into my neckline to pull her out. She was blue and shivering. Uh-oh, she hadn't liked phasing.

I carefully called fire to my fingertips and held it near her. She raised her little head and let out a purring, chuffing sound then climbed into the flames and let them dance around her. I kept the flames on her for a good five minutes before calling them back into me. 'Are you okay now?' I asked. She was warm to my touch and making happy noises.

There was a bunch of flowers on my dressing table that Emory had given me as a 'yay, we're getting married soon' gift. They were mocking me. 'If you're hungry,' I said to the salamander, 'you can go nuts on that bouquet of flowers.'

She made a sound that I took as agreement, so I placed her carefully amongst them and she started nibbling.

I didn't want to ask Nate to unbutton the row of buttons at the back of my wedding dress –I'd been dreaming of Emory doing that – so I took Glimmer and carefully sliced down the front of the dress. The tattered remains fell to the floor like my hopes and dreams. Tears threatened.

Turn that frown upside down. I heard my mum's voice in my heart and blew out a breath. She was right; there was no point crying over spilt milk. My perfect wedding day had been ruined but I was alive, Emory was alive and we would have another day. Maybe we'd look back on this and laugh. It didn't seem possible now, but maybe it would be a funny story to tell our children – the sanitised version, of course – about the day Mummy got arrested instead of married.

I turned the shower to hot and stepped into the water. I was so grateful for my clean bathroom, with its lights and shower gel and hot clean water. A little deprivation does a world of good in helping you to appreciate the good things in your life. And I *was* grateful, so grateful I was still alive and that Holt hadn't had the chance to act on that gleam in his eye. One way or another, I was going to make sure he could *never* act on it.

Chapter 12

My almost-wedding day had been the longest day ever and I was bone tired, but I didn't want to go to sleep without seeing Emory.

Nate had made us a batch of tomato and meatball pasta. By the time I'd devoured it, I was crashing hard from the adrenaline bomb-out. Nate wrapped me in a blanket and plied me with cookies and tea. He'd put *Friends* on the TV so I could zone out and giggle at their shenanigans. It was the perfect balm to the soul. I had no objections to being looked after.

Finally I felt Emory coming closer and I went to the front door to wait for him. Impatience got the better of me and I pulled the door open. My mouth dropped open when I saw that my house was surrounded by brethren and the dark seraph. I spotted Shirdal and Bastion among the small army that lined the whole street. Thank goodness it was dark.

'You can't all be here!' I exclaimed, eyes wide. 'What will the neighbours think?' No one moved. I let it go because at that moment a Mercedes was making its way through my guards. 'Move out of the way! It's Emory,' I shouted.

'The Prime.' The assembled group whispered the title, even though it wasn't his anymore, then they parted to let the car through. When it stopped, Emory climbed out followed by Tom, Gato, Indy and Lucy. Chris stayed behind the wheel, ready to make a quick getaway if we needed to.

Emory ignored the crowd and covered the distance between us with vampyric speed. There was a murmur of surprise. His eyes swept over me and I saw his jaw working as he spotted the black-and-blue skin on my cheek.

He drew me into his arms and kissed me gently; apparently he no longer gave a shit about public displays of affection. I pressed my mouth forcefully to his. I didn't want a gentle peck; we'd been kept apart and I wanted the reassurance that we were together again now and that nothing would tear us apart ever again.

Emory relented and kissed me with a hot passion that set my pulse to racing. Finally he tore his lips from mine and his eyes swept over my bruised face. 'I shouldn't have let them take you,' he snarled.

'It's done now,' I murmured.

'It's not done until they're dead. Give me names,' he demanded.

'Holt and Randall.'

'They are dead men walking.'

I smiled. 'I know.' I gestured to the gathering around us. 'Can you sort this spectacle out, please? What will the neighbours think?'

'Tom,' Emory called without taking his eyes off me. 'Sort this.' Then he lifted me into his arms and carried me bridal style into the house.

'I can walk you know,' I whispered.

'Shush. Let me hold you.' He cradled me to his chest, carried me effortlessly into the living room and settled me on his lap. He held me tightly and I hugged him back just as hard.

Lucy, Indy and Gato let us have a moment before intruding. Lucy went to pull me up to give her a hug, but it took Emory a few beats to release me and the look he gave her was unimpressed. 'Are you all right?' she asked, searching my eyes intently.

'I've been better,' I confessed. 'But I'll get there. I was supposed to get married today.' I tried to keep the petulance out of my voice.

She hugged me again. 'I know, love, I know. We'll have another wedding for you, a *better* wedding.'

'This one would have been perfect,' I complained. 'Stupid fucking Randall.'

'He's a dead man walking.' Lucy repeated Emory's words. 'Esme and I will rip his throat out.'

I smiled. 'You guys are the best.'

'I have dibs on ripping his throat out,' Emory growled.

'He burnt her,' Nate spat.

'What?' Emory's nostrils flared.

'The bastard burnt her hand.'

I rubbed my left palm, worrying at the spot that had been blistered. 'Yeah. That wasn't fun. I'm glad to be home.'

Gato came and gave me a big lick. 'Hey, pup.' He went as if to send me back to the Common realm but I shied away. 'Thanks, but no. I need my magic for a while tonight. Sorry. I'm not ready to go without it.' His big eyes were understanding. Indy came for a full body cuddle, before settling down nicely. She was on her best behaviour.

Manners strode in. 'Hey, Jinx. Glad you're back home okay.' As always, he was master of the understatement.

'Thanks. Me too.'

'Lucy, we've got an issue,' he continued.

'Don't we always?' She sighed.

'A big one. A Jimmy Rain one.' Manners stated.

Lucy frowned. 'Jimmy Rain is a blight on werewolves everywhere. He's the werewolf symposium member—'

'Um, shouldn't that be you? You're the Queen?' I pointed out.

'Removing him was on my to-do list. You wouldn't believe how much admin rulers have to deal with. I just hadn't gotten around to it yet.'

'Well, we're going to have to get round to it now,' Manners said grimly. 'Rain is as Anti-Crea as they come, full of werewolf-supremacy vitriol. Archie sent word he's trying to stage a coup while you're gone.'

'Fuck,' Lucy swore. 'He's such a slimy bugger, doing it behind my back.'

Emory frowned. 'We're hip deep in Anti-Crea here too and we think a daemon is stirring things up. It wouldn't surprise me if the same culprit were behind your situation. Check Rain's hands and eyes – if his hands are shaking and his eyes look feverish, then he's under a daemon's influence.'

'I hope he's not,' Lucy said, 'because if he's being influenced then we can't just end him once and for all – not if it's not his fault.'

'There's a lot of shit that *is* his fault, but I agree,' Manners said. 'We'll have to see what the situation is when we get home. It's going to be a mess. I'm sorry we have to leave you now, Jinx, but we need to go.'

Lucy rubbed her tired eyes. 'When it rains, it pours.' She turned to me. 'I don't want to leave you,' she admitted unhappily.

'Go,' I told her. 'You've got stuff to do, and I have no idea how quickly all of this will shake out. It may well be linked. Anyway, I'm going to bed now.'

A yawn cracked Lucy's face. 'Yeah that's not a bad idea.'

'I'll drive us,' Manners offered. 'You nap.'

'Deal.' She kissed my cheek. 'Call me tomorrow? I need to know you're okay.'

'I'm fine.' *Lie.*

'Did it ping?'

I grinned and said nothing; that in itself was answer enough. Her lips tightened. 'Call me tomorrow,' she re-iterated.

'Call me when you've dealt with Rain,' I pressed back.

'Will do.' Lucy waved goodbye and she and Manners ducked out to deal with their own emergency.

'I have something to tell you.' Emory rubbed a hand over tired eyes. 'But not now, okay? It's late and it's been a bloody hard day. Right now, I just need to hold you.'

I nodded. I knew that I still wasn't quite myself because I accepted what he said and curiosity didn't tear through me. Hopefully a good night's sleep would screw my head on straight.

I had expected nightmares to chase my dreams but perhaps even my subconscious was just too exhausted. Instead I woke leaden-limbed and drowsy. Unusually, Emory was next to me; usually he got up and started to buy companies while I slept on. But today he was wrapped protectively around me. I snuggled in and relished the feeling of being home, warm and safe.

Emory pressed a kiss to my shoulder. 'Good afternoon, my love.'

'Afternoon?' I asked in surprise.

'We went to bed late and I let you sleep in. You needed the rest.'

I catalogued myself and my body. 'I'm okay.' I studied his haunted eyes. 'Are you okay?'

He considered his answer. 'I'm something,' he replied finally.

I pushed up on one arm. 'Talk to me.' I could feel the emotions warring in his heart; there was guilt in the mix.

'I've been too soft on the Anti-Crea. They've targeted you more than once. Action is needed – I see that now. No amount of conversation with these bastards will convince them I'm not an animal. If they want a beast, I'll give them a beast,' he promised grimly.

'Not all of them deserve death,' I argued.

'Perhaps not, but now more than ever we need to send a message. We cannot let this shit slide again or they'll keep on coming.' He grimaced. 'My detractors in the dragon court were whingeing that I was too soft. Now I find it hard to disagree.'

'You're not soft.'

'No, but I've let this go on too long, and look where it's gotten us.'

'Not married?' I tried to joke.

'You were kidnapped and hurt. They should fear my wrath, but they do not. We'll be changing that today.'

'Today?'

'There's no time like the present.'

Another thought wriggled into my brain. 'You said you had something else to tell me?'

'Ah yes.' He licked his lips and cleared his throat.

There was a knock at the front door and Gato and Indy started to bark. 'I'll get it,' I said, hastily throwing on my dressing gown.

'Jess – wait—' He pulled back the covers and started searching for his clothes.

I ignored him. This was my house and I'd open the damned door. If Randall was standing there, this time I'd blast him with my fire before he could breathe. I hopped quickly down the stairs.

'Dammit, Jessica, just wait!' Emory called after me.

I opened the front door and my mouth dropped open as I stared at the man on my doorstep. All thoughts sputtered to a stop. 'What?' I said, my mind totally blank. 'How?'

Zachary Stone smiled. 'Hey, Jinx.'

Chapter 13

My mind stumbled towards a thought, then it stuttered and died again. Stone. How was Stone here? 'How?' I repeated dumbly again.

He looked different, even though he was dressed much the same in a charcoal-grey suit, with black cufflinks embossed with silver triangles. But his light-brown hair was flecked with grey and his once-youthful face carried extra lines that hadn't been there when he'd ... died? His warm brown eyes were the same, but they carried a wariness I'd never seen before. Stone had always been confident both of his abilities and his absolute authority. In the few months he'd been dead and gone, he'd really aged.

'What?' I said again.

Stone's lips turned up in a smile. 'Glad to see I can still make a woman speechless.'

'That's what I was trying to tell you,' Emory said from behind me. 'Before we were interrupted.' He glared at Stone.

'You could have told her yesterday,' Stone bitched. 'I gave you plenty of time.'

'I was more concerned with letting her sleep after all she'd been through.' Emory paused, his jaw clenched, before he ground out, 'Randall tortured her.'

I opened my mouth to object to the term torture then closed it again. Randall had inflicted pain on me for no reason other than because he hated me, so perhaps Emory wasn't wrong. I was grateful the ordeal had ended when it had. It had been horrifying. If I thought about it for too long I'd start to cry, so I shoved it into a box of horror in my mind, closed the lid and tiptoed away. It was a totally healthy way of dealing with it.

'He what?' Stone's eyes flashed red.

I stepped back and pointed to his eyes. 'Um, red eyes are never a good sign.'

Emory moved me behind him protectively. 'Get control of your daemon,' he ordered Stone.

'I'm not a pet,' red-eyed Stone said drily.

Daemon. Stone was being subsumed by a daemon and Emory was fine with it? 'Can someone explain what the fuck is going on?' I snapped.

Stone's eyes returned to brown. 'When I leapt into the portal, your mum's soul had already been accepted as the sacrifice so I was surplus to requirements. I found myself still alive in the daemon realm. Luckily, I stumbled across Khalt and he healed me and saved my life. We became friends. He's a prince of one of the factions, and he took me in and kept me safe from the other daemons. His father wasn't overly impressed with his son's human pet, but he let it go as an eccentricity.'

I was struggling to understand this new information. 'But why didn't you just return to the human world? You look ... older.'

'I *am* older. Time moves differently there. I lived there for years and, without access to the Third realm, I aged naturally.'

I studied his grey hair and something clicked into place. 'It *was* you. In Portmeirion. At the diner. I saw you!'

Stone grimaced. 'Yes,' he admitted. 'I've been back for a few weeks. I've checked in a time or two to look after you.'

I stifled the urge to point out that I didn't need looking after. His words would have had greater impact if I hadn't just been arrested and tortured in a black-ops site by the Anti-Crea bastards, Randall and Holt. Thinking about them made something else click into place. They had admitted to breaking into my office but not to placing

Stone's prints there. 'You broke into my office! Your prints were there!'

He scowled. 'Yeah, I should have worn gloves, but I had no reason to expect that your office would be broken into again later that day. I was checking to see what information you'd stored on me, if any. I used your computer program to run a few searches. Because I was planning on officially staying "dead", I didn't have access to the Connection's resources.'

'Hold on!' My brain was working now. 'If you *do* come back from the dead officially, you can make a statement and get my arrest warrant rescinded!' This whole nightmare would be over.

Stone smiled gently. 'I've already done it, Jinx. I came here to tell you in person that you're no longer wanted by the Connection. The charges have been dropped.'

Relief washed through me, though it was tempered by the knowledge that Randall wasn't done with me – not by a long shot. 'Thank you. However, I might not be wanted by the Connection but I'm still wanted by the Anti-Crea, so I'm not totally in the clear yet.'

I frowned and cast my mind back. 'Randall was talking about attacking the centaurs. I should have said something to you sooner. Emory, can you get word to the herd master? I don't know anything more than that, but the centaurs should move out of their current location and they should be wary. Bronx was selling information to Randall.'

Emory nodded grimly. 'I'll call him. I'll leave you two to catch up.' He nodded at Gato and my dog nodded back, stood up and bristled to attention. Emory might be leaving me with Stone, but Gato was on guard-dog duty.

'Thank you,' I said softly to Stone now that we were mostly alone.

'For what?' He quirked an eyebrow.

'For introducing me to the Other realm. For saving my life when you were fighting with Ajay. For making a statement and freeing me now. Pick whichever you like best – or take them all. You changed my life and I'll never forget that.'

He shifted uncomfortably. 'No problem.'

'But it is, isn't it? Is Khalt with you here? Was he the reason your eyes flashed red?' I asked.

He nodded, 'Yes.'

'Don't take this the wrong way, but how *are* you here?' I probed.

'Ah, well.' Stone rubbed the back of his neck. 'One of Khalt's rivals, Jadin, managed to open a portal to the Other realm. We followed him through before he closed it. That's why we're here, to capture Jadin and take him back.'

'Jadin is the daemon that's been fucking things up? Making Farrell kill? Making Hardman punch me? This may be a bit self-involved, but it seems like Jadin's a bit obsessed with me. What gives?'

'He was involved in Sky's attempt to get the portal open. His brother, Limbal, was one of the thirteen daemons that got stuck here. He seems to blame you for closing it.'

'Why me?' I objected. 'Surely he should blame Amber, if anyone?'

Stone looked sympathetic. 'It was your mum who closed the portal. He can't seek retribution on her, so I guess he settled for you.'

Great: second-hand retribution. Exactly what I needed. I didn't even *deserve* this shit.

Emory came back in, his phone in his hand. 'All good here?' He stared a little too hard at Stone.

'Yes,' I reassured him. 'Stone was just explaining why one of the daemons has his knickers in a twist about me.' Emory's lips tightened.

'I'm here to take him back,' Stone reassured us both.

'And how is that working for you so far?' Emory snarked.

'It's been harder to identify his host than you'd think – but I'm almost sure that it's Elliot Randall.' Jonathan Randall's dad.

'What makes you say that?' Emory quizzed.

'The Anti-Crea have been escalating things lately, more than is usual for them. They like spouting Anti-Creature rhetoric and feeling smugly superior – but actually harming other creatures? That wasn't in their repertoire before.' Stone would know; he'd been an Inspector for more than a decade.

I thought of Dave and Jackie, the brethren guards who'd had their throats slit. 'It's in their repertoire now,' I said grimly.

'I know. I heard about the Elder, Darius. I'm sorry you had to kill him.' Stone cast a hard look at Emory. 'That shouldn't have been on you, Jinx.' He wasn't even trying to hide his criticism of Emory. Emory glared back and the tension ramped up.

'Boys. Enough. I know you're rivals or whatever, but can we set that aside for a minute? We need to find this Jadin and stop his influence. I know you think that it's Elliot Randall, but all you've got is conjecture. Yes?' I asked Stone.

'Yes, and the fact that he was seen near the circus before Farrier went on his killing spree. I think Jadin hoped that Farrier would kill other members of the circus and cause a scene. Instead, Farrier managed to channel the urges to something else.'

'Farrier still killed people,' I pointed out.

'Yes, but not innocent ones,' Stone stated.

'Well, that's all right then,' I threw back sarcastically.

'It wasn't his fault!'

'No,' I agreed, because it really wasn't. 'It was Jadin's.' I thought for a moment. 'You said his brother – Limbal – was one of the thirteen trapped here. What happened to them?'

'I've no idea,' Stone admitted. 'That was the elves' purview. Amber DeLea worked with them on containment charms and then they took over.'

'I guess we'd better go and see the elves,' I suggested. 'Emory, do you have my phone somewhere?' I hadn't had it on me when I'd been 'arrested'.

He chucked me the phone he'd been holding. 'Here. This is yours.'

'Thanks.' I caught it neatly and sent him a grateful smile. I opened it and searched for Leo Harfen's home number. He was old enough and old-fashioned enough to still have a landline. I found the number and hit dial, then listened to the ring tone over and over again.

He wasn't answering. I hung up. 'It's ringing out,' I said, my voice grim. My gut did not feel happy about this turn of events.

Chapter 14

'We'd better get over there,' Stone suggested.

Emory didn't look happy at Stone's use of the word 'we'; he wanted Stone and his daemon ride-along far away from me. 'I've got to go and meet the herd master,' he admitted, sounding frustrated. 'I said my personal brethren and I would help him secure the herd. The centaurs are under my protection. If you're going to Leo's, you're taking backup – Shirdal, Reynard and some of the other brethren.' His tone brooked no argument, but with my ordeal fresh in my mind I wasn't going to give one.

'How many personal brethren do you have?' I asked. 'I mean, you were an orphan so...?'

'Some dragons have bigger families than others; some brethren just want to leave their family sphere. Audrey and Cuth have had a lot of descendants over the years and they gifted me some brethren when I was young. They and their family lines have served me ever since.'

'Tom?' I guessed.

'Yes, he's been a part of my brethren since he was born. I saw his first steps,' Emory said with obvious fondness. Huh.

I tried to return to the issue at hand. Emory had made one notable omission. 'Am I not taking Bastion?'

'He's still not a hundred-percent fighting fit. I'll take him with me.'

'And Tom and a few others?' I was ready to insist; if I was taking backup, so was he.

'Yes. I'll take a strong contingent of brethren and dark seraph with me,' Emory promised. 'They can secure the herd between them.'

'What the hell are dark seraph?' Stone frowned.

'They used to be gargoyles, but Emory used some ancient dragon magic to save their lives and they became black-winged creatures instead. They've chosen to call themselves the dark seraph,' I explained quickly.

'Black-winged angels?'

'Yeah – but still with some gargoyle manners,' I admitted.

'They've kept the swearing thing?' Stone raised an eyebrow.

'Mostly by choice,' I replied.

Stone looked at Emory. 'All right, so you're taking some flying, potty-mouthed angels with you. What good will they be to the centaurs, besides being more cannon fodder if the Anti-Crea come knocking?'

'They're more than that, but their secrets are not mine to spill,' Emory replied, his tone steely. 'Nor do I need to justify myself – or them – to you. Rest assured, no brethren of mine are unable to defend themselves.'

'Or their dragons,' Stone muttered cynically. Emory's eyes narrowed.

I let out a sigh. 'So you were able to work together for what – five minutes? But now you've managed to free me from the Connection's crosshairs, you're back to bickering?'

'Absolutely,' Stone nodded.

'Yes,' Emory agreed, folding his arms.

I rolled my eyes. 'Wonderful.' I gave Emory a quick kiss. 'I'll take Gato, you have Indy. Go secure the herd. I'll go and see Leo. I'll be in touch.'

'Stay safe,' Emory said. He often said it to me but now it had an emphasis, and an underlying anxiety flowed down our bond.

'I will,' I promised. *True.* 'You stay safe too, love.' We separated and I ran outside to find Shirdal.

Mike was heading a team of brethren. They were all dressed like a SWAT team, fully weaponed up and with guns on hips. Shirdal and Reynard were sitting near another car but they stalked forward when they spotted Stone. 'Inspector Stone,' Shirdal greeted him evenly.

'Shirdal,' Stone replied tightly.

'You appear to be alive,' Shirdal noted coolly.

'Rumours of my death were greatly exaggerated.' There was a hint of humour in Stone's voice.

Reynard's hands grew into claws. 'We can rectify that,' he growled.

'No, no, no!' I protested. 'Stone is on *our* side. He's come back from the dead and made a report to the Connection, so the warrant for my arrest has been dropped. We *like* Stone.'

'*You* can like Stone all you want. I have nothing but fucking hatred for him,' Reynard snarled.

'Reynard—' I started.

'No,' Stone interrupted me softly. 'It's okay. I killed one of Reynard's compatriots who kept singing at the humans and causing road rage. He'd been warned several times. I should have just arrested him but I was told to make an example of him. So I did.'

'He sent his head rolling,' Reynard sneered. 'It bounced. I still remember the sound of it.'

Stone grimaced. 'I'm sorry.' *True.*

'It's a little late for apologies, swine, unless you know how to reanimate the dead.' Reynard's hands were still in claw form and they were twitching to do damage. I moved closer.

'No,' Stone admitted. 'I don't.'

I inserted myself between the two men. 'I'm sorry for your loss, Reynard, I really am. But we have to work together to send this daemon back to his realm.'

'And what about *his* daemon?' Reynard asked pointedly. 'The Prime told us all about him.'

'One thing at a time?' I suggested dryly. I turned to Stone. 'You were told to make an example of the gargoyle? Who by?'

'My father,' he admitted uncomfortably.

'When he was the wizard symposium member?'

'Yes.'

'So you could have been court-martialled if you hadn't followed his instructions?' I asked, drawing it out.

'Yes,' he agreed. 'But even so I regret my actions.'

I turned to Reynard. 'His father is dead. The true perpetrator of the crime has paid for it.'

'The true perpetrator of the crime stands right there,' Reynard shot back.

'Stone was following orders,' Shirdal interjected.

'That's just the kind of sophistry that I would expect from an assassin.' Reynard glared at Shirdal.

'Whoa, whoa, whoa. Cool it, Reynard. Can you work with these two men? If not, I'm leaving you behind,' I threatened.

Reynard grimaced but he simmered down. 'I can work with them. The Prime has asked me to, so I will. I won't disappoint him, or you.'

'Emory is not Prime,' Stone muttered.

I glared. 'Really?'

Stone gave a one-shouldered shrug. 'Well, he's not.'

'You can be not living, if you like.' Reynard threatened. 'He's *my* Prime, and nothing some old dragons say will change my mind.'

I cleared my throat. 'Right. Thank you. Let's focus on the actual issue, shall we? We need to get on the road – I just need to grab something before we leave.'

I left the men to sort out their differences and do some masculine posturing, and ran up to my room to rifle through my bedside drawer. Most people keep sex toys and tissues in their bedsides drawers but I keep knives and a number of lockpick sets. I put one of them in my bumbag, then slid a tension wrench and a rake into my sock. Paranoid? Probably, but I wasn't going without my tools again, not after what happened last time. Maybe in a week or two I wouldn't feel the need to walk around with lockpicking tools jabbing my ankle, but today wasn't that day.

Feeling better having the tools of my trade with me, I bounced back downstairs. I hoped everyone would still be alive when I got there.

Mike touched my arm as I headed back out. 'I'm glad to see you're okay, Prima.' His eyes were clouded. 'We failed you. I'm sorry.'

I hugged him. 'Don't be silly. I went willingly.' I paused. 'I won't be doing that again. Lesson learned.'

'Summer sends her love,' Mike said. 'She was so worried for you.'

I couldn't help smiling. 'Oh, she does, does she?' Those two had been flirting on and off for weeks and I was excited that they might finally be pulling their heads out of their asses.

Mike gave me an awkward pat. 'This time I swear I'll keep you safe, Prima.'

I nodded, swallowing down my instinctive protest that I didn't need to be protected because clearly I did. Look at me, having some personal growth. All it had taken was a spot of torture.

I left Mike to prepare the brethren while I went to find my rabble. They were piled into a car with Gato in the sizeable boot. I climbed in the back and Shirdal started the engine. He drew forward, waited until the several carloads of brethren were behind us then we motored off.

Tension hummed in the car for five long minutes until Gato let out a monstrous fart. 'Gato!' I gasped, unwinding the window. 'Don't gas us all.'

'What are you feeding him?' asked Reynard, looking green, also hastily winding down his window.

'Just the usual. Lots of sausages.'

'That is not normal. He should eat dry dog biscuits,' Shirdal said.

'Sure. You go right ahead and try and feed that crap to a hellhound. See how long you stay in one piece,' I shot back.

'Fair point,' he conceded.

Stone sat quietly in the back trying to be unobtrusive. I wasn't used to seeing him like that; before he'd always been front and centre, pushing in suspects' faces. I guess a decade as a human in a daemon realm would teach you to keep out of the way, but somehow it hurt to see him shrinking in on himself. It was a hard reminder that he wasn't the same man. I didn't know *this* Stone at all.

The drive to Caldy didn't take long. We drove up to the stunning Edwardian manor house, which was rendered cream and had a slate-grey roof. It reared out of several acres of woodland; a slice of perfection. I loved this place. It had seven bedrooms and sprawling outbuildings I had once suspected held a pool or a gym. I knew better now.

We parked on the wide gravel drive and I let Gato out of the boot. There were some forlorn-looking bushes in the centre of the circular driveway and Gato looked at me as he peed on them like they were his own territory. 'Gato!' I chastened, but there wasn't much fire in my voice. A few years ago he had lived here and this *had* been his territory. Dogs never quite let these things go. Gato looked at me, big tongue lolling. He wasn't sorry.

I waited until he was back at my side before I knocked firmly on the front door. I waited for Erin to open it but she didn't come. My gut was clenching with dread as I told myself that maybe they were out.

'Damn it,' Stone swore. 'I don't have my lockpick set with me.'

Before I could confess that I had mine, Shirdal beat me to it. 'I have mine,' he reassured us with a mischievous grin. Then he shifted into griffin form and threw himself at the white door with all of his might. With a loud whump, it burst open.

The smell of death assaulted our noses. Oh shit.

Chapter 15

We found Erin first. She was in the hallway, her throat slit, her pale-blue dress soaked with blood. Her golden hair was spread about her shoulders and her pointed ears protruded. Her eyes were wide, her face twisted in anger. Her staff lay a couple of feet from her side, tossed aside as if it were nothing.

Mike and the brethren insisted on sweeping the building while we stayed put. Shirdal and Reynard both had their claws out ready to defend me, but it wasn't necessary. I'd swept out with my empathy and I knew that nobody else was there. Even so, I let the brethren do their thing; it would make them feel better to do their jobs.

Stone examined Erin. 'She's still warm to the touch and rigor mortis hasn't set in. She's not been dead long – three hours at most.' I guessed if anyone knew death, it would be him or a pathologist and I didn't have the latter handy, so I'd take his word for it.

The recriminations in my mind wanted to start: *we should have come here sooner*. But shoulda, woulda, coulda wouldn't help us now, so I set them aside. They would haunt me later but now we had a job to do.

'All clear,' Mike confirmed. 'There's no one else present – except Leo Harfen.'

I could tell from the tone of his voice that Leo wasn't sipping a cup of tea and eating a biscuit. 'Show me,' I ordered grimly.

Leo Harfen was in his office, dead at his desk with a small vial in his hand. His face was bright red. Regret and remorse swamped me; the elf had been a good friend to my parents and to me. He had protected me on numerous occasions, and now he was gone. I hadn't loved him, hadn't known him well enough to do so, but I had *liked* him. I should have seen more of him.

I tried to study the body clinically. The red face was a giveaway. 'Poison?' I asked the room in general.

Stone nodded. 'I'd say so.' He moved closer to sniff the vial. 'Bitter almonds. Cyanide.'

'He killed himself when the intruders came in?' I hazarded. 'Why?'

'The elves have been maintaining the wards on the daemons,' Stone explained. 'The witches paint them but the elves sustain them, and they take turns letting the wards feed off their magical energy. I guess that Leo didn't want to be forced to let the daemons go.'

'Let them go how?'

'If he released the wards, the daemons could walk the realms in their physical counterparts,' Stone explained.

'So now Leo is dead, the daemons just have to wait for the wards to fall?'

'If the wards were fully charged, that could take a day – even two. Jadin won't have the patience to wait for that,' Stone's tone was grim.

'So what will he do?' Mike asked.

'Kill the hosts and free the daemons to go back to the daemon realm. Limbal will be free, albeit not in this realm though that was his aim. Man, Jadin will be pissed.' Stone grinned a bit at that; there was no love lost between the two of them.

I sighed. 'Give me a moment, then let's check the outhouse.' The outhouses were used for daemon containment rather than the nice pool I'd once expected.

Everyone else filtered out, giving me a moment alone with Leo. Call me nuts, but the moment alone wasn't for me: it was for my dagger. I called Glimmer to my hands. As its familiar weight settled there, its song filled my mind and this time it was a dirge: melodic, haunting and full of loss. Glimmer was mourning the death of its creator.

I laid my dagger on Leo's hand to give them one last moment together. It felt right. Eventually, when Glimmer's song quietened in my mind, I picked it up again.

'I'm sorry for your loss,' I told my dagger awkwardly. It hummed back; if it had been human, it would have been weeping. I tucked it carefully away in a loop on the waistband of my jeans, gave it a pat, and went to find the others.

Mike and his team entered the outhouse first. The metallic tang of blood and the underlying scent of defecating bodies wafted out. We were too late.

He turned on the fluorescent lights and they shone harshly down on the miasma of death cloaking the room. There were thirteen open cages and thirteen now-human bodies. The werewolves that had been forced to house the daemons had transformed back into human form upon their deaths.

'Christ. This is a mess.' I muttered. I pulled out my phone.

'What are you doing?' Stone asked with a frown.

'Calling it in.'

'To whom?'

'The Connection. If I'm off their radar, I want to give them someone else to gun for. Let's give them the damn

Anti-Crea. It's time to use the Connection to our advantage instead of running from it.' I dialled Elvira.

'Jinx? Are you okay? I am so sorry about—' Elvira babbled.

'I know,' I interrupted. 'It's fine. We'll talk about it another time. For now, I need you, Bland and anyone else you trust who isn't Anti-Crea. I've got a lot of dead bodies you need to see.'

There was a pause. 'Thank you for calling me,' she said honestly, 'and without a stupid fake accent this time. Jinx, I'm so sorry about the arrest. The warrant has been dropped now – I'm guessing Emory greased some palms. Honestly, I would never have been a part of it if I'd known they were going to take you to the hotel. It's supposed to be out of commission. It's owned by Linkage LLP, and it's been shut down since Stone died.'

I cleared my throat. 'About that...'

'What?'

'Stone.' I didn't quite know how to say it so I went with bald facts. 'He didn't die.'

There was a moment of silence. 'What do you mean, he didn't die?' Her voice was hard, like she suspected me of a prank.

'I know it's unreal, but he's alive. He's here. He made a statement to the Connection and that's why the warrant for my arrest was dropped.'

The silence on the other side was heavy. When she finally spoke, I could feel her agitation through the phone. 'Are you shitting me?' she asked finally.

She wasn't going to believe me without proof. 'No,' I promised. 'I wouldn't joke about something like this. Here,' I passed Stone the phone, 'talk to Elvira.'

'Hi, Elvira,' he said casually. 'How have you been?'

I couldn't hear her response, and I wished I had a dragon's sensitive hearing so I could hear what she was saying. I was betting there were some expletives in there. Looking at Stone's slightly shocked face, I knew I was betting on a certainty.

Eventually he hung up and passed me the phone. He cleared his throat. 'She's on her way here with a few people she can trust.' He frowned. 'Elvira didn't seem like herself.'

'The man she loves has just come back from the dead. Give her a moment,' I suggested.

He blinked. 'She doesn't love me. Her parents and my father planned an arranged marriage for her. Feelings weren't involved.'

Was he really so dense? 'On your part, maybe. But on hers? There were feelings, lots of feelings.'

'She's just mourning the loss of my money,' he said cynically.

'I thought that once,' I agreed. 'But she's been grieving ever since you died. She's not gone out with her friends, she's thrown herself into work, and she never once visited your lawyer to ask if she got something from your estate. And besides, I'm a truth seeker, remember? You can trust me when I say that she loved you.'

Stone looked genuinely surprised and his eyes flashed red. 'See? I told you so,' Khalt laughed. 'Dim-witted human.' He spoke the insult affectionately.

Stone's eyes flashed back to their usual brown. 'Quit it,' he said firmly to the daemon inside him. 'I'm in the driving seat while we're in the Other realm, remember? That was the deal.'

The eyes turned red again. 'Yes, yes, you're in control, Igneous.' Stone's eyes turned back to brown.

I smirked as the daemon called Stone by one of my annoying nicknames for him. 'I love that the name stuck.'

'I regret ever telling him about you.' *True.* 'If I'd kept my mouth closed, Jadin would never have learned what had happened to Limbal.' He grimaced.

'Yeah. I wish you'd kept your mouth shut about Limbal, too.' I sighed. 'But it's done now.' And the bodies had quite literally hit the floor. There was nothing we could do about it now. As I'd watched it, Leo's body hadn't flickered or looked like anything else for even a second. There was no illusion rune on it; it was what it was – a dead body. I couldn't go to the Third Realm to rescue him because I'd already seen him dead. I felt a pang of loss. Leo and I hadn't been close but I'd owed him.

The very least I could do was destroy the fuckers who had caused his untimely demise and also killed Erin.

Chapter 16

When Elvira finally arrived, she was all cool professionalism. She stared at Stone perhaps a beat too long, but then she turned and started barking orders to the detectives around her. Randall wasn't on the team, nor was Holt.

I saw Stone clench his fists as he watched the others working; he was struggling with not barking out orders of his own. I also saw a number of wide-eyed detectives watching him with hero-worship in their eyes.

'What's the deal with a return to work?' I asked Stone. 'Can you become an inspector again? They held a real nice funeral for you, and there's even a plaque in St George's Hall to commemorate your bravery. I bet they're a bit pissed off that you're actually alive.'

'It caused waves,' he admitted. 'The Connection offered to reinstate me as an inspector, but I thought it best that I turned them down while I'm trying to sort out Jadin's mess.'

'But you want to go back? Eventually, I mean.'

'Being an inspector is all I've known. It's the only job I've ever had.' Stone ran a hand through his short hair. 'It's the reason I moved ahead with selling Linkage LLP to Emory. I don't want to be the wizard symposium member, and I don't want to own and run Linkage. I just want to be an inspector again. Besides, I should have destroyed Linkage when I had the chance. Its history is chequered, to say the least.'

'You okayed the sale of Linkage LLP to Emory?' I asked.

'Yes. By then I'd informed the board of my safe return and ordered them to sell the company. The board approached Emory on my behalf. There's information in Linkage that he could use to do some good.' He grimaced. 'Like shutting down the hotel.'

'Has the sale been finalised?' I asked.

'Not yet. That's why Emory didn't know where you were. It should go through this week, if the solicitors pull their fingers out. If I'd known that you'd been taken there, I would have rescued you myself.' He swore.

I sniffed. 'I didn't need rescuing. I got out by myself.' With the aid of a magic dagger, a salamander and a vampyr. But *mostly* I'd rescued myself.

'Yes, you did,' he agreed, pride shining in his voice.

I gave him a nudge. 'You're proud of me.'

'I'm in awe of you,' he corrected. He smiled awkwardly. 'But I'm not in love with you.' *True.* 'Not any more. You have to realise that for me you've been gone for more than a decade. I had time to realise what I felt was ... illusory, at best. I hope I didn't make you feel uncomfortable with my infatuation.'

I am a truth-seeker, so I had known that he meant it when he told me that he loved me. But he meant it just as much now when he told me that he didn't.

'Feelings change,' I offered with a gentle smile. 'And that's okay. You and I had chemistry and real affection for each other. In another life maybe it would have been more. I don't regret our time together. You helped introduce me to the Other realm and I'll always be grateful to you for that.'

'I'm glad,' he said softly.

The Connection crime-scene people arrived in vans. It was getting busy and we were surplus to requirements. 'Let's go and find Elvira then we can give a statement and get out of here,' I suggested to Stone.

He nodded. Elvira was kneeling by one of the changed shape shifters. 'Hey,' I said. 'Sorry to interrupt, but if you don't need us for anything else we'd better head off.' I was getting itchy with all of the Connection people around me. Even though I knew that the warrant for my arrest had been cancelled, I still couldn't shake off my unease.

'Let me just take a brief statement.' Elvira stood up from the body and moved us away from anyone else. 'Okay, give me the full story then we can pare it down to what we actually put in the report,' she instructed briskly.

Guilt twinged my heart. I should have trusted her last time and told her the truth about the circus and Farrier. She would have done the right thing by them, and our friendship wouldn't have fractured. And maybe if we'd been talking on my wedding day, she would have called ahead to warn me that the Connection was coming rather than riding in its vanguard.

I decided to lay it bare. 'Stone escaped from the daemon realm with a daemon prince called Khalt riding around in his skin.' Stone's eyes flashed red and, as Khalt, he gave a jaunty finger wave. 'My honour to meet you, Elvira. I've heard a lot about you.' He winked. When his eyes opened again they were back to Stone's brown.

'Quit it, Khalt,' Stone growled.

I ignored their interruption and pushed on. 'Stone had some issues with a daemon called Jadin. He kept quizzing him to find out what had happened to his brother, Limbal, who had been summoned here by Sky.'

Stone took up the narration. 'I didn't appreciate that time moves differently in the daemon realm to the human one. I thought it had been two decades before I inadvertently told him the truth. Once he learned his brother was *trapped* here rather than having the naughty daemonic time of his life, Jadin vowed to come here to free him and cause trouble for those who had encased him and his compatriots.'

'Unfortunately,' I said drily, 'Jadin blamed my mum for closing the portal. Without her around to wreak revenge on, he settled for me. The sins of the mother and all that. That's why he got Hardman to punch me in the face and Farrier to bomb my car.'

'Farrier?' Elvira asked sharply, eyes narrowing.

'You were right.' I admitted unhappily. 'Cain Stilwell is Clark Farrier.'

'From the Other circus?' she clarified, tone grim.

'Yes. I didn't lie to you, and my report was wholly accurate. I didn't see anything Other about the circus the whole time I was investigating it for you,' I protested. 'But it turns out the circus is manned by runaways from the Other realm. They joined together for safety in numbers, and they travel up and down the country helping others that want to escape from the Other realm. Farrier runs the circus with the witches' help. You remember that I got hired to find a kid who was missing from the circus? It transpired that he was a centaur on the run from his abusive father. When the Anti-Crea broke into my office, they sent the son's file to the father who came to reclaim him. But he got killed instead.'

'Byron Bronx,' Elvira murmured. 'The herd said his death was an internal matter.'

'Well, it was, kind of, but the herd master agreed not to reveal the circus. It's a safe haven,' I explained.

'From the Connection,' she said flatly.

I contradicted her. 'From the Other. Most of the people in the circus aren't running from the Connection but from another supernatural person or faction who has threatened them. They just want to feel *safe*,' I said passionately.

'And they give up their magic to do so?' Her tone was incredulous.

'They give up everything – their magic, their family and friends, all ties to their past life. But when I rescued the centaur and Byron Bronx ended up dead, it allowed the young centaur to return to the herd. Apparently that inspired Clark Farrier to kill a few more miscreants that had forced his members into hiding. He was being influenced by Jadin – he would never have come to that crazy conclusion without the daemon's influence. The same thing applies to Hardman – he would never have hired me to find out about the satyrs' deaths and he would never have punched me if it hadn't been for the daemon. We're lucky that I had the IR and could hold him back, otherwise Hardman's injuries would have been much worse. Jadin was responsible for all that, too.'

'And we think Jadin's influencing the Anti-Crea,' Stone added. 'They have been escalating their demonstrations and attacks. They used to be happy with a few shitty slogans and placards but recently they've really upped the ante.'

'They killed two brethren members in Emory's castle,' I said. 'They slit their throats while they were on duty. And ultimately the Anti-Crea were behind my arrest and mistreatment.'

'Fuck, this is a mess,' Elvira swore. 'And the dead bodies here?'

'Jadin came here to rescue his brother Limbal so that they could walk this realm together,' Stone explained. 'Leo Harfen killed himself before he could be forced to release Limbal from his wards. Jadin killed all of the daemon hosts so that the daemons could at least be freed back to their realm.'

'Well, at least one good thing came of all this – we have thirteen fewer daemons in the realm.' Elvira pinched the bridge of her nose.

'One walking about freely is causing enough trouble,' I pointed out.

'And Prince Khalt, what's his skin in the game?' Elvira asked Stone.

'He's a good man,' Stone said firmly. 'He doesn't want to be in the human realm, he wants to wait for his time to rule in the daemon one.'

'And yet, here you both are,' Elvira said cynically.

'He's not trying to influence anyone, not even me,' Stone promised. 'Working together like this was the only way we could follow Jadin.'

'And how did Jadin get into the Other realm?'

'He was summoned.'

'By whom?' Elvira demanded.

'By Elliot Randall, we think,' I asserted.

'That's who you think he's possessing?'

Stone nodded. 'Yes.'

'Christ, this is a clusterfuck,' Elvira sighed. 'Elliot Randall is rich and has a lot of political friends. He also has a lot of Connection people in his pockets.' She slid me a pointed look that I didn't need. I was all too aware of what clout he had; it had landed me in an unofficial black ops site.

'We know,' I said firmly, 'But it's time they were weeded out.'

'You're going to war with the Anti-Crea?'

'It sure looks that way,' I admitted, squaring my shoulders.

'This is going to get messy.' Elvira grimaced.

'Yup. So choose what's going in your report but leave the circus out of it. Please.'

'Of course.' She paused and met my eyes. 'I would have left it out of the report last time.'

'I know and I'm sorry. I do trust you, but – I couldn't be sure,' I explained. 'Farrier was being influenced by a daemon, as was Hardman. They weren't responsible for their actions. I got them runed by a witch, the influence stripped, and let them carry on with their lives. The guilt they'll have is enough. They didn't need to be arrested.'

She sighed. 'I guess it will *have* to be enough,' she said unhappily.

'See?' I said in frustration. 'This is why I didn't tell you! Now you're in a shitty position.'

'I'd rather be trusted and be in the know and be in a shitty position,' she said firmly. 'Next time, tell me the truth. We'll pick the path that works for everyone.'

'Okay,' I agreed. 'After all, that's what I did this time,' I pointed out.

She nodded and the tension left her shoulders. 'Yeah, you did and I appreciate it. And now I need to tell someone higher up that we suspect Elliot Randall has been subsumed by a daemon.'

'Pick your confidant carefully,' Stone suggested.

'No shit. Thank goodness I have your advice, otherwise I was going to send out an organisation-wide email,' Elvira bitched, eyes narrowed. She was still pissed that he was back from the dead and hadn't contacted her.

'I guess you know what you're doing,' Stone conceded.

'Oh thanks, boss.' Her voice was heavy with sarcasm.

'I'm not your boss anymore,' he pointed out.

'No. You're not. You're not my anything anymore.' She walked away before he could respond.

'Ouch,' I said for him.

To my surprise, there was a soft smile on Stone's lips and he was watching Elvira walk away with a speculative look in his eyes.

The next second, Emory rang. 'Hey,' I said. 'How is the herd?'

'Anxious – and with good reason. We're near Bangor and there's a whole army massing on their doorstep.'

'Shit.'

'Yeah.'

'What magic do the centaurs have?' I asked. As far as I knew, they had none.

'Next to nothing. They have four legs and extra strength, but that's it. They're vulnerable – that's why they have me and the brethren.'

'What do you need?' I knew he wasn't calling just to chit-chat.

'I need you to go to the dragon circle and ask them to send help. Dragons, preferably.'

'Do you think they will?' I asked dubiously. They hadn't seemed the most helpful, progressive bunch when I'd met them.

'Some of them ... maybe. Veronica would come. Tobias. Samara.'

The dragons he named were the ones whom he trusted most; I noted that Elizabeth and Leonard didn't make the cut.

'It's disappointing to see how many Anti-Crea there are here,' Emory admitted unhappily.

'Are they definitely Anti-Crea?'

'Well, they're carrying banners and chanting bullshit.'

Damn. 'Okay. I'll go now and send reinforcements as soon as I can.' The dragons would go and help, even if I had to frogmarch them there myself.

'Thanks. Stay safe.'

'Isn't that my line?' I quipped. 'You're the one facing an angry mob.'

'I can breathe fire,' he said in a hard voice. 'They should be fearing me.'

'They think you're – placid.' I selected the least offensive word.

'Maybe I was, but that was before they kidnapped my fiancée at the altar. Now they can burn.' He hung up without any 'I love yous', which made me a bit grumpy, but I guessed he had more pressing matters than making kissy noises at me. Like saving an entire species.

I turned to Shirdal. 'I need you to fly me to Caernarfon Castle as fast as you can. Reynard, you go and help Emory.' God knows, he needed it.

'What shall I do?' Stone asked impatiently.

'Go to Bangor with Reynard. Take Gato. He can help fight.'

'Someone should protect you,' he argued.

'No, someone should protect the centaurs. Besides, I have Shirdal and I'm literally riding into the dragon's stronghold – I couldn't be safer. Go. All of you. Help Emory,' I ordered.

Shirdal had shifted onto four legs and was waiting patiently. I climbed onto his back; I was getting so used to it that I hardly balked at climbing onto the deadly predator. Gato barked at me. 'I'll stay safe,' I promised. 'You too.'

Shirdal flexed his huge wings and we took off. I hadn't secured my phone in my pocket and the force of our ascent flung the device from my hand. I watched it smash on the hard ground below us. Dammit, now I needed a new phone. I cursed, then leaned down low on Shirdal's body to make us more streamlined. Shirdal had taken me at my word; never had I regretted saying 'as fast as you can' so much.

He flew as the crow flies, over the seas and the hills. All the while I was plastered onto him like a limpet on a whale and feeling just as small. I wanted to be going towards Emory, not away from him, but more dragons could turn the tide on a battle against the Anti-Crea.

But the thing that I couldn't quite ignore was the niggle at the back of my mind that kept asking, *Why haven't they attacked yet? What are they waiting for?*

Chapter 17

When we arrived at Caernarfon Castle, it was immediately clear that something was very wrong. Firstly, the castle was surrounded; secondly, I could hear gunshots ringing out. The castle was under attack – so that was why the Anti-Crea in Bangor weren't attacking Emory and the centaurs. They were simply a diversion to make us to split our forces.

Randall's comments about the centaurs had been a trick, designed to pull some of us away. And if that were true, it meant that they'd let me escape so I could relay the set-up to Emory. We'd been played. The real attack was here at the castle.

Shirdal landed on the castle turret and I flung myself off him. I concentrated on my bond and did my best to transmit my panic at Emory; hopefully that would make him come running. Shirdal shifted into his human form and we ran into the castle. It was in disarray, and brethren were running around armed to the teeth.

'I need a phone,' I said to someone I didn't recognise.

'They used an EMP,' he confirmed grimly.

'A what?' I asked.

'An electromagnetic pulse. It knocked out all the electricity in the area.'

'No phones?'

'No. No security cameras, either.'

'Fuck.'

'That sums it up. I have to go, Prima. I'm needed on the walls.' He turned away.

'I'm not Prima,' I called out of habit more than anything.

'You are to us,' he chucked back over his shoulder as he ran towards the fighting. It made my heart do funny things.

I turned to Shirdal. 'You've got to get to Emory. Tell him that the castle is under attack. He can be here in minutes with the brethren close behind. It could turn the tide of the battle.'

Shirdal frowned unhappily. 'I don't want to leave you here, sweetheart.'

'The castle will still be standing when you get back,' I insisted. 'Go, Shirdal!'

'It's not the castle I'm worried about,' he muttered mutinously.

'I have fire, water, the IR and a magical dagger. I'll be fine.'

'If you're close enough that you need Glimmer, you're already in trouble. Can you make Glimmer invisible? If they can't see it coming then you'll stand a better chance.' Once a sneaky assassin, always a sneaky assassin, I guess.

I wanted to argue that it didn't seem like I'd be fighting fair if I made my dagger invisible, but I wanted Shirdal to get to Emory. I pulled out Glimmer, gathered my intention and wrapped the blade with magic, willing it to disappear from sight. It seemed like a waste of magical energy, but what did I know? I tied off the magic, so that Glimmer would stay invisible until I changed it back to visible, then I carefully plunged the invisible blade into my belt. I hoped I'd remember to be careful when I sat down.

'See? All gone. Go! Now!' I shooed Shirdal with my hands.

'I'm going, Prima, I'm going.' He turned and leapt out of an open window in human form.

I had seen him do it before but I still ran to the window to check. I got there in time to see him shimmer into his winged form and fly away. That man was going to give me a heart attack one day.

I ran down the corridor to the main hall. The dragon circle were sitting. Literally. They were sitting at their circular table, sipping cups of tea. 'What the fuck are you doing?' I exclaimed. 'The castle is under attack. You need to be out there, fighting with the brethren.'

'The castle has stood for seven hundred years. It's not going to fall now,' Leonard said calmly.

'It's faced humans and rifles before, not a magical attack,' I pointed out. 'This is different.'

'We're fine,' Leonard said firmly. 'We have men manning the walls and we have the hoard runed up to the hilt.'

'This isn't about money,' I said incredulously.

'It's always about money,' he shot back.

'Have you at least evacuated the younglings?'

'Of course,' Veronica huffed. 'That was the first thing we did.'

'Then why aren't you out there breathing fire on the attackers?' I asked.

'Because we can't agree on a course of action and darkness hasn't fallen yet,' Elizabeth explained. 'We need to wait for night to cover us, otherwise everyone in the Common realm will suddenly see a lot of dragons and there'll be a massive clean-up job for the Connection afterwards.'

'But in the meantime the brethren will die for you,' I spat out.

'It is what they are bred to do,' Leonard said calmly.

I stared at him, horrified. 'That is a terrible attitude. Why are their lives worth less than yours?'

'Their lives are significantly shorter,' he shrugged.

'That means their lives have *more* value, not less. They have to cram in every moment of living. You have no right to take even a second away from them. You can't simply stay here drinking cups of tea while your men die all around you. It's not right.' I was getting on my soapbox.

Veronica tried to placate me. 'Darkness falls in half an hour, then they will see our might.'

'You're all fucking crazy! Emory doesn't care about being seen, he cares about doing what is right.'

'Emory is no longer the Prime,' Elizabeth said coolly.

'No. Instead you are now Primeless, and you're sitting here and quibbling about what to do and who will be the next leader. You're more concerned with your power vacuum than your people. Your men and women are dying. Order the dragons out! Now!' I half-pleaded, half-ordered. Silence greeted me.

I stared at each of them in turn. Elizabeth was looking at me with a strange glint in her eye, like she was *pleased* about this turn of events. Veronica wouldn't meet my gaze but the others simply stared back at me. I shook my head. 'You should all be ashamed of yourselves.' With that, I turned on my heel and left them to argue amongst themselves.

I went down through the castle to join the front lines. I had fire and I had the IR; I could be an asset for as long as my magical energy kept going. I was running across the courtyard when I spied Evan. 'Evan?' I called. 'What are you doing here? All the children are supposed to have been evacuated.'

He looked hugely relieved to see me. 'Jinx! Thank goodness you're here. I didn't think I'd be able to find you.'

'What's the matter?' I asked.

'I heard something in the catacombs. I think they've found a way in!'

'Shit. Let me grab some men.' I looked around.

'We don't have time for that,' Evan said urgently. 'Everyone is needed on the walls!' *True.*

I hesitated a second before nodding and following him into the catacombs. The gate was already unlocked. 'Do you have a key?' I asked, surprised.

'Yes. I stole one for the prank, remember?'

I nodded. 'The Eye. Yes. Lead me to where you heard noises – but quietly.'

'I know what I'm doing.' Evan's tone was truculent.

I didn't like taking him with me but the catacombs were vast and sprawling; with the cameras down, it would take me ages to find the intruders. It made sense to let Evan lead me to the right spot, even if my gut didn't like it. If someone was in the catacombs, we needed to stop them before they attacked our forces from behind. Maybe I could collapse part of the roof; at the very least that would delay them and give us time to raise the alarm. But I still hoped Evan was wrong and he'd heard a mouse or something.

'This way,' Evan called as he scurried ahead of me. There was an edge of fear in his voice, and his anxiety and dismay swirled around me in the corridor. His terror was so thick that it was cloying. I focused on the sound of the ocean to drown it out so that I could still operate at my best. He was being so brave, helping me when he was so scared.

'Evan! Not too fast!' I called. I was losing sight of him. It was almost like he was trying to lose me. I put on an extra spurt of speed, rounded the corner – and ran straight into a trap.

Fuck.

Chapter 18

It was easy to figure out that the man standing before me was Elliot Randall. He closely resembled his son Jonathan, who had taken such pleasure in torturing me, and I wasn't going to forget his face in a hurry.

I twisted on my heels and whirled around, ready to bolt, but Jonathan Randall stepped out of the shadows. Of course he was with Daddy Dearest. 'Stay,' he barked at me. It wasn't a dog-like command but a release word as he wrapped the IR around me. Panic flooded me. I couldn't move.

'Good job, Evan, my clever little brother,' Jonathan Randall praised Emory's ward. 'I knew you had it in you.' He reached out and tousled Evan's hair. Evan looked down at his feet.

My mind went blank. As Evan stood next to Jonathan, the family resemblance was clear. Evan didn't look a damned bit like Elliot but he did look like his half-brother,

Jonathan. Their mother must have had an affair with a dragon and Evan was the result. I should have realised something was up when I saw Evan because Veronica had said all the younglings had been evacuated.

My mouth was dry with fear. I was being held immobile in the catacombs and no one knew I was there.

I might have been immobile but I still had magic. I couldn't speak to say a release word so I couldn't use the IR, but I could still summon fire or water. I tried to pull some fire out of me and a tiny flicker of flame appeared in front of me, but somehow it was harder to grow it without using my hands.

Elliot Randall looked over my shoulder and frowned. 'Someone else is coming.'

I felt hope surge at the exact same moment that Jonathan Randall struck me over the head. It was lights out for Jinx, and my flames fled with my consciousness.

I awoke groggy, in pain and with a strange sense of déjà vu. My magic was gone and so were my bonds with Emory and Nate. My arms were secured behind me, presumably with magic-cancelling cuffs.

I looked up and took stock of my situation. I wasn't alone. Elizabeth hung opposite me, shackled to the wall, her feet in irons that were linked to the cuffs around her wrists. She was hanging by her arms and looked as uncomfortable as hell. The room was even more barren than the one I'd been kept in at the hotel. This one had all the hallmarks of a dungeon. There were more runes than I'd ever seen on the walls and they seemed to be painted in blood. Brilliant.

'Elizabeth,' I hissed. She didn't respond.

'Elizabeth!' I called more loudly.

She stirred and her head lolled. Finally she opened her eyes. 'Jinx? What's going on?' Her voice sounded groggy and disorientated.

'Did you follow me down to the catacombs?' I asked.

'Yes. I was coming to say that you were right and that I would use my influence to get the dragons to fight, and to hell with the consequences. But then you went into the catacombs and I started to worry why you'd go there in the middle of a battle, so I followed you. That's the last thing I remember.' She looked around at our cell but, to my surprise, didn't collapse into hysterics. She methodically started to test each of the chains securing her.

'Evan told me that there were interlopers in the catacombs,' I explained.

'Evan? He was evacuated hours ago. I saw him get on the coach.'

'Well,' I said grumpily, 'he got off it.'

'He'll regret that,' she promised.

'He betrayed us.'

'What do you mean?' She frowned.

'He betrayed us to his Anti-Crea father. You didn't think it was worth mentioning that his father is Elliot Randall? That Evan Randall is brother to Jonathan Randall, the man who kidnapped me?'

Elizabeth paled. 'To be fair, I didn't know Evan's pedigree. He started using Donna's surname when he joined us – he was called Evan Caddie. I didn't think any more about it. But I remember from his file that his father had tried to kill him, so why would Evan join forces with him?'

'Because blood is thicker than water? Or maybe he's still trying to earn some damned affection from his father. Whatever his motives, he lured me straight into Elliot Randall's clutches. And, by default, you too. Although ...' I mused, 'I could feel Evan's fear. Maybe he was threatened. Whatever happened, this is a mess.'

Elizabeth didn't disagree. 'I wonder how everyone else is doing?' For once she seemed almost human.

'Do you care?' I asked, somewhat brusquely.

'Of course I care,' she responded, looking a little taken a back.

'A lot of the time you don't seem to. You were mad at me for saving your son's life.'

'What?' She was genuinely surprised. 'Who told you that? Of course I'm not mad that you saved Greg's life. How absurd.'

'But ... I made him a werewolf!'

'So? Being a werewolf is better than being dead. I'm *grateful* that you saved him.'

'If you're grateful, you show your gratitude in weird ways.'

'My attitude towards you as a prospective Prima has nothing to do with my opinion of you as a person. The traditions must be observed. I was hoping you would be the true Prima, the one in prophecy.'

'Of course there's a prophecy floating about,' I muttered drily. Bloody prophecies. Retrieving Lucy's had been a total pain in the ass.

Elizabeth closed her eyes, and started to recite the prophecy from memory.

'Born a wizard, raised a human,
Tested by truth, tempered by lie
The true Prima to rule us all.
To save dragons, she must first die.

The first Prima to his Prime Elite,
Destined to love, yet marked for death,
Scorched by hot flame, by daemon cursed,
She'll save us with her every breath.'

She met my eyes. 'That's not all of the Revival Prophecy. It goes on for about ten more stanzas about how the true Prima will help the Prime Elite usher in a golden age of prosperity. When I discovered that you were a truth seeker, I was convinced that the ancient prophecy was referring to you – "*tested by truth*". A true Prima to Emory's Prime Elite.'

'If you thought that, then why did you depose Emory?' I asked, totally exasperated.

'I didn't think he'd *be* deposed. I thought Geneve would vote in his favour – and Darius was always a fan of his. I thought it would cement Emory's position.'

'But I killed Darius.'

'Yes, and his brother wasn't too forgiving about that.' She sighed.

'*You* voted nay!' I said harshly.

'Well, the circle's vote doesn't count when the Elder's number is uneven, so it didn't matter. I wanted to see how Fabian would vote. I'd told him to vote yay.' She frowned. He hadn't.

Politics. Great. 'Fabian voted nay. If you thought I was the one in the prophecy, then you bollixed that up, didn't you?'

'I was so sure it was you,' she admitted. 'That's why I insisted on the proper challenges. The prophecy goes on about you suffering trials by fire so I made you light the wicker man and face the phoenix flames. I really thought I was helping us all. Besides,' she frowned, 'the Eye of Ebrel is tied to the Revival Prophecy. It shouldn't have shone red for Emory, not if he really is the Prime Elite of the Revival Prophecy. I'm convinced it's been tampered with. I've asked Leonard to summon a witch to do some testing on it. It's just not right. It doesn't make sense.'

She looked so dejected that I couldn't help but comfort her. 'Never mind. It's done now. Let's not focus on the past – we need to focus on the present, and work out a way to get out of here. Luckily, I have a set of lock picks shoved into my socks—' sock picks? '—and I can still feel them. Unfortunately, I can't reach them.'

'That's a pickle,' Elizabeth agreed.

The door to our dungeon clanged open and in strode Elliot Randall and Evan. 'Well, well, it was a two-for-one-special,' Elliot sneered. He was tall, with greying hair and a beer belly. His skin was reddened and he looked like he was someone's grandfather. He should have been kindly, propped up next to a fire with a good book, not shackling women to his walls. But I'd learnt a long time ago that appearances could be deceptive.

I hoped to hell that he hadn't heard my confession about my sock picks before he burst in or my one chance of escape would be over before it even began.

Chapter 19

'It's a shame that we have to kill you,' Elliot Randall said to me in a conversational tone. 'You're human, after all, and a wizard and an empath. A powerful one! But you pissed off the daemon and he's given me so much power. We can't risk him taking it all away, can we?'

'Just let us go or Emory will destroy you all,' I threatened.

His hands clenched. 'Your disgusting lover seems quite determined to destroy us all in any event. We had to run from the catacombs while he was barbecuing our good men and women. It didn't seem right to leave them, but we got what we came for. Jadin wants to extract some revenge, for keeping his brother here for so many years. Decades. He's petty about things like that.'

'My mum closed the portal and I was part of a team,' I pointed out. 'It wasn't just me that secured Limbal and the other daemons.'

'Yet it is your name that keeps coming up.' He smiled nicely at me. 'I've promised to deliver you some pain.' He moved so quickly, so unexpectedly, that I hardly had a chance to blink before he started to hit me. He snapped my head back into the wall. I was in so much pain that I barely registered Elizabeth and Evan shouting at him to stop.

Finally the beating stopped. My head was woozy and I struggled to follow what was going on.

Elliot was solemn. 'It seems only fitting that you should burn like my people did. Hold her arm,' he instructed Evan. 'Stop being a pussy and move!' he roared suddenly.

Evan swallowed hard before he stepped forward and loosely held my arm. I could feel his fingers trembling. 'It's okay,' I said to him. If my lie detector had been working, it would have been pinging away. It wasn't okay and I wasn't okay. I didn't want to be set on fire.

'Tighter than that, boy, or she'll pull her hand free,' Elliot snarled. When Evan didn't act immediately, he slapped him around the head. Evan stumbled. He looked up at me and tears filled his eyes.

'Don't worry,' I said. 'Just do what he says.'

Elliot laughed. 'Are you consoling him? The boy that betrayed you? The boy that showed us the entrance to the catacombs and gave us the key to the gate? And led you right to us? He even helped us do a little dry run when he hid the Eye of Ebrel. We used the time when the cameras were out to check out the entrance from the city. If it wasn't for Evan, you'd probably be safe in your bed next to your dragon. Instead, you're here.'

'And where is here?' I asked. I had to keep him talking.

'Never you mind. It's time to make you burn.' He flicked a lighter. Like father, like son, I thought inanely. He held the flame to my arm and I started to scream.

When he finally let go of me, both my arms were burnt and blistered. I'd screamed myself hoarse and Elizabeth was begging Elliot over and over again to stop. Evan had thrown up and was rocking in the corner.

'I would burn you,' Elliot said to Elizabeth, 'but you fucking dragons are immune to fire –though you can feel the pain of a living flare. I've already summoned a lovely little rogue fire elemental to cast a living flare on you both until your hearts give out. Horrifically painful for you, though I like the smell of scorched flesh.'

Elliot sniffed my arms loudly. 'Like chicken,' he murmured and his tummy growled. 'But we do what we must. I'll be back – and soon. Then we'll get started on some other parts of you. Your legs, perhaps, or your stomach.'

He clapped his hands in delighted anticipation. 'Jonathan has been begging me for another turn with you. I think I should say yes, don't you? He's been such a good boy, sowing discord in the Connection, deleting naughty bits of evidence against us, siphoning off information on the creatures that we could use against them. Yes, I should definitely let him and Holt have some time alone with you.'

Fear rocketed through me. I couldn't feel my magic or Emory, and once again, I was at some crazy asshole's mercy. Unlike last time, though, this time I had lockpicks in my sock and Glimmer lying invisible on my hip. I just needed my hands free and I could *do* something.

'Secure her, you pathetic piece of shit,' Elliot ordered Evan. 'I should have realised you weren't my son years ago. You're pathetic.'

I looked at Evan with pleading eyes but he wouldn't make eye contact with me. He clicked the iron cuffs so that they locked around the magic-cancelling cuffs and pulled me tight to the wall. He pushed me back a little – and this time he met my eyes. His were wide with meaning but I had no clue what he was trying to say, so I stayed still and hoped he hadn't re-shackled me properly.

Elliot's eyes flashed with temper. 'Despite his betrayal, you do seem to like the boy,' he said to me. 'Isn't that fun?

He is *such* a disappointment. He's not even my son.' His expression never changed as he reached out and snapped Evan's neck. Then he dropped the boy's body so that it crumpled to the ground.

'No!' I screamed.

'Evan!' Elizabeth cried.

Elliot laughed. 'His usefulness was done. I did the same to his mother when I discovered her faithlessness. Snap. Necks are so pathetically vulnerable – they're ridiculous, really. I'll send Jonathan along to keep you both company until the fire elemental arrives.'

'You must want something,' I said desperately, trying to delay the inevitable. I didn't want Jonathan and Holt back in the room with me.

'The only thing I want is for you to burn,' Elliot said. 'The daemon was very clear on that. Being deprived of his brother's protection deprived him of a great many other things, too, and he's very cross about it. The least that I can do is deprive you of your skin.'

As Elliot Randall turned to leave, he paused and looked down at the corpse of the boy he'd called his son. I saw not a flicker of remorse. 'Dragon scum,' he said roughly, kicking his son's body.

'Leave him alone! Haven't you done enough?' I shouted hoarsely.

He laughed. 'Not by half, my dear. Not by half.'

He left the door slightly ajar; I guessed he didn't need to worry about locking it with us chained to the wall. But was I secured as tightly as he thought? I waited until the sound of his footsteps receded from the hall and then pulled myself forward. As I'd thought – hoped – Evan hadn't fastened the shackles properly to my handcuffs. My hands were behind my back in the magic-cancelling cuffs, but at least I could do something.

With a bit of manoeuvring, the shackles fell away. Without my arms properly secured behind me, I slumped down and carefully pulled the lockpick tools from my sock, thanking all that was holy that these twats hadn't seen fit to pat me down properly.

Although I couldn't *see* Glimmer, I could feel its weight at my hip. Thank goodness for Shirdal's paranoia. With my hands free, my magic and my blade, we'd have a fighting chance.

I inserted the pick into the lock on the cuffs. It took a painfully long time to get the tension right. I raked the lock for five long minutes, cursing that I couldn't see what I was doing, before they finally came free.

Emory and Nate snapped into existence into my mind. They weren't near but they weren't too far way. Emory was lost in a towering rage and I tugged at him with all my might, hoping to make him realise I needed him. His rage faltered and was replaced by determination.

Next I tried to drag Nate to me, but he couldn't come. Fucking runes. Still, I had my magic; I could feel it swirling in me. I let out a sob of relief as I showed my hands to Elizabeth. Having freed them and my magic, I was feeling a lot more optimistic. I had no doubt that Emory would come.

I gathered the intention and willed it to break the chains around my feet. 'Break,' I ordered. Nothing happened and I frowned. I gathered the intention again. 'Break!'

Nothing. 'What the hell?'

'The runes,' Elizabeth said in a small voice. 'The runes will stop you using the IR. Too many people have the IR for it not to be runed against. You can probably still use your empathy, though.'

'Great,' I said sarcastically. 'We'll care them to death.' She didn't reply and I bit my lip. 'Sorry – I'm sorry. This is awful. I'm upset.' Upset was an understatement for how I felt. My arms were in agony and my heart wasn't in much better shape. And neither of us could look at Evan's young body, near the door.

'It's fine,' Elizabeth said calmly, and her voice anchored me. 'Free your legs with the lockpicks. We'll worry about magic after that.'

I unfastened the locks quickly; it was so much easier when I could angle the tools and see what I was doing. As soon as the ankle shackles clicked open, I scurried across to Elizabeth's side of the room to work on her magic-cancelling cuffs.

When they fell off, there was a moment's silence before Elizabeth swore. 'I can't shift. I'm sorry. I can feel my magic but I can't reach it. Bloody runes.' She swore again, colourfully.

'That's quite the potty mouth you have there,' I joked as I made short work of her ankle shackles. 'Okay, we've got our hands and feet.'

'And magic we can't access.'

'We're still better off than before,' I said determinedly. 'Do you have any idea which of these runes cancels the IR? Maybe we can rub it out somehow.'

Elizabeth shook her head. 'Cancelling the IR, or not allowing someone to shift, are highly illegal runes. They're not something you see often. This is black-witch territory.'

'Then we need to get out of here.'

We edged closer to the door, opened it and tried to walk out – but we couldn't. Damn Elliot Randall: he'd definitely been toying with us when he'd left the door open.

'Why can't we leave?' I asked Elizabeth desperately.

'I think they've painted runes on *us* somewhere. We need to find them.' She rolled up her trousers to reveal pale legs. No runes. We were both frantically checking our bodies when we heard the sound of a door open. Steps echoed down a corridor.

My heart started to hammer and I grabbed Glimmer from my hip.

'What on earth are you doing?' Elizabeth hissed, frowning at my hand which was clenched around some air. She couldn't see Glimmer, didn't know what I was going to do. Hell, *I* didn't know what I was going to do.

I considered my options. I could attack whoever came in, but if it went wrong I'd imbue our enemies with essence of dragon shifter. The last life that Glimmer had taken was Darius's, so now my dagger was primed to make someone a dragon. If Elizabeth hadn't recited that stupid prophecy maybe the idea wouldn't have been in my head, but she had and it was.

But I had to do something. I couldn't let those bastards burn me again – the thought of that made fear well up so thick and terrifying that it almost choked me. Then I realised that wherever Emory was, he must be feeling my terror and I tried to claw it back down, to think rationally.

I had a chance to escape, one chance, and at least this way I'd be immune to flames – if I survived. There would be consequences. Emory needed me to be human to carry his children; if I took this step, I wasn't so sure that I'd still qualify.

I took a deep breath, doubting everything and wishing for a life that was slipping away from me.

'What are you doing?' Elizabeth hissed.

'Making a prophecy come true,' I breathed.

And then I plunged Glimmer into my heart.

Chapter 20

I felt the moment that my heart stopped and my bond with Emory shattered. It was the moment that I died.

My body fell to the ground and landed with a thump. My eyes were wide, unseeing, and for a moment I thought that it was over. For a split second, I felt excitement – I'd get to see Mum again. But then I took a shuddering breath and suddenly my hands were moving of their own volition. Glimmer was in control.

Magic surged into me, foreign and mighty, like fire being accelerated by a fierce wind. My hands pulled the blade from my heart. As it came free, my flesh closed leaving no remnants behind of the insanity of my decision.

My death had shattered my bond with Emory but not the one with Nate. Perhaps a master-slave bond continued even in death, or perhaps the fact that Nate was already dead changed things. Either way, I hoped he was with Emory. To feel our bond shatter – I knew what Emory must be thinking. I tugged on Nate's bond as hard as I could and prayed that he would find a way to tell Emory that I was still alive before he succumbed to despair.

'What the fuck?' said Jonathan Randall as he strode in and saw me on the floor next to the body of his brother. 'Evan?' he said in disbelief.

'Your father killed him.' I sat up. 'Just like he'll kill you. He doesn't care about anyone but the daemon and his power. You need to let us go so we can send the daemon back.'

I got to my feet as Jonathan's face twisted in a bitter snarl. 'Nice try, bitch. You killed Evan, and now I'll kill you.' He swung a fist towards me but this time I wasn't bound and helpless. Adrenalin kicked in and I evaded his clumsy blow easily. He was used to beating helpless foes but I no longer fell into that category.

I brought my fists up to guard my face and shifted my weight onto the balls of my feet. Jonathan recognised a fighter's stance and sneered dismissively. That was his next mistake. 'Stupid dragon whore,' he spat at me. 'I'm going to enjoy killing you.'

Focused as he was on me, he wasn't prepared when Elizabeth swung a loose manacle at his head. He went down like a tree. Blood spilled from his head – though he was still alive, for now.

I grinned. 'Nice one.'

'You died,' she said, eyes wide. 'I saw you die. And now you're not dead.'

'It's better than that.' I winked. 'Technically, I'm now a dragon shifter.'

'A dragon,' she said reverently. 'We just call ourselves dragons.'

'Right. I'll get the lingo with time.'

Before we tried to escape the room again, I swept outwards with my empathy. To my shock, I sensed not three people in the room but four. 'Evan's still alive!' I exclaimed. His neck was broken but his heart was still beating.

'He needs to shift then he'll heal,' Elizabeth said urgently. 'He can survive this.'

He might survive it, but we still didn't have a way out; something was keeping us in the small dungeon. I was getting desperate. I needed to get to Emory; I needed to let him know that I wasn't dead.

If we couldn't leave by the door, we'd have to use the window. Unlike my last place of incarceration, this window didn't have bars over it – I guessed there was no need if the Randalls kept their prisoners shackled to the wall. I grabbed the manacles and flung one end towards the window with all my might. Maybe I used a bit too much might; the window exploded into a mass of shattered glass and the noise made me wince.

My throbbing arms were a distraction but I pushed aside the pain of the burns. I pulled Jonathan Randall's jacket roughly off him and wrapped it around my ruined arm, then cleared the broken shards from the frame. I looked outside. The window was a decent size so we could climb through it, but we were high up, higher than I'd anticipated. We couldn't do a drop and roll from here.

Elizabeth joined me and looked down. 'We'll have to shift mid-air,' she said confidently. 'I hope they didn't rune the window, too.'

'Shift mid-air? That's easy for you to say. How the hell do I shift?' And what if I couldn't? Glimmer gave me certain powers but there was always a twist. Lucy could shift incredibly fast; Hes didn't need to drink blood. What had Glimmer done to me?

'You just have to relax and surrender to the dragon within,' she instructed.

'I can't feel any dragons within,' I huffed. The only dragon I'd ever had within me was Emory.

Elizabeth tried to explain. 'Your dragon isn't a separate being, like it is for the werewolves. The dragon is *you* – it is your hunter's instinct, your mothering instinct. It is flight and freedom. Just relax into it.'

'You want me to relax as I plunge towards the ground?' I asked doubtfully.

'Yes, well, obviously the circumstances aren't ideal for a first-time shift. Normally a youngling would spend some time meditating and focusing on their dragon shape before attempting their first shift, but obviously we don't have the time for that. Clear your mind and calm yourself. Meditate,' she suggested. 'Quickly.'

Luckily for Elizabeth, I cleared my mind and meditated every single day; it helped to keep me level, to keep my empathy powers at bay so I didn't go mad from sensing everyone around me. I could do this. Probably.

'I'll go first,' she said. 'I'll carry Evan in my arms then shift him to my claws. Then we must get to the castle. There's a potion there that can force a shift on us. If we can get that into him, there's no reason why he shouldn't survive.'

'As long as his broken neck isn't jostled too much,' I pointed out, biting my lip.

'It's a risk we have to take,' she argued. 'We can't leave him here.'

She was right. I hated risking Evan, even after what he'd done to me. He'd been so scared. I really hoped he'd betrayed us because he'd been threatened and not because he still believed the Anti-Crea vitriol he'd been raised with.

'Okay,' I said. 'Climb into the window then I'll pass him to you. We'll try not to knock him around too much.'

For an older lady, she was spry. The window ledge was nearly a foot in depth so she could stand on it comfortably. She stuck an arm experimentally out of the window, and then a leg, until she was half in, half out. 'No rune!' she crowed triumphantly.

No rune, so it was go time. We had a way out. I looked dubiously at Evan's body. He was a skinny teenager but even so he would be hard to lift. I braced my body, bent my knees, slid my arms under him ... and lifted him easily. Whoa. This shifter strength thing was cool. At least I'd now got that. Maybe I'd survive if I didn't manage to shift when I dived out of the window. I grimaced. Way to think relaxing thoughts, Jinx.

I hefted the unconscious boy and carefully transferred him into Elizabeth's waiting arms. She took him easily and turned. 'Watch,' she instructed, and then she jumped out of the window feet first.

I leaned forward to look down. A moment later, her magnificent wings were flexed and she had somehow transferred Evan into her claws. 'Hurry!' she called urgently. 'I've been seen.'

She was right; I could hear cries of alarm. Damn. I climbed quickly into the window.

'I'll try and catch you with my body if you don't shift,' Elizabeth shouted. That offer was a big deal because she'd be letting me ride her, and that was an honour only afforded to a dragon's mate or closest family in whom they had paramount trust.

No time to get soppy. 'Thank you,' I said, trying to imbue my voice with the gratitude I was feeling.

Unlike Elizabeth, I couldn't face the thought of going feet first, so I turned until my back faced the perilous drop. I closed my eyes and imagined the sea and the beach, then I flung my body backwards and concentrated on relaxing. I was falling, but that was okay. I'm a skydiver; I do this all the time.

I concentrated on my breath. I relaxed. I surrendered.

I hit the ground hard.

Chapter 21

'That wasn't so bad for a first try,' Elizabeth consoled me as I lay winded on the ground. 'I could see you shimmering almost immediately.'

'Thanks,' I wheezed as I tried to catch my breath. I pushed myself up – and almost screamed as I saw that I no longer had hands. I had wings. Silver wings. I was a dragon! 'I did it!' I squealed.

Elizabeth hovered in the air beside me, gently moving her wings back and forth in micro-movements to stay aloft. She was still holding Evan gently in her claws; she didn't want to waste time laying him down and picking him up again. 'You did,' she said. 'A little too late, but still. We need to get out of here, Prima.'

'I'm not your Prima,' I huffed reflexively.

'You are. You will be. Get to your feet and flap your wings – you'll find it comes naturally. We need to get above those clouds quickly. The daemon's forces are coming out of the keep.'

I stood, my body significantly larger than usual though it didn't feel lumbering or cumbersome. It felt strong. Mighty.

I extended my arms – my wings – and instinctively tried to move them. I knew that the movement I'd made would not be sufficient to get me off the ground so I made a stronger movement – and resisted the squeal of excitement when I felt my claws lift. Holy hell, I had claws! I flapped my wings harder and felt myself being propelled upwards. 'Which way to the castle?' I asked Elizabeth. 'I have no idea where we are.'

'Let's get up above the clouds first. I'll find my bearings when we're further away from the keep.'

I agreed and we both hauled ass to get up above the clouds. 'This is amazing.' I grinned at her.

Elizabeth smiled indulgently. 'It's been a while since I did my first flight. Watching you reminds me of the sense of wonder I used to have. It *is* amazing. Follow me.' Her usual unflappable calm was back.

I had no idea how she was navigating, but she ducked and dived under the clouds to check the land then came back up. 'This way. We're not far from the castle at all. Ten minutes' flight, if we push.'

'Then let's push,' I said. 'Emory felt me die.'

She missed a flap of her wings and stared at me with wide, shocked, eyes. 'Oh, shit.'

'Yeah.'

We flew as fast as we could which, it transpires, is really fucking fast. When Emory and I had flown to Lucy's aid, he'd been taking it easy because I was on his back and he didn't want me to fall. Elizabeth and I powered on, far faster than I'd ever moved freely in my life. It was exhilarating, and it could have been amazing, but anxiety was curling in my gut. I was missing Emory so much and I had to get to him. The bond between us was gone, and emptiness reigned where he should have been. It was horrifically wrong.

It felt like a moment and a lifetime before our castle suddenly came into view. The moon was high, lighting up the night, but even without it I would have seen what was going on. Emory was in dragon form and he was on a rampage.

I couldn't see any signs of the Anti-Crea that had been storming the castle, only a lot of blackened earth and soot. Emory had destroyed them all and now he was screaming his rage into the night. I watched as he scorched a field then came back towards the castle with more destruction in mind. There were no enemies left. Shit.

'Emory!' I shouted. 'Emory!' But the wind took my voice away and he didn't hear me. I flew towards him, but he was a more experienced flier and he let the wind carry him up and over the castle. 'Emory!' I screamed. 'It's Jinx! I'm here! I'm all right! Stop! You've got to stop!'

He didn't hear me – or he didn't listen – as he plunged towards his castle. All reason was gone.

I tucked my wings into my body and dived straight at him, just as if I were tracking on a skydive. I flew towards him and whumped into his side. He roared and reared towards me. *Now* I had his attention. His emerald eyes slid towards me but there was no recognition in them. The kettle was on but the tea was gone. 'Emory! It's me, Jinx!' I shouted to him.

He faltered for a second and I pressed home my advantage. 'It's Jinx! I used Glimmer to turn myself into a dragon. I'm alive, Emory.'

The towering rage seemed to lift and he blinked at me as if he were coming out of a daze. 'Jessica?' he said uncertainly.

'Yes, my love. It's me, Jessica. I escaped. I'm okay.'

'Dragon.' He was dumbfounded.

'I am, yes. Will you land with me? Let me see you?' I entreated desperately. I knew he wouldn't believe it was me until he saw me in human form.

'Yes,' he agreed, still monosyllabic.

We coasted into the castle's courtyard. Elizabeth joined us now that Emory seemed a little more sane, though she still landed a good distance away. 'I need a shift potion,' she barked. I had no idea who she thought she was ordering about because the courtyard was totally deserted. Everyone was hiding in the castle, and with good reason. Emory had been on a murderous rampage and I doubted whether he'd been able to tell the difference between the brethren and the Anti-Crea.

Someone was listening to Elizabeth: Mike. It should have been difficult to make him out in the darkness because he was dressed in his all-black uniform, but I saw him easily. Amazing; I didn't know the dragons could see so well in the dark.

'Hurry!' Elizabeth ordered.

'I'm coming, I'm coming,' Mike muttered under his breath. I shouldn't have been able to hear him from where I was, but with my hearing heightened to dragon level it was as if he were speaking right next to me instead of muttering quietly thirty feet away. Wow. This could totally up my surveillance game.

Elizabeth laid Evan gently on the ground. Mike opened the boy's mouth and carefully tipped in the potion, then stepped back hastily. As I watched, Evan shimmered and changed into a small green dragon. His neck looked fine and I let out a sigh of relief.

'Is he going to be okay?' I called to Elizabeth.

'He'll be fine now he's shifted. Let's take him into the warmth of the catacombs. He's had a lot of trauma and he needs to be bundled.' She turned to Mike. 'Run ahead and get the hoard antechamber warm. And fetch extra food.' She looked at Emory and me. 'Lots of extra food.'

'We need to secure the breach where the Anti-Crea got in,' I pointed out.

'Already done,' Mike promised. 'Emory sealed up the exit when he saw you'd been taken through it. The brethren teams have swept the catacombs and there are no other areas of weakness.'

'Weakness?' I queried.

'Ingresses or exits that have not been secured.'

'Okay. Fine. You go ahead, we'll follow.'

I darted a quick look at Emory. He was watching everything but his expression was flat, still and completely placid, like nothing was truly reaching him. I swallowed hard. *I* would reach him.

Flying as a dragon was incredibly quick but walking as a dragon was a bit more languid. I felt a bit like a duck waddling from side to side as we went into the catacombs. I led the way with Emory behind me. Elizabeth slung Evan onto her back and followed us in. It was easy to follow the pitter of Mike's steps through the long, echoing corridors. Despite it being dark in the catacombs, I could still see. I understood now that the lighting was for the brethren rather than the dragons.

It had been a long-ass day and suddenly I was bone tired. I kept going through sheer force of will.

Tobias greeted us at the antechamber. I had always thought the catacombs were ridiculously spacious but they were suddenly far less so with five dragons lumbering about. Emory's continued silence bothered me. It wasn't like him – he didn't do apathy.

Mike had started fires at both ends of the antechamber – gas fires. Handy. The chamber was still cool but soon it wouldn't be. He was stretching out big pieces of hessian to cover the cold flagstone floor. I eyed it cynically; it didn't look at all comfy.

Before she shimmered into human, Elizabeth carefully laid Evan down on what passed for a blanket. Emory finally moved of his own volition and wrapped himself protectively around his ward.

More brethren arrived and laid food on a table, a lot of food. This wasn't Mrs Jones' finest food; this was the proceeds of many hunts. Cooked meats – there must have been two whole cows and, my nose told me, at least one pig. Yay. Bacon.

'Feed Emory,' Elizabeth said to me in a low voice. 'Give him plenty of food while you're in your human form. Let him see that it is you. Feeding your mate is one of the things that starts a bond forming.' I suddenly remembered Emory kneeling before me and feeding me at Audrey and Cuthbert's house.

Elizabeth continued, 'Once you're done and he's had enough to eat, shift back into dragon form if you can. Get some rest and sleep – together.'

'What's wrong with him?' I asked quietly, though knowing it wasn't quiet enough. Emory could hear us; he just didn't care.

'His mate bond has snapped, he was in the throes of the murdering madness, and then you popped up. He's struggling to accept what his eyes are telling him because it contradicts what's in his heart and the broken bond. Just be here, feed him and talk to him. I'm confident he'll come back to you.'

I bit my lip. She was wordsmithing. 'But you're not sure?'

'No,' she admitted. 'I'm not sure.'

'Has it happened before?'

'Someone coming back from the brink like this?' She hesitated before shaking her head. 'No. But then, there's not been a Prima who's died and survived. We're lucky your bond wasn't fully formed. It was probably about eighty percent there, but that remaining twenty percent may save us. We're in unchartered territory here. Rest, Prima. I think all will be well.'

'I'm not your—'

'Yes, so you keep saying.' She smiled. 'But you're wrong. You are the Prima of the Revival Prophecy. The Dragons' Revival is at hand.' She beamed before gesturing for the brethren to leave us. Then she retreated, leaving me with an unconscious Evan and a very conscious Emory.

Chapter 22

Emory was watching my every move, my every breath. His huge dragon eyes were locked on to me and he barely blinked, like he didn't want to take his eyes off me even for that microsecond. Like a blink would be too much time without seeing me and knowing I was still alive. At least, I assumed that was what was going on – but maybe dragons just didn't blink that much.

Elizabeth had left without giving me instructions about how to turn back to my human form. Great. I moved closer to Emory's giant red head. 'I need to shift to human. Any advice on how to do that, love?'

'Relax,' came the soft instruction. He was there; my Emory was still in there. I'd get him back. But first, I needed to get into my human form.

Relax: I could do that. I sat down next to him, closed my eyes and concentrated on my breathing. Something in me eased and, when I opened my eyes, I found I had hands once more. 'Hey! I did it! And I have my clothes! Cool.' I examined my arms. All marks, all hints of the burns I'd suffered, had disappeared. 'The burns are gone!'

'Burns?' Emory growled, and suddenly his green eyes were lit with rage again. *Shit, Jinx.*

'I'm okay,' I babbled. 'All fine. Look!' I held my pale arms out to him. 'Not a mark on me. Everything is good. I'm fine.'

Emory settled down. 'Perfect.'

'Thank you. I think you're perfect too. But I could really do with you cutting out this monosyllabic thing. I miss you. Come back to me,' I pleaded.

'Mate,' he growled.

'You're my mate, yes,' I agreed. 'And I'm yours.'

'Dead.' The word was ripped from him and grief contorted his features.

'I died,' I agreed, 'but only very briefly. Seconds, really, and then my heart started again. So I'm fine. I'm not dead. I'm alive,' I babbled.

He watched me but said nothing.

Right. Food.

I went to the table, grabbed a leg of lamb and brought it over to Emory. 'Eat,' I urged. He did so with surprising delicacy, then held the bone out to me with his lips.

'Sure. I'll just take that.' I took the slobbery bone out of his mouth and carefully set it aside, resisting the urge to wipe his spit from my hands. I wondered suddenly if his dragon spit still had magical vampiric healing properties; it would certainly be an easy way to get huge quantities of it in a hurry. Maybe I should get Evan to swallow some.

As if I had summoned him to consciousness, Evan stirred. His eyes opened and he stared around the room in confusion. I bit my lip; I needed to handle this delicately. 'Hey Evan. You're okay. You're safe with Emory and me in the catacombs under the castle.'

He opened his mouth to talk and I held up a hand. 'Be careful what you say. Emory felt me die and our bond has snapped. He descended into madness and we're trying to get him back. Aren't we, love?' I said to Emory. He watched but still said nothing. 'So ... don't say anything triggering, okay?' Like apologising for betraying me and tricking me into walking into his father's torturing hands.

'Emory?' Evan said cautiously to Emory. Emory was still curled protectively around the boy but he didn't respond.

You died? Evan mouthed at me silently.

Later, I mouthed back. 'I'm going to keep feeding Emory,' I said aloud. This time I dragged over a huge leg of a cow.

Evan's tummy rumbled. 'I'm kind of hungry, too.'

'Of course you are. You're a teenager – you have hollow legs,' I teased.

He smiled a little but didn't want to meet my eyes. Something between us was damaged and my heart ached.

I know, kid, I know. We needed to talk about shit and clear the air, but we couldn't do that with Emory in this state. One wrong move and he'd go Rambo again.

For the next hour I took turns lugging pieces of meat to the two dragons who were curled up together. When Emory finally turned his head away from a piece of food that I offered him, I knew that his appetite was fully sated.

The fires had been burning for a while now and the room was toasty warm. Normally I'd have been sweating, but now the heat was comforting and not a single bead of sweat adorned my forehead. This would be so handy next time we went to a tropical location. No sweating on holiday. Hurrah, I'd save a fortune on antiperspirants.

'Have you had enough food?' I asked Evan.

'Yes, thank you,' he confirmed sleepily.

'How's your neck?' I risked asking.

'Fine,' he said tightly.

'Good.' I turned to the table of food. Emory and Evan had made a sizeable dent in the offerings but there was still a good amount left. I decided that I would enjoy it more in dragon form, so I closed my eyes, concentrated on the ocean around me and relaxed. I gave in to my inner dragon – and let out a happy noise when I opened my eyes and saw silver scales.

I'd have loved to see what I looked like in dragon form but selfies were nigh on impossible with claws. I'd have to wait until someone else was around.

Rather than moving the food to me, I went to the table and fell on it. I ate ravenously until I was so full I could have slept for a year. With my belly feeling like I was nine-months pregnant – a thought that caused a painful pang – I waddled over to Emory and Evan and happily collapsed with them both.

I awoke to the sensation of being watched and snapped open my eyes. 'You're okay,' Emory soothed as he stroked my back. 'You had a bad dream.' His words were comforting but his voice was tight. I turned to examine him.

He was in human form again and his eyes were hard in a way that I had never seen before. He was dressed in his customary black suit and black shirt; they seemed incongruous against the backdrop of the darkened catacombs antechamber and the hessian sacks we were sitting on. Sometime in the night I had also shifted back into human form. Let me tell you, hessian sacks over hard flagstones don't work so well as a bed for humans.

I stretched, making my back crack. 'Did I?' I shrugged. 'I don't remember.'

'You didn't seem too upset,' Emory confessed. 'There was just a lot of tossing and turning.'

I was so happy he was using more than one word at a time, even if his eyes still looked like he was containing something. 'That might have been the hard floor,' I joked.

Evan was still sleeping and he was also in human form again. I was grateful Emory and I could have these few minutes to talk. I searched Emory's eyes but I couldn't get a read on how he was feeling. 'Hi, my love,' I greeted him properly with a warm smile. 'You're back.'

He moved away from me. 'As are you. From the dead.' His tone was hard, accusing.

I winced. 'I'm sorry I put you through that.' I reached out again; though he allowed me to close the distance between us, his body was rigid. 'I can't even begin to imagine how horrible it was thinking I was gone ...'

'It was indescribable.' His jaw clenched. 'All of our dreams, washed away in an instant. To think I would never see you again, never hold you in my arms ... ' His control snapped and his voice broke as he pulled me to him. We held each other tightly as he cried. When the tears finally stopped, I kissed him gently.

'You're alive,' he murmured wonderingly. 'You're really alive.' He clutched me like I would disappear if he didn't hold me tightly enough.

'I'm alive,' I promised.

He hunkered down and rested his head against my chest to listen to my heartbeat. I stroked his hair, letting him do whatever he needed to absorb the knowledge that I was alive.

'Thank God,' he said finally. 'You're alive,' he repeated then he crushed his lips desperately against mine, letting me feel with his touch how happy he was.

But the silence of the bond between us made my heart ache; I hadn't realised how much I would miss it until it was gone. Nate hummed in my head, louder than ever. He was close by, too, and concerned. I sent him a pulse of reassurance and felt him relax.

Emory was studying me. 'You're a dragon now. Do you know what that means?'

'I can fly?' I joked.

'Only a dragon and a human can have a child together. Two dragons ...' He trailed off.

'We won't be able to have children together,' I confirmed in a small voice. God, I hated that my actions had taken away the future that Emory had desired so much. I'd started to think of it, too, a child with his blazing green eyes ...

'Emory, I'm so sorry.' A sob slipped out and I had to battle not to break down, not here, not now.

At my sob, Evan stirred a little. I took a few deep breaths; when I knew I could talk without my voice breaking, I continued. 'At least we have Evan,' I said weakly in an effort to lift the mood.

A trace of a smile painted Emory's lips. 'Danny and Sophie mostly have Evan.'

'We have half of him, at least,' I argued. 'The legs, maybe.'

Emory's smile widened; he was letting me cope with this by joking. Another day I'd cry about it but not now. Now I wanted to be grateful for what we still had.

'I don't want his bottom half,' he objected. 'I don't want to be responsible for his male appendage. I was a male teenager once.'

'Yeah, but the top half has his smart-ass mouth.'

'True. But I don't think it's the done thing to saw your ward in half. Unless you have some hidden magician skills that I don't know about?' Emory's eyes glazed over as he undoubtedly imagined me in a magician's assistant's skimpy outfit.

He was giving me levity, letting me brush over this, but my smile faded. It was too soon. 'I'm sorry, Emory,' I offered again. 'I couldn't see another way out at the time – and I wanted very much to be immune to fire.'

All the humour faded from his face. His jaw tightened and his nostrils flared. 'They burned you,' he said in a gravelly whisper. A shiver ran down my spine; seeing the dark look on Emory's face, I wouldn't want to be Elliot Randall right now.

'Yes, my arms. It was horrible. I think it was too close to what had happened in the hotel and fear kicked in big time. Elizabeth had just recited the Revival Prophecy and it gave me some hope that everything might be okay, but I needed to be immune to fire. Maybe I wasn't making good choices, but I was really scared.'

'I know. I felt it. And I'm not surprised. I don't blame you at all. When Benedict held me under the living flare, I would have done anything to make it stop,' he confessed. I squeezed his hand to offer comfort and to be comforted in turn. 'None of this is your fault,' Emory growled. 'It's Randall's.'

'Did you know that Randall raised Evan?' I asked. 'Evan is Jonathan's half-brother. I *knew* there was something familiar about Jonathan.'

Emory sighed. 'It was such a busy day when Evan was signed across to us. I remember his family were self-proclaimed Anti-Crea. As soon as he was adopted, he went by Donna's surname – Caddie.' He shrugged. 'Elliot Randall only rose to the top of the Anti-Crea ranks in the last six months or so. Before him, it was someone called Graham Flannigan. I didn't connect the dots.' He frowned and nodded towards Evan. 'What happened?'

'Evan led me into the catacombs where I was captured,' I admitted reluctantly.

Emory reared back as if he'd been punched. 'He betrayed us? Betrayed *you*?' he hissed, turning furious eyes on his sleeping ward.

'I don't think he wanted to,' I explained hastily. 'He got me into the catacombs and then he ran as fast as he could. I think he was trying to lose me, but I followed him too quickly – and fell straight into a trap. I could feel how anxious Evan was. At the time I thought he was upset because the catacombs were being broken into, not because he was about to hand me over to his father.'

'He's not really my father,' Evan said bitterly as he opened his eyes. He swallowed hard. 'I'm sorry. I'm so sorry. I was so scared. Elliott Randall is an awful man – he's the monster, not us.'

He started to cry and I instinctively wrapped my arms around him and rubbed his back. I looked over his head at Emory; I could see him warring with himself but finally his empathy won out and he also reached out to comfort Evan. That made Evan cry even harder and we hugged him until the worst was over. Finally, he tried to pull himself together.

'Just cry until you're all done,' I murmured. 'Don't stop until you're ready.'

'I'm done crying over that asshole. He snapped my neck!' he said. 'He tried to kill me and he thought that he'd succeeded. That bastard. I called him father for fifteen years and he tried to kill me.' His voice was thick with disbelief.

'I'm so sorry, Evan,' I murmured. Never had I been more grateful for my own love-filled upbringing.

'People can be awful,' Emory offered. 'But you never have to see him again.'

'He came in to the castle one day,' Evan explained. 'As a guest, like he was Common. I was sitting by the rock on my lunch break from school, and he came up to me. He told me that if I didn't help him get you, he'd kill my sister. She's only eleven. God, what if he kills her now?'

'He won't,' I assured him. 'He has no reason to. And remember, he and Jonathan both think you're dead.'

'Yeah, that's true. But we have to rescue her, we have to rescue Harriet,' he pleaded desperately.

'We'll do what we can,' Emory promised. Which, honestly, was not a whole lot. Elliot was Harriet's father and her legal custodian; he also had the Connection so deep in his pocket that they were nearly dropping out of his trousers.

'I'm so sorry,' Evan offered to me again. 'I'll never ever do anything that would harm either of you ever again.' It was *true*, for now.

'It's okay. I forgive you.' *True.* 'But next time, trust us. Tell us what's going on. We would have come up with a plan to rescue you *and* Harriet.'

'When you got captured at the wedding – It was awful, but I thought I was going to be off the hook.' Evan's voice warbled.

'And then you weren't.'

He shook his head. 'No, then I was back *on* the hook. Ready to be fed to the fishes.'

I slung an arm around him. 'Well, the fishes aren't biting. We're cod rather than piranhas.' I turned to Emory. 'Wait – do cod have teeth?'

'Yup,' Emory confirmed. 'Lots of little ones.'

'Well what fish doesn't have teeth? We'll be like one of those ones. Like a guppy fish or something.'

'Did she bang her head?' Evan asked Emory with a ghost of a smirk.

'She thinks she's funny.' Emory winked.

The smirk broke out. 'Oh. Is that what she calls it?'

I rolled my eyes. 'Ha. Ha. You guys are hilarious.'

'Someone should be,' Evan muttered cheekily, but with none of his usual bite.

'Come on, we should emerge from our catacomb lair,' Emory suggested.

'It's not a lair,' I protested. 'The bad guys have lairs. We're the good guys.'

'Depends on who's writing the story, I guess.'

'I am,' I said firmly. 'So we're the good guys. And this is … a den. Hey, do I need to start my own hoard now I'm a dragon?' Important things first.

'Yeah.' Emory grinned. 'Why not?'

'Awesome. I'm going to hoard books. I'm going to stockpile them on my Kindle and then I'll have the biggest mobile hoard ever.'

Emory smiled. 'That's actually pretty brilliant. It'll get your hoarding urges out and you won't have to pay loads in security.'

I frowned suddenly. 'What do you hoard?' I asked Emory. 'You do hoard, right?'

'Haven't you worked it out yet?'

'Money?'

'Nothing so prosaic. I hoard companies.'

I blinked. 'You do! You hoard companies. Huh. That's why you went on such a spree when your Primeship got ... before you relinquished being Prime.'

He gave me a wry look which said I wasn't as smooth as I thought.

'Anyway, books. Awesome.' I clumsily changed the subject. 'Do I get my own brethren?'

'Sure. I'll ask among my men and see if there's any volunteers. I'm sure Mike will be keen.' A thought occurred to Emory and he suddenly stiffened in panic. 'Shit, what happened to all of my men when I lost it?'

'They made it to the safety of the castle,' I reassured him. 'Our foe did not.'

'What happened to our foe?' Emory asked.

'You smote them. Or flambéed them. Whatever you want to call it. There were ashes.'

He examined his emotions about that. 'It's hard to feel bad,' he said finally. 'They were attacking my home, they had killed my people.' He shrugged. 'I don't think I regret it.'

'What happened to the centaurs?' I asked.

'When Shirdal arrived with news that the castle was under attack, the Anti-Crea forces melted away. I presume that was right about when you got kidnapped.' He said grimly. 'The centaurs were nothing more than a diversion. When I left, they were moving themselves to a safe secondary location.'

'That's good. All's well that ends well. Look at it this way … ' I started.

'What?'

'No one is going to call you soft for a good couple of centuries!'

Chapter 23

We emerged from the catacombs into daylight. Straight away, Nate, Gato and Indy rushed towards us. 'The brethren wouldn't let me come in to the catacombs,' Nate bitched. 'Never mind that I'd been there before.'

'I'm surprised and impressed that you asked permission,' I said.

'I'm trying not to create a diplomatic incident. I could feel that you were calling me but I couldn't phase to you while you were on the move.'

'I was only trying to call you so you could tell Emory that I was still alive. It's a good thing you didn't phase to me – I was flying and you might have fallen to your death.'

'Yeah. That's not my preferred way to go,' Nate admitted.

'Which would be?' I asked nosily.

'Death via exhaustion after too much sex,' he offered in a matter-of-fact tone. 'I think that's how most blokes would like to go.'

'What about peacefully in your sleep?'

'No,' Emory interjected. 'He's right. It's the sex thing.'

'Yup,' Evan agreed.

'No,' I said firmly to Evan, wagging a finger in his face. 'You are twelve—'

'Sixteen.'

I continued as if he hadn't spoken, 'and you do not have sex. If you do, I don't need to hear about it.' I paused. Oh hell. 'But if you do have sex, practise safe sex. We don't need dragon babies crawling around.' My cheeks were bright red. 'Oh man, I sound like my mum.'

'Did she threaten you with dragon babies, too?' Evan asked, amused.

'No, just normal babies, but it worked. She'd bang on about teething and the spit up, and the sleepless nights.'

Evan pulled a face. 'I'm good.'

'You better be,' I mock-threatened, but I reached out and gave his shoulder a squeeze.

'Let's go and find Elizabeth,' Emory suggested. 'We can assess the damage and then we can work on finding Randall.'

'Do you need me?' Nate asked.

'Not right now,' I said. 'Sorry to drag you all this way for nothing.'

'No problem. But vampyrs aren't exactly welcomed with open arms in the dragon stronghold so I'll head off. Consider me on standby. Call me when you need me and I'll help you bring down this bastard daemon.'

'Thanks. I appreciate that.' I gave him a quick hug. 'Hey, did you ever find out about that vampyr that accosted me?' I asked before he headed off.

'What's this?' Emory frowned. 'You didn't tell me you were accosted.'

'It was when I was with Lucy on our hen do. Then there was the whole wedding arrest situation, so it fell down my list of things to chat about,' I explained.

'I get that – but tell me now.' Emory folded his arms.

'Just a vampyr dude spouting Ante-Crea rhetoric. We threatened him and he left. So did we. No biggie.'

'You're under Volderiss's protection, so yeah, it is a biggie,' Nate argued. 'He violated clan law. If he wanted to speak with you, he should have petitioned my father first.'

'He didn't want a tête-à- tête,' I said, amused. 'He wanted to threaten me. That shit doesn't go through proper channels.'

'I guess not,' Nate conceded. 'My father didn't recognise him, nor did anyone else we've asked. If he's so off-grid,

Dad suspects he's part of the Red Guard.' His tone was grim.

'That's not good.'

'No, but it's vampyr business so leave it with me.' Nate gave me another hug goodbye, Emory a friendly nod and Evan a curious look before stepping into the shadows and phasing away.

I brushed a lock of hair off Evan's face. 'No one needs to know about your part in my capture. There's no reason to tar you with that brush.' I met Emory's eyes. 'We can keep it to ourselves.'

'If Elizabeth will keep her mouth shut,' Emory said dubiously.

'She will if we ask her,' I said firmly. 'She believes that we've triggered the Revival Prophecy.'

Emory froze. 'Born a wizard, raised a human...' He trailed off. 'It works.' His eyes went wide. 'You died. Fuck, it *really* works.'

'And you're a Prime Elite,' I pointed out. 'Which is apparently incredibly rare...'

A shadow passed over his face. 'I'm not the Prime any longer.'

'Elizabeth will have you reinstated before they can say "sorry we kicked you to the kerb",' I predicted.

'We'll see.'

He didn't want to get his hopes up but in my view the dragons would be mad to stay Prime-less, especially after the recent Anti-Crea attack that Emory had vanquished almost single-handedly. Of course, I'd thought they were mad to boot him at the time; he was the best thing that ever happened to the dragon community – albeit I may be a teensy bit biased.

When we walked into the formal hall, it was heaving with brethren and dragons. Elizabeth and the rest of the dragon circle were sitting on the dais that they'd used for Emory's trial. Despite the number of people milling around, the hall fell silent as we entered.

'Emory Elite,' Elizabeth called, voice full of pomp and theatre. 'The circle recognises you. Please approach.'

The crowd parted as Emory strode confidently forward. He joined them on the platform and raised an elegant eyebrow questioningly.

'The dragon circle recognises the strength that Emory Elite displayed last night in destroying our enemies,' Veronica said in a clear voice.

'The dragon circle recognises the wisdom that Emory Elite displayed last night in destroying our enemies,' Fabian announced.

'The dragon circle recognises the bravery that Emory Elite displayed last night in destroying our enemies,'

Leonard confirmed, though I fancied his voice sounded grudging.

'The dragon circle recognises the loyalty that Emory Elite displayed last night in destroying our enemies,' Elizabeth concluded. 'Strength, wisdom, bravery and loyalty. Those are the characteristics the dragons value in their Prime. Long has the circle sat and mulled over the issue of succession. Our castle – our stronghold – was attacked. Foes circled us like sharks – and they circle still! But last night Emory Elite did not hesitate. He did what had to be done and he saved us all!' The room erupted into wild cheers that Elizabeth made no effort to calm down.

Eventually the crowd fell silent and everyone leaned forward in anticipation of Elizabeth's next words. She waited until it was completely quiet before she continued. 'Emory Elite was removed as our Prime, so he is our Prime no longer. He violated our laws by making true brethren, and the Elders laid down their judgement.' She paused dramatically. 'But the laws must change with the times in which we find ourselves. This morning the dragon circle voted to remove the restriction on made-brethren and the law is now duly changed. Consequently, Emory Elite has not broken current law.'

It was pure sophistry on the circle's part but I didn't care. Emory was holding my hand tightly and my heart was in my throat. I didn't even care about Elizabeth's damned dramatics; I just wanted to hear what was coming next. Surely …

Elizabeth cleared her throat. 'In light of the recent heroics of Emory Elite, the dragon circle would like to extend an invitation to him to become our Prime.' I liked how she made it seem like an entirely new position, like she wasn't just giving him back the job they'd so recently stolen from him. 'What say you?' she called to the assembled crowd. 'Yay or nay?'

'Yay!' the crowd roared.

She held up a hand. 'Silence!' Elizabeth ordered, and they fell silent.

Elizabeth smiled at us. 'And what say you, Emory Elite? Yay or nay?' There was deathly quiet as everyone held their breaths and waited for Emory's answer. If he was a petty person, he'd say nay and fuck them all.

But he wasn't. 'Yay,' he confirmed with a small smile.

The crowd erupted in cheers; some were crying with happiness and hugging each other. It was unreal. I knew that they had loved Emory's rule, but I was still taken aback at the joy and happiness that was buffeting my mental shields. I took a moment to shore them up. I knew that if I were still bound to Emory, I'd be feeling joy from him too. I missed that.

Elizabeth gave a nod to Tom and he stepped forward carrying a red and ermine cloak. Tom passed it to Leonard who fastened the cloak around Emory's shoulders. Fabian stepped forward with ceremonial slowness, carrying a sceptre. All eyes were on Fabian as he made his way to his new Prime Elite. Fabian stopped before Emory, giving him a deep bow before he held out the gold sceptre in offering. Emory took it, thanking him. Fabian shrank away and it was Veronica's turn. She stepped forward, holding a sword encrusted with more diamonds than I had ever seen in my life. Veronica paced forward slowly, until she, too, bowed and held out the sword to Emory. Emory gave my hand a squeeze before he relinquished my fingers to take up the sword.

While Fabian and Veronica had been doing their stately marches, a host of musicians had been thrown together, grabbing their musical instruments, and as Emory held the sword aloft, the music began.

The drums began first, reverberating around the room. Then someone started to sing, and my scalp prickled as the song struck some hidden primeval chord within me. The ancient song was undoubtedly Celtic in origin, and triumphant in nature. The strains of the song and the music wound round the room, hypnotic in its potency. We all listened in rapt attention until the strains of the song faded away.

Elizabeth spoke triumphantly into the delicate silence. 'The age of the Revival of the Dragons is upon us. Long live Emory Prime Elite, and his Prima, Jessica Sharp.'

'Long live Prime Elite. Long Live Prima Sharp.'

Well now, there's nothing quite like having a roomful of people reverently chanting your name. I'd thought I'd hate being Emory's queen, but I could get used to being universally adored. And I understood now what being Prime meant to Emory and what having it taken away had involved. He was *meant* to be the Prime Elite – and maybe I was meant to be Prima.

'The circle will retire to the anteroom while important matters are discussed,' Emory spoke clearly across the sounds of celebration. 'We have dealt a significant blow against the Anti-Crea movement but our work is yet to be completed. Eat – and ready yourselves. War is brewing and the day is not done.' His voice carried around the hall, leaving it buzzing with anticipatory energy.

Mrs Jones and her staff leapt into action. The doors opened to the kitchen so that they could start bringing in food for the masses. Despite Emory's words of warning, the feeling in the hall was celebratory. Tobias was hugging a woman, and I wondered if it was the mysterious Samara I had yet to meet.

Evan quietly excused himself to go and see his friends. I watched him go, concerned; he'd been through the mill. I couldn't even begin to imagine the psychological damage it would have done to me if someone that I loved had tried to kill me. It was a heavy weight for one so young to carry.

Emory strode confidently forward to the anteroom and waited until the remaining circle members joined us. 'Shall I leave you to it?' I suggested.

'Nonsense, Prima,' Elizabeth said firmly. 'Please come and sit with us.'

'I'm still not Prima. I'm not married to Emory,' I pointed out.

'Not yet, but you have been recognised by the circle as Prima. You *are* the Prima now, whether you decide to mate with Emory or not. You are one of the dragons' rulers from this day forth.'

'Unless you decide to summon the Elders to boot us out of the role,' I said drily.

'With hindsight, we should have dealt with the gargoyle issue differently,' Veronica said. 'To ensure that issue is wholly settled – even with the change in the law – I hereby vote that Emory Elite is cleared of any wrongdoing in respect of the creatures now known as the dark seraph.'

'Seconded,' Elizabeth called.

'And passed,' Fabian noted.

Some residual tension drained out of Emory's shoulders. 'Very well. I am grateful to the circle for clearing up that little matter.' He managed not to let any sarcasm drip into his tone. Masterful.

'What's to stop it being raised again?' I asked belligerently.

'Once he's cleared, he can't be re-tried on the same grounds,' Veronica explained. 'The gargoyle issue can't legally be brought against him again. The circle's ruling is absolute.'

'What if the Elders disagree?' I asked, thinking of Geneve and her woman-scorned feelings.

'The Elders have not been invited to adjudicate. In any event, they cannot counter a circle vote of wrongdoing,' Elizabeth said.

I folded my arms. 'So – what? It's just back to business as usual?'

'Not quite. We have a daemon to get rid of. What can you tell me about the keep where you and Jessica were imprisoned?' Emory asked Elizabeth.

'It's not too far from here. I could lead us back by wing. I've had Fritz working on identifying it by using my directions and—'

The doors burst open and in marched Fritz with his laptop. 'I've got it!' he said triumphantly. 'Is this it?' He showed us an aerial picture of the keep and I felt my stomach lurch at the sight of it.

'Yes,' Elizabeth agreed. 'That's where we were held.'

Emory barked out orders. 'Take the co-ordinates to the brethren teams and let's get some vehicles on the roads doing reconnaissance. Elizabeth, take Samara with you, do some aerial passes and feed what we can expect back to the land team.'

Elizabeth raised an eyebrow. 'And what can we expect? Are we going into battle or to negotiate?'

Before my kidnap, and before our bond was severed, the answer would have been negotiate. 'Battle,' Emory declared. 'We've let them fester long enough. Sometimes the fist is all the bastards understand, so we'll show it to them.'

Elizabeth grinned triumphantly. 'Yes sir.' She was getting the version of Emory that she'd always wanted: one dressed in black and ready to draw blood.

Chapter 24

I insisted on returning to the keep, mostly because I personally wanted to oversee it being razed to the ground, but also because if I didn't face what had happened it would haunt my dreams for the rest of my life. I thought I was going to die in there – and, in a way, I had.

Stone and his daemon, Khalt, came along for the ride. I gave Elvira a heads-up but, for obvious reasons, she wasn't attending the party. Amber didn't answer her phone, so Emory called Kass Scholes to come as our witch of choice. She turned up in jeans, a hoodie and carrying her electric-blue backpack. She obviously wanted to be comfy while she defeated evil.

The elves were also on board. I didn't know them well, but Summer had reached out to their new leader, Caleb Smythe. They would meet us at the keep and, from what Summer said, they were baying for blood. I didn't blame them.

We left Evan at home with Veronica and Leonard. He wanted to come; I suspected that, much like me, he wanted to face his daemons. Quite literally. However, I pointed out that if Elliot Randall realised he wasn't dead, it would put his sister Harriet at greater risk. He reluctantly agreed to stay put.

We rolled out in force, fixing for a fight – but when we arrived the keep was empty. Abandoned. Fuck. 'Let me go first,' Kass called, climbing out of the car. 'There may be—'

Fire sprang up around us when one of the brethren touched the front door. 'Traps,' she finished drily.

I used my elemental powers to summon water from a nearby creek and poured it onto the flames. In seconds, they were doused.

Mike grinned at me. 'Nice.' He cleared his throat. 'Emory has asked if I would like to become your first brethren.' I held my breath. 'I would be honoured to serve you, as would my brother, Robbie.' He bowed.

'Thank you,' I said earnestly. 'I can't think of anyone I would rather have by my side.'

'I won't let you down Prima,' he vowed.

A stray spark landed on his jacket sleeve and I flicked a small pool of water towards him to put it out before it could take hold. Mike beamed. 'You're a handy person to have around, Prima.'

'I aim to please.'

Shirdal landed with a whump next to me. 'Don't say that around Emory or you'll find yourself in a sexy maid's outfit before you can say "roleplay". Hello, sweetheart.'

'Hi, Shirdal. Are you okay?' I ignored the maid thing.

'Better than you were,' he said grimly. 'I have failed you twice.'

I blinked. 'How do you figure?'

'Once by allowing Hardman to punch you. The second time by leaving you and allowing you to be kidnapped.'

'If you recall, I ordered you to fetch Emory. In doing so, you probably saved a great many lives that were at risk in the castle.' I dropped my voice and whispered, 'the dragon circle weren't listening to me – they weren't fighting. The brethren would have been killed. They're excellent warriors, but having no magic and taking on a bunch of Anti-Crea wizards is a sure way to get your brains splattered up a wall.'

'You have such a way with words,' Shirdal said cheerfully. I resisted the urge to tell him the mermaids called me Jinx Wisewords.

'You saved their lives,' I insisted.

'And risked yours. I will not let anything happen to you today. You have my word and honour. The rest of the world can burn, but you will not,' he vowed.

I smiled. 'You say the nicest things.'

'Griffins aren't natural bodyguards – guarding is a different skillset to killing – but I'm going to guard you to my last breath today.'

'It looks like you won't have to,' I admitted glumly. 'It doesn't look like anybody's home.'

'That's disappointing. I was ready to go down in a blaze of glory so they can sing stories of my heroics in the centuries to come.'

'You and your songs. Your dirge isn't going to make it on Spotify.'

'Who said anything about a dirge? I want a pop hit. *Sh-ir-ir-ir-dal*,' he sang as if to a beat.

I grinned and shook my head. 'Let's check this place is actually empty, then we can raze it to the ground. I'm in the mood for some razing.'

Shirdal smirked. 'You've been spending too much time with me. I love it.'

The brethren were doing their SWAT-impression and clearing the keep room by room. Mike stayed glued to my side. I went in when we got the all clear. It was eerie. The place was full of trinkets and artefacts, there were even plates of food on the tables, but there were no men or women. They'd left in a hurry.

Good. Let them run.

Emory appeared next to me and startled the hell out of me. Usually our bond warned me of his proximity, but our bond was dead and gone and that made my heart ache. It had been the symbol of our future together – and it had also been very handy. I had felt his emotions like my own, which was useful when he was playing poker face. The bond had worked at a distance, too, allowing me to keep tabs on him while he was off ruling and I was on a stakeout. I felt a pain in my chest where it had resided.

'Take me to where you were held.' Emory's eyes flashed with barely restrained fury.

'I don't know exactly—' I started.

'This way,' Elizabeth interjected. She led us up some stairs and then up some more, guided us into a tower and to the high turret where we'd been imprisoned. A shiver ran through my spine.

Emory's nostril's flared when he saw the bloodied manacles lying on the ground. The wind whistled through the solitary window we'd broken out of. There was no sign of Jonathan Randall, and it was too much to hope that he was dead and gone.

'You died here?' Emory asked tightly.

I nodded, fearful that saying anything else would send him into a tailspin of despair again. He stalked around the room, soaking it in, and with every step his rage grew. 'You jumped from here?' He pointed at the window.

I nodded. 'Well, I jumped and tried to shift into dragon form, but it was a bit of an ask.'

'You managed it,' Elizabeth argued.

'As I hit the ground!'

'Well, the shift probably saved your life. You would have gone splat from this height.'

I winced at Elizabeth's bluntness and cast a sidelong glance at Emory.

He was grinding his teeth. 'Get everyone out of the building,' he snarled. Whoops. There was no arguing when he was like this.

We evacuated the keep. Tom did a headcount as we left and retreated a dozen feet from the brick building. Then he called to Emory, 'All clear!'

From within the keep we heard a deep answering roar and moments later Emory burst through the roof. His spiked tail swung at the turret where Elizabeth and I had been held. The ancient building stood little chance against a raging dragon; his tail hammered into it and bricks flew.

'Everyone back a bit further,' Tom called when a stray brick landed much too close. We retreated several more feet as Emory roared again and let a plume of fire kiss the air. Breathing flames he dived into the ruin, setting the many trinkets and knick-knacks on fire. In a way it seemed wasteful, but on the other hand I didn't want any reminders of my incarceration here. Besides, they probably had bad juju. This wasn't a holiday resort. The dungeon in the turret had seen a lot of use; bad things had happened here.

Gato gave a growl of discontent. He wanted to be marauding too, destroying the building that had seen my death. I gave his ears a scruffle. 'Emory needs this.' I murmured to him. He tapped his tail twice in agreement and reluctantly sat down by my side. Indy was careening around the field like a nutcase, darting this way and that. I didn't mind if she got the zoomies out, as long as she didn't get too near to the building.

Elizabeth had taken out her phone to record Emory's destructive rampage. 'Will that work?' I asked curiously. 'The footage, I mean.'

'If you're in Other, you'll see exactly this. If you're in the Common realm, you'll see a gas explosion or something similar.'

'And you're recording this why?'

'PR.'

'A roaring dragon doesn't seem like the best public relations' footage,' I pointed out.

'It depends what sort of relations you're trying to engineer,' Elizabeth disagreed.

'And what sort of relations are you engineering?' I asked.

'Deadly ones,' she growled. 'Let them know what will happen if they dare attack our Prima again.'

'But no one is in the keep,' I clarified. 'Emory's just attacking a building.'

'But they will be when we tell the story again. Hundreds of Anti-Crea will have gathered here plotting against us,' she asserted smugly.

'Dragons can't lie,' I protested.

'No.' She winked. 'But the brethren can.' She was sneaky, and she was really starting to grow on me.

Shirdal sidled up and let out a baleful sigh. 'What's up?' I asked.

'It looks like Emory is doing all the razing himself. He gets all the fun.'

I watched the keep burn. 'Don't worry. The day isn't done yet.'

Chapter 25

When the keep was so much rubble and rock, Emory strolled out to meet us. He had shifted back into his suit and looked as civilised and urbane as ever. It was a sharp juxtaposition to the burning destruction behind him. 'Feeling better?' I called out.

He gave me his charismatic grin, which I recognised with relief. I hadn't seen that smile since our bond had snapped and something eased in me now it was back.

'Much.'

'You know that building was probably Grade 2 listed? The windows were all old school.'

'So?'

'So we're supposed to *preserve* history. You're not supposed to damage Grade 2 listed buildings, let alone demolish them.'

'There was nothing here that needed to be preserved.' He spoke with zero remorse.

'You're not even a bit sorry are you?' I asked.

'Not even a little bit. You *died* here. It's only right that the building should perish too.'

'It wasn't the building's fault,' I pointed out. 'Architecture is rarely responsible for death.'

He grinned at that. 'No, but Randall isn't here and I had my rage on. Something had to give – and it was this building.'

Gato and Indy went to examine the remains of the keep. Gato cocked his leg and pissed on the rubble. There was no doubt how he felt about that particular building.

Kass strolled over. 'I've got to go; I've been summoned to heal someone. I've got other witches readying themselves to assist you. They'll join you shortly.'

'Can't someone else heal the person?' Emory asked. 'I'd rather keep a witch on hand.'

'No, I owe a favour, personally. Someone will be with you soon, I promise. I won't leave you in the lurch.'

Emory touched his hand to his heart and gave her a micro-bow. 'I appreciate that Ms Scholes.'

She returned the gesture. 'I look forward to working with you more in the future.' She gave me a smile before she walked away. Kass wanted to be the next Symposium Member for the witches. She was making allies. I hoped

Amber knew who she was up against. Amber had coveted the role for as long as I had known her.

Tom approached, interrupting my thoughts. 'Prime, the building has been destroyed and the area secured. What are your orders?'

'Randall isn't dead and we don't stop until he is. Get Fritz on it. Get me another location.'

'I've got another idea.' I pulled out the replacement phone Tom had gotten for me earlier. He was nothing if not efficient. I rang Evan. 'Hey kid, how are you doing?'

'I've been better. Is it done?' he asked tightly.

My stomach lurched as I realised he was asking me if his dad was dead. 'No. I'm sorry, the keep was empty when we arrived.'

'They'll be at the cabin,' he said tightly. 'It's our final stronghold.'

'Can you give the location to Veronica so she can let us know where it is?' The question shouldn't have been *can* but *will*. I was asking a lot from Emory's ward, and I knew it. 'Otherwise, I can get it from Fritz, but that will give them longer to prepare for us.'

'No, it's okay. I'll tell you. Harriet will be at the cabin.' His voice warbled with emotion. 'Will you get her out first?'

'We will,' I vowed.

'Do you promise, Jinx?' he asked desperately.

'Pinkie swear,' I responded seriously.

'Okay. If someone gets me a map, I'll give Veronica the co-ordinates.'

'Thanks, kid,' I said softly. I knew what this was doing to him.

'Stay alive this time, Jinx.' He hung up.

I pocketed my phone. 'Evan is going to tell Veronica where we need to go. It's their final stronghold.'

'No doubt it will be well defended,' Emory surmised.

'We've got a freaking army,' I pointed out.

'They've got a daemon,' he countered.

'So do we.' I pointed to Stone, who was standing several feet away. Reynard was keeping a suspicious eye on him.

'Good point – but can we trust him?' Emory asked.

'We don't need to trust him, we just need to point him at Jadin and let their feud do the rest.'

'Khalt, yes. But what about Stone?' he said softly. 'They've been linked now and I've never heard of a host surviving a de-coupling.'

'Stone will be different,' I said confidently. 'He has to be. I can't tell Elvira he's died again.'

'MOVE OUT!' Tom hollered. 'We've got co-ordinates. Everyone back in the cars.'

'We could fly,' I suggested to Emory.

'To where?' he asked.

'Good point. Okay. Hop in a car with me?'

'Of course.' He took my hand and led me to a car. Gato and Indy jumped into the boot and settled down. Shirdal took the wheel and Reynard sat on the roof – like a gargoyle.

'Is he not adjusting to his new circumstances?' I pointed to the roof so it was clear I was talking about Reynard.

'He's fine.' Emory smiled at me. 'He just wants to protect us both. There's a whole bunch of dark seraph in the skies above us. I bet the Common realmers will see a flock of crows.'

'A murder,' I corrected.

'What?'

'The collective term for crows is a murder.'

'Of course it is. That's probably why Krieg has his little flock.'

'Murder,' I corrected again.

Emory laughed. 'I'm so glad I have you back to browbeat me.'

'Don't be wrong and I won't have to.'

'I'm rarely wrong.' His smile faded. 'I've destroyed the keep but it's not enough. The rage inside me needs more. The broken bond is jagged inside me.' He rubbed his chest.

'You're not going back to being monosyllabic, are you?' I asked, concerned.

'No, but I am having some pretty caveman urges right now.' There was a look in his eyes that I recognised.

I smiled. 'We can neck on the way to the cabin.'

He leaned forward. 'What a good idea.' His lips brushed mine.

'I have good ideas all the time,' I said breathlessly.

'You do,' he agreed, leaning down and meeting my lips again. It was the last thing either of us said for the rest of the journey.

Shirdal cleared his throat loudly. 'If you two are done with your tonsil hockey,' he said, 'we've arrived at the rendezvous point.'

It took some work for both of us to get our mindset back on murder and mayhem. Emory stayed in the car for a few moments to cool off.

'Why are you looking so fucking flushed?' Reynard asked me.

The red in my cheeks darkened. 'There was no fucking! Who said that?' I accused, looking around. Reynard grinned at me.

Shirdal rolled his eyes. 'They were exchanging saliva the whole journey. It was very distracting.'

Reynard smirked. 'That's because you're pansexual. *I* wouldn't have been distracted at all if I'd been the driver.'

'You can't even drive!' Shirdal bitched back.

'Do you two have to bicker right now?' I sighed.

Shirdal cocked his head, considering. 'Why, yes, I believe we do? Reynard?'

'Yes, we do.' Reynard agreed. 'The day we stop bickering is the day the sun doesn't rise.'

'The day you stop bickering is the day you two fuck,' I interjected.

Reynard's checks pinked and Shirdal looked away. Ah-hah – no denials. At least the quip stopped them arguing.

Emory stepped out of the car. 'What did I miss?'

I grinned but took pity on my two followers. 'Nothing much. Let's find Tom. We need to rescue Harriet before we go in – I promised Evan.'

'Of course you did,' Emory said drolly. 'Because attacking a highly defended cabin wouldn't be hard enough without having to do a silent penetration first.'

'I expect Shirdal's an expert on silent penetration,' I offered innocently. For the first time ever, Shirdal blushed. He cleared his throat and his eyes briefly landed on Reynard's face before dancing away. 'I'm happy to lead an extraction mission,' he confirmed carefully. 'As long as Jinx stays safely behind.'

'Nope, not happening. I gave Evan my word so I'm going in and I'm getting his sister, and you can't stop me. I'm Prima.' For the first time in my life, I pulled rank – of course, it was the first time in my life that I'd had a rank to pull.

Emory studied me. 'That's her stubborn face, so she won't be dissuaded. The four of us will go in – me, Jessica, Shirdal and Reynard. A small team can get in and out more easily.'

'I'll come with you,' Tom said quietly, startling the hell out of me.

'Crikey! Wear a bell or something,' I said to him.

'And I'm coming too,' Stone confirmed.

'No,' I said firmly. 'Not you. We don't want to risk Jadin finding you this early. This is a snatch and grab. We're going in, we're snatching, we're leaving. Once Harriet is safe *then* we let the hammer fall.'

'Am I the hammer in this scenario?' Stone asked.

'We're all the fucking hammer,' Reynard sniffed. 'They're not going to know what hit them.'

Chapter 26

The brethren had set up a staging camp a mile or so from the cabin that included a tent, which Tom had set up for a council of war. Someone had brought in a table and some chairs. He spread out a copy of the cabin's blueprints. 'Cabin' was a wildly deceptive term for the Anti-Creas' refuge: 'stronghold' or 'fort' would have been more accurate. Even so, there were a couple of points of ingress.

We crowded around the table and pored over the map before deciding to go in through the old servants' entrance. It was guarded by only a couple of men who appeared to be wizards.

I zoned out of Tom's plan as he droned on because my plan was a little different to the official one. He had outlined the strengths and weaknesses of the cabin, and he'd said that we'd need a diversion to get in because it was well fortified and crawling with Anti-Crea. His plan was good but mine was better.

'I just need the loo,' I fibbed. *Lie.* Hey! Even though I was a dragon, I could still fib! Maybe that was Glimmer's gift to my dragon-self; Glimmer always makes you Other with a twist, like Hes becoming a vegan vampyr.

Nobody would expect it. I promised to use my super-powers sparingly; if I didn't, I'd be found out lightning fast. I grabbed Gato and slipped away. Emory watched me leave with narrowed eyes; he knew I was up to something.

Once Gato and I were alone, I hastily explained my plan to my hound. 'I promised Evan we'd rescue Harriet. Right now, this place is Fort Knox, protected by the usual guards *and* the men from the keep. I propose we go back to the time before the second set of reinforcements arrived. We can sneak in, get Harriet and sneak back out before they come.'

Gato looked at me for a long moment then gave a tap of agreement. He didn't like taking me into danger but perhaps he agreed that this would be *less* dangerous than waiting for the place to be flooded with enemy warriors.

'Let's go,' I ordered. 'You send us to the time that you think best.' I always give Gato complete freedom as to the *when* that he sends us to. He is the one that can play with time, so I leave it to him.

We hid behind a car so no one would watch us wink out of existence then Gato touched his cold, wet nose to my forehead.

The sun leapt in the sky. We were back in the morning. Again.

Tom had showed me reconnaissance photographs of the cabin, so I knew what to expect, even from our position a mile or so away. 'Do you know where to go?' I asked Gato.

He nodded and trotted forward. I followed. Another day, the walk in the woods around the cabin would have been pleasant, but just then I was feeling nervous. Back in the day, I'd sneaked into my fair share of locked buildings when I was 'recovering' heirlooms and artefacts for Lord Wilfred Samuel but that was a while ago, and my incarceration was fresh in my mind. *If I was discovered and taken...*

I blocked the thought from my mind. I couldn't allow fear to cripple me, not now. I acknowledged that it was there but I refused to let it control me. I was more than my fears.

When we were closer to the building, I took a moment to wrap the IR around Gato and me. 'Invisible,' I said and released the magic. It surged around us and I felt the tug that meant it was working. Gato disappeared from my sight.

We had worked together for years, albeit the invisibility thing was a new string to my bow. He knew to wait for me. I moved to where I thought he might be – and abruptly gave myself a head thunk.

The good thing about the IR is that its limit is the amount of magic you have and the extent of your imagination. I gathered the intention again and said, 'Invisible to everyone except each other.' I concentrated on the fact that Gato and I needed to see each other but be invisible to everyone else. Gato winked into existence a metre away and wagged his tail.

'Hey. That works better – I hope.' Now that we could see each other, I feared that others could also see us. It was something we'd be testing very shortly.

'Before we go any further,' I cautioned Gato, 'there are bound to be runes guarding the cabin. We need to focus on the fact that we don't mean harm to anyone, we are only here to help Harriet. We have no malintent.' I had to hope that the Anti-Creas' runes were similar to the ones protecting the dragon hoard in the catacombs. 'Keep your intentions at the forefront of your mind,' I ordered Gato and he gave a clear nod.

'Okay.' I blew out a breath. 'Let's do this.'

As we crept forward, I winced at every single crunch of a leaf or snap of a twig. There were two guards on the back door where Tom planned to enter and create a diversion. I didn't want to be so flashy; ideally, no one would know we'd been there at all. We had time to wait for the perfect opportunity, but we needed to know that we were invisible to the guards.

Biting my lip, feeling my heart pound at doing something completely against all my instincts, I stepped into their line of sight. Neither man looked at me. I prowled forward as quietly as I could with Gato padding behind me on silent paws. We were close to both men but they didn't acknowledge our presence.

The two didn't appear to be friends; there was no chatter between them. I sat down on my heels to wait.

'I'm going for a piss,' one said after fifteen long minutes, and strolled off into the woods. The other guard watched him go patiently before opening the door, reaching into a backpack and pulling out a packet of cigarettes. His movements were clandestine so I guessed smoke breaks were forbidden. Once he had his cigarettes, he shoved the backpack inside the cabin. At the last minute, I reached forward and pulled it so it jammed the door open slightly.

While the guard was standing with his back to the door, preoccupied with lighting his cigarette, I slipped behind him and cautiously opened the door wide enough for Gato and me to sneak in. I pulled the backpack inside and care-fully let the door close slowly with a soft snick.

This wasn't our first rodeo, so we waited a beat or two for a cry of alarm. When none came, we carried on into the house. Given how bustling the property would be later in the day, it was eerily quiet.

Tom's blueprints had been sent to Evan, who had iden-tified the rooms that Harriet could be in. If we were lucky, she'd be in her bedroom; if we were unlucky, she'd be in one of the common rooms surrounded by a bunch of suspicious adults. I prayed for the former as Gato and I moved towards the Randalls' rooms.

I toyed with cancelling my invisibility because someone invisible opening the door would cause far more alarm than someone they simply didn't recognise. Fear of bump-ing into Elliot or Jonathan Randall kept me invisible, though. I didn't want to examine that feeling too much – was it cowardice or just being sensible? It didn't matter what label you applied, I wasn't up for tangling with either of them right now. Harriet was my sole objective; she had to be.

The suite of rooms was supposed to be behind the fifth door on the left. When I got there, I paused and pressed my ear against it. With my dragon hearing, I could hear someone snoring inside. Snoring was good – as long as we didn't wake up the snoozer. I turned the round handle carefully and it gave a light click as the door opened. I paused, heart hammering, but thankfully the snoring continued unabated.

I opened the door wider and tiptoed in with Gato at my heels. The source of the snoring was none other than that bastard, Jonathan Randall. He was sprawled on a sofa, an arm flung over his head. I froze as fear curdled my breath, making the air thick and hard to breathe. Everything inside me was tight with anticipation.

This man had held me against my will and burnt me. His father had been the one to do the real damage, but the echoes of the pain from Elliot's bullying son were strong, too. Fear and hatred are powerful motivators, and for a moment I seriously considered smothering him in his sleep. I wasn't proud of that thought, and the horror of what I was considering helped force me onwards. I swallowed hard and inched my way past his slumbering form. His head bore not a single mark from its encounter with the manacles that Elizabeth had swung at him. Shame.

This suite was always used by the leader of the Anti-Crea. While Evan had known its position, he couldn't say which bedroom Harriet would be in. It would be just my luck to open the door into Elliot Randall's room instead of his daughter's.

I kept a wary eye on Jonathan as I tried another door. This one was a bedroom but not Harriet's. From the Connection uniform strewn on the floor, my money was on it being Jonathan's. He was a bully *and* a slob.

The next room was an office, no doubt Elliot Randall's. Thankfully it was empty. I shut the door and turned to the next one. As I stepped closer, I heard soft sobs and my heart wrenched. Bingo.

I wanted to knock, to give her a moment to collect herself but that was a bad idea, so instead I slid the door open and sidled inside with Gato padding after me. Once we were in, I spoke softly. 'Evan sent me.'

The girl sobbing into her pillow shot upright and looked around wildly as she hastily wiped away her tears. 'Who's there? My father will kill you if you hurt me.'

'I'm not here to hurt you.' I promised. I let the IR go and Gato and I winked into sight. Her eyes widened at the sight of us. 'I'm Jinx, Evan's—'

'Stop saying his name,' she demanded sharply. 'He's dead, and I can't hear his name right now.'

'He's not dead.' I shook my head emphatically.

'He is. Father broke his neck.' Her bottom lip trembled. 'He told me so.'

'Evan is a dragon-shifter,' I pointed out. 'They're hardy as hell. One shift and he was good as new. I promise.'

Her eyes filled with hope and she scoured my eyes for the truth. 'You're not messing with me?'

'No. I swear he's alive. He's sent me to get you out of here.'

'Why now? He's left me here in this hell for a year. Why come and get me now?' Her eyes seemed far older than those of an eleven-year-old as she demanded the truth.

I shrugged helplessly; I had no idea what Evan had been thinking. 'It's not easy to remove someone from a parent's care. Legally, it could have repercussions.'

'What's different now?' she asked, eyes narrowed.

The truthful reply was, 'because hopefully your dad will be dead soon', but that wasn't something I could say. 'Because a conflict is coming and I promised Evan I'd keep you out of it.'

She opened her mouth to argue but I held up a hand. Something had changed. 'Shush a minute,' I whispered urgently. She obeyed and I listened to the silence – the total silence.

The sound of the snoring had stopped. Shit.

Chapter 27

I whirled around to face the door and gathered my intention. 'No,' Harriet hissed. 'Hide.' She pushed me towards her desk as if to make me get under it but I shook my head. I flung the IR to Gato and made us invisible to everyone but each other.

Harriet blinked as we disappeared. 'Huh. That works.'

I wanted to hush her, but I held my tongue and was glad that I had. The next second her door flew open and Jonathan strode in. 'Who were you talking to, squirt? I know Mum took your phone off you.' He looked around cynically. The 'squirt' wasn't said with any affection but a fair amount of bite.

'I was talking to myself. I do that a lot now that Evan is gone.' She folded her arms and lifted her chin pugnaciously.

Jonathan sneered at her. 'That's the first sign of madness, you know.'

'Screw you,' she threw back with a sneer. My tummy clenched. He wasn't going to like that.

Jonathan crossed the room in two steps and backhanded her. And that was it – I was in the game. I let the invisibility go so that I could use the IR for something else if I needed it, grabbed him and hauled him off her. 'You're a fucking bully, even to your kid sister. You're a disgrace.' I reared back and punched him in the face as hard as I could. There was a satisfying crunch.

He let out a growl and threw a punch back at me. I wasn't tied to a table this time so I ducked out of the way. 'I'm not such an easy target when I'm not in cuffs,' I snarled and hit him again. Yeah, this was good therapy.

'Dragon-whore,' he spat. 'You're a dead bitch walking.' He drew something from his hip and flipped out a blade. I wished for Glimmer – and there it was. God, I love magic. I smirked as I pulled it out.

Harriet had scrambled back from the bed; she was eyeing her brother with disdain but not surprise. This wasn't the first time he'd hit her. Asshole.

'You just love to hit vulnerable women, don't you? Well, I've got news for you. I'm not vulnerable now,' I taunted him. His eyes were fixed on me, ignoring his surroundings. 'And another thing,' I said as we circled each other.

'You talk too much,' he snarled.

'You listen too little,' I countered. 'And you're not aware of your surroundings,' I said in a sing-song voice.

'I don't need to be aware. I'm going to kill you.'

I smiled. Gato had shifted into battle cat form, spiked, huge and deadly. Gato is my bound hellhound and he's very protective of me; not only that, my dad is part of Gato and he had listened as I sobbed in Emory's arms about everything this prick had put me through. Parental rage is a real thing.

With his eyes fixed on me, Jonathan hadn't registered the threat prowling behind him, but Harriet had and her eyes widened at the sight of Gato's glowing red eyes. They were full of hate and fury and the brimstone of hell. I guess that's where the hounds get their names from.

Seeing Harriet's wide eyes, Jonathan whirled around – but he was too late. Gato was thundering towards him, spikes protruding. He slammed his hard, spiked head into Jonathan's vulnerable gut then wrenched it viciously sideways. Blood sprayed.

I pivoted on my heel and covered Harriet's eyes. 'Don't look,' I murmured. 'You don't need to see this.'

Jonathan let out a surprised gurgle and blood welled from his mouth as he slowly slid to the floor. He pressed his hands to the mess of his stomach, as if to shove his entrails back inside. Gato had been messy.

Harriet tore my fingers from her eyes. 'Yes, I do. He bullied me and beat me virtually every day for the last year. The only regret I have is not killing him myself.'

'You're a child,' I said, horrified.

'I wasn't allowed to be one,' she countered bitterly. 'I may not have had the courage to kill him, but seeing him die will definitely help with my nightmares. They call it closure.'

'I'm sorry,' I offered weakly.

'Why? You didn't burn me or beat me.' She shrugged nonchalantly but her eyes were full of tears.

'I'm sorry you had to live through that.'

'Me too.' She rubbed at her red eyes.

'Let's go.' I tugged her to the door. 'Are there any other kids in the compound?'

'No, just me. I'm the only kid Daddy Dearest would bring to this hell hole.' She tugged back against my hand. 'Wait. I need to see him die to know he's not coming back,' she insisted.

It seemed macabre, but I'd had an idyllic childhood full of love and joy and I couldn't imagine how hard it had been for Harriet. She was only eleven; I hoped we could rescue some of her childhood. She deserved that. Every child did.

Jonathan let out his last breath and Harriet swallowed hard. Then she reached out and kicked him. He slid over and his face struck the carpeted floor. 'Definitely dead,' she pronounced. She paused. 'I thought I'd feel better when he died.'

'I don't think it's an instant thing.'

'No. Maybe not.' She shrugged. 'I'll probably need therapy.'

No shit. She would need a butt-tonne of therapy. 'Shall we go?'

'Please. Get me out of here.' It was an order but there was a note of entreaty in her voice.

I needed to do something with Jonathan's body; it wouldn't do for someone to find him before we were ready. I dragged him into the closet and made him and his blood invisible for the next four hours for good measure. I tied the magic around him and released it. That should do the trick.

'Stay close. I'm going to make us all invisible now,' I said. I wrapped the IR around all three of us, making sure we could still see each other.

The corridors were still empty and I congratulated myself on my decision to go back in time to rescue Harriet. As we crept forward, we passed what must have been Elliot Randall's office. With my dragon-sensitive hearing, I could hear him talking even through the thick door. 'Make sure the daemon is ready,' he said imperiously. 'The pathetic Prime won't stand a chance against the daemon.'

I frowned. We'd been so sure that Elliot was the daemon's host, so that didn't seem right.

'Just do your part,' a familiar voice sneered, 'and I'll do mine. Lure the Prime here and I'll destroy him.'

My stomach lurched. Holy fuck, I knew that voice.

Chapter 28

I hustled us out of the cabin as fast as I could. Before I opened the door, I created a hasty illusion of a cigarette butt starting a fire a few feet away. While the guards were swearing and stamping it out, we slipped out from behind them and made a beeline for the trees.

I giggled a little as Guard One started to shout at Guard Two about his smoking habit. The way Guard Two was looking at him ... I guess smoking really does kill.

'Shit, that was scary.' Harriet finally breathed out when we were in the relative safety of the woods.

'Language!' I chastened.

'Seriously? I just watched your dog maul my brother to death and you're worried about my swears?'

She had a good point. 'He's not a dog, he's a hellhound,' I corrected lamely – because *that* was what was important here.

'Obviously. The spikes and red eyes are a giveaway,' she sassed, though she was eyeing Gato cautiously.

'He's normally very even-tempered,' I assured her. 'But your brother arrested me and beat me, and my hound took it personally.'

'Sure. I get that. Jonathan is – *was* – a wanker.'

'Language!'

She rolled her eyes. She might have been a pre-teen but I was getting total teen vibes off her. She was eleven going on eighteen; eleventeen.

'Come on. Let's hunker down here to wait.' I let the IR go and made us visible again. I didn't want to waste my magical reserves before the main fight started.

'To wait for what?' Harriet asked.

'The cavalry.' I winked.

When I was certain that Emory and the others had arrived, I started us forward again. 'Keep low and out of sight,' I instructed Harriet.

'I thought these were the good guys,' she complained.

'They are,' I confirmed. 'It's complicated.' You're not supposed to tell people about the Third Realm because timey-wimey stuff is supposed to be super-secret. So naturally at least half of the Other realm knows all about it.

I crawled forward and dropped down to do a military crawl.

'Seriously?' she said incredulously, staring at the dry ground with distaste.

'Seriously. Get your backside down.' It was almost certainly unnecessary but, hey, it gave us something to do. Harriet had been looking a bit lost, and sometimes when your mind is being a dick doing something physical helps. Hence army crawling.

With some muttered swearing – which I ignored – she did as I said. We looked ridiculous, but the lost look vanished from her eyes so it was worth it. Together we slowly and laboriously approached the camp of the dragons and brethren.

'Is Evan here?' she whispered, gesturing to the hive of activity.

'No, sorry. He's back at our stronghold. You'll see him later.' When there was only one of me running around, I'd send her away from the warzone. The shit that she'd seen today was enough for any kid. A battle was coming and it was going to be messy and bloody, no place for a child.

We crouched behind some thick foliage to wait. Peering through the leaves, I saw the car that I'd hidden behind when I trotted back in time. Other Me didn't leave us waiting long; I'd timed it to perfection.

Next to me, Harriet frowned. 'Hey, do you have a twin?'

'Nope.'

'Then who is—' Other Me winked out of existence. She turned to me, eyes wide. 'Where did you go?'

'To get you,' I answered lightly. 'Come on.'

'But how were there two of you? There was one there and you here.'

'Don't think too hard about it,' I suggested. 'You'll get a headache.' I tugged her up. 'Come on.'

I took her to the tent where Tom, Emory, Reynard and Shirdal were still poring over blueprints. 'New plan,' I announced as I walked in. 'I got Harriet out.'

Harriet gave an awkward wave. Emory grimaced but said nothing, though he didn't look surprised. He knows me well. Apparently, Elizabeth, Stone and Mike had come in when I had left the tent, but I ignored them for a moment. 'Tom, can you get a brethren team to escort Harriet to Evan?'

Harriet opened her mouth to object. 'You absolutely cannot stay,' I said firmly. 'Go and be safe with your brother.' She huffed but obediently left with Tom.

Emory was looking at me with narrow eyes. 'The Third?' he asked evenly, like he wasn't hopping mad. I missed our bond so much; Emory has a great poker face, but at that moment I was sure steam was coming out of his ears.

'Yup,' I confirmed simply.

Shirdal swore loudly and vociferously.

'Nice,' Reynard complimented him. 'I liked the inventive swear with the donkey and courgette.'

Shirdal ignored him. 'I am flabbergasted. Bamboozled. Bowled over. I am *supposed* to be your guard and you slipped into the cabin without me?' He glared at me and his voice rose an octave. 'Is that blood I spy on your shirt?'.

That is why black is the *couleur du jour* in the Other. 'I spy with my little eye, something that looks like Jonathan Randall,' I joked, as I looked at the splash of blood on my shirt. I grimaced. It was only small but I didn't want to wear a shirt with blood staining it. Especially as it was that prick's blood. But now wasn't the time to be squeamish. That one little splash was going to be joined by others. Soon the ground would be soaked with it.

'You killed him?' Emory tilted his head to study me. I couldn't read his expression. Damn it, I missed the damn bond so much. Was he mad at me? I guessed so.

'Nope.' I shook my head. 'Gato did the killing. He headbutted Jonathan with his spikes.'

Shirdal gave Gato a pat. 'Good man.' Gato pranced smugly, tail high.

'Then they'll know we're fucking coming now,' Reynard asserted, tone grim.

'Possibly, but not necessarily,' I argued. 'I hid the body.'

'Bodies can be found,' Reynard stated pugnaciously.

'I made it invisible for another hour or so. He's wedged in Harriet's wardrobe until then.'

'How did you do that?' Reynard asked, eyebrows shooting up.

'Magic.' I waved my fingers. 'I have the IR as well as my fire and water,' I pointed out.

His expression cleared. 'I forgot about that. You've been stabbed by Glimmer a couple of times.'

'Technically a few times,' I corrected. The first couple of times had been mere nicks and I'd been awarded with fire-elemental and water-elemental powers. The last time had killed me and made me a dragon – a dragon that could lie. Glimmer let me collect powers like other people collected wealth. I did my best not to advertise it because the stronger I became, the more likely it was that someone would try to kill me either because they perceived me as a threat or because they wanted Glimmer for themselves.

'So we've got time.' Reynard relaxed.

'What we've got —' I said grimly '— is a traitor.'

Chapter 29

Shirdal raised an eyebrow. 'Name them and they'll die.'

'Well, shall we talk to them a bit and find out the craic first?' Stone countered evenly, his roots as an officer of the Connection showing. Stone believed in due process.

Shirdal considered it and dismissed it just a quickly. 'Nah, let's just kill the bastard. Who is it?' he asked me.

'We've been operating on the assumption that Elliot Randall is hosting Jadin, but that's wrong. While I was in the cabin, I overhead Randall talking with someone. I recognised the voice straight away.' I turned to Emory. 'It was Leonard. Maybe I wasn't so wrong with my nickname, NotLeo. Leonard is sometimes Jadin. You'd think one of us would have seen his red eyes one time or another.'

'The red eye thing is an affectation – the daemon can be in control and keep the host's eye colour if they want to. They use the natural colour when they want to be incognito and red eyes when they want to intimidate,' Stone explained.

That made sense. When I'd met Lord Cathill, he'd been the vampy member of the symposium. He'd been subsumed by a daemon but he hadn't been red-eyed the whole time.

Emory ignored the by-play and he didn't insult me by asking if I was sure about Leonard's betrayal. His expression never changed and he made no exclamation of shock. I was so used to being privy to his innermost thoughts that it hurt now to be excluded. And it was my own fault, damn it.

'You never liked him,' Emory noted calmly.

'That doesn't mean I'm wrong about this,' I insisted, begging him to believe me.

Emory smiled. 'Of course not. I just meant that you were on the money, as usual. We should always trust your gut. On some level, you knew there was something hinky about Leonard.'

Shirdal held up a hand. 'Can we just take a minute to appreciate the Prime Elite using the word "hinky"?' he chortled.

'This isn't the time for jokes,' Elizabeth said primly and shot Shirdal a disapproving glare.

'We're about to go battle with a daemon and a host of Anti-Crea wizards,' Shirdal said, 'If we don't joke now there won't be time later, and I'm always up for some banter.'

'Pre-battle jitters, ma'am. Some men deal with them by humour,' Mike explained deferentially to Elizabeth.

'Others deal with it with bravado,' Reynard asserted, sliding a look at Shirdal.

'And others deal with it by fucking,' Shirdal replied just as blandly. 'Elizabeth, are you game?'

She sighed and put her head in her hands for a moment. 'Okay. Joke away.'

'Why, thank you for your permission, your high dragon-ness.' Shirdal sketched a bow. Despite herself, Elizabeth's lips twitched.

Tom brought in a bag full of granola bars and started to hand them out. 'Everyone eat something, keep your energy up. Harriet is en route to Caernarfon Castle. What did I miss?'

'Leonard is a traitor,' Shirdal said.

Tom stilled and looked to Emory for confirmation. Emory nodded. 'It appears that he is housing Jadin.'

Tom hauled out his phone and dialled. 'Where is Leonard right now?' he demanded when someone answered.

I heard Veronica's voice. 'He's on his way to help you. He's bringing the Eye of Ebrel, like the Prime requested.'

Tom grimaced and flicked his eyes to Emory. Emory shook his head; he hadn't requested the Eye.

'Leonard is a traitor,' Tom declared. 'He's willingly been subsumed by a daemon.'

Veronica gasped, then there was a pause as she connected all the dots. 'Darius didn't go mad, he was daemon influenced...'

'I suspect so, ma'am. Yes,' Tom agreed.

Veronica swore loudly. 'I'll shore things up here. You be careful. He knows you're coming, and he knows who you've got with you.' She hung up.

'She's right,' I agreed.

'What did she say?' asked Mike. I'd forgotten that not everyone has dragon hearing.

'Sorry. She said Leonard is on his way and he's taken the Eye of Ebrel "like the Prime requested". And he knows exactly how many dragons and brethren we have with us.'

'Then we'd better get some allies he's not expecting,' Mike suggested.

'Got any spare in your pocket?' Shirdal asked drily.

'We've got the dark seraph,' I said. 'He doesn't know about *their* capabilities.'

Elizabeth grimaced. 'Yes, he does. As part of our investigation into the made-brethren, Reynard demonstrated their usefulness by showing us that they could shift their hands into claws.'

I turned to Reynard and studied him carefully. 'Is that all you can do?'

He sent me a wolfish grin. 'No, ma'am.'

I grinned back. 'And I'll call Nate. Leonard won't be expecting any vampyr support.'

'The cabin is owned privately by Randall so they won't be able to phase in,' Shirdal pointed out.

'That's fine. I don't expect the fight in the cabin to last long, not if Emory's destructive rampage earlier on is anything to go by. He'll be Hulk-smashing the heck out of that building before they can say "earthquake".'

Shirdal took a bite of his granola bar and promptly spat it out. 'This tastes like shit.'

'I've always found that phrase funny. Like, who has gone around eating poop to check that it tastes bad?' I asked. '*Does* it even taste bad?' I was genuinely curious.

Emory cleared his throat. 'We've gone off topic. Leonard is heading here with the Eye. Why is the Eye relevant? What can it do?' As one, we all looked at Elizabeth.

She shrugged helplessly. 'I'm not an Elder. I know it's mentioned in the Revival Prophecies and it's supposed to

contain a mighty power. When it turned red for Emory...
' She frowned. 'I wondered then whether it had been in-
terfered with. Leonard would have had plenty of opportunity to toy with it. It was his nephew, Luke Caruso, who
fixed the cameras when the children hid the Eye. Maybe
Leonard took it for his own nefarious purposes, but I've
no idea what purposes those might be.'

'Death's head upon a mop-stick,' Reynard swore.
'Knowing that is as much use as tits on a bull.'

'It tells us to be wary,' Stone noted.

'I'm already as wary as a meerkat on a date with a lion,'
Reynard snorted. 'We're about to go into battle with a
daemon.'

I'd only fought a daemon once before, and I hadn't
known enough to be wary then. But then Cathill had
rained lightning down from the sky and tried to compel
me, and I'd learnt better. Fighting a daemon wouldn't
be easy. 'So what are we waiting for?' I asked lightly. 'An
engraved invitation?'

'No, we're waiting for the elves and the witches,' Emory
said.

I frowned. 'Does Leonard know they're coming to help
us?'

Emory's jaw tightened and that told me the answer.
'Tom,' he ground out, 'get them on the phone. Now.'

Tom hauled out his phone and we listened as the ring tone rang and rang. Nobody answered.

Chapter 30

Reynard and his dark seraph cast into the skies to see if they could ascertain what was keeping the elves and the witches. Fingers crossed it wasn't death because we needed them; they were our only hope of containing the daemon. If containment was out, the only other option was killing the host body – which in this case was an immortal dragon. I'd managed to kill Darius with a stab into his eye, albeit with some difficulty, but he'd been influenced by a daemon and wasn't in his right mind. Leonard wouldn't be so easily dispatched because he wasn't influenced, he was *subsumed*.

Elizabeth was trying to get hold of one of the Elders to find out what the Eye could do, and the brethren were arming up, pulling on guns and ammo. No one bothered with camo paint – we weren't going in stealthily, we were going in hot and heavy and hard. All the H's.

While we waited for things to get moving, Gato sent me to the Common realm so I could have a quick mini-charge. I didn't feel itchy but I didn't want to have to hold anything back. Now I was a dragon, I had no idea whether I even *needed* to recharge but it wasn't a good time to experiment just before a battle.

I ate granola bars and waited impatiently for news.

News didn't arrive but the dark seraph did, carrying the few survivors of the Anti-Creas' attack. So many dead. First Leo Harfen and Erin, and now this. When the elf Caleb Smythe was brought into the staging site, he was vibrating with barely contained fury. Black anger rolled off him in waves. I kept my distance and battened down my mental shields.

Of the fifteen elves Caleb had brought with him, he had four survivors including himself. That was the absolute bare minimum number he would need to contain a daemon. If one of the elves was killed, it was game over.

Reynard and three of his dark seraph, plus a team of ten brethren guards, were tasked with keeping the elvish team alive. For once, Shirdal and Reynard weren't arguing. We all knew that the odds weren't stacking in our favour; Leonard might be a bastard, but he was a smart one.

Of the seven witches – a powerful number – only three had survived. None of them were known to me and I thanked my lucky stars that neither Amber nor Kass had been summoned. I guessed daemons weren't their speciality, or maybe they were off doing other things; whatever it was, I was grateful they hadn't been involved.

The survivors had sent for reinforcements and we sat tight waiting for them. We were on the back foot; every moment meant that Leonard had more time to prepare.

Emory wrapped his arms around me. 'You look pensive, love.'

I rested my head against his shoulder. 'It's going to be messy and a lot of people are going to die.'

'Yes,' he said simply. 'But it's still the right thing to do. We can't let this stand; we can't let their evil flourish just because it's easier to walk away. Every man and woman here knows that they could pay the ultimate price.'

'And you? Would you pay the price?' I asked quietly.

'To keep you safe forever? In a heartbeat,' he said simply.

'Don't you dare,' I ordered. 'We still have so many things to do together.'

'Like getting married and going on the honeymoon to end all honeymoons?'

'Exactly.' I snuggled in. 'It's going to be okay.' *Lie.* I kissed his neck.

'I will do everything in my power to make sure it is,' he promised, using his wordsmithing skills. He hugged me back and I was grateful that we had this moment of calm together.

'I miss our bond,' I admitted. 'I miss having you in my head, knowing what you're feeling. You use your poker-face a lot more around your people.'

'Yes, I miss it too. I miss you. We'll fix it. Elizabeth thinks it might reinstate itself when we marry.' He tucked some loose hair behind my ear. It was telling that he'd missed the bond too and he'd discussed it with Elizabeth.

'Does she really?' I asked hopefully. 'That would be great.'

'Something to look forward to.' He kissed the tip of my nose, making me smile.

Tom poked his head around the tent flap. 'The vampyrs have arrived and they've brought the witches with them.'

Amber pushed past him. 'It seemed expedient at the time – but good gravy, phasing is cold. It'll take me a week to feel warm again.'

At the sight of Amber, I was instantly conflicted. I was glad to see her brusque competent ass, but I wanted all of my friends and loved ones far from this conflict. I recognised, though, that it wasn't up to me to dictate their actions. 'I'm glad to see you Amber.'

'Can't let you get all the glory, can I? I managed to contain Cathill. I'll get Jadin too.' She looked confident.

Stone walked in. 'Cathill's daemon was low level but Jadin is a Lord. This isn't going to be easy.'

Amber looked at him. 'You're looking remarkably well for someone who's dead.' She paused. 'It's good to see you still breathing, Stone.'

'Back at you, DeLea.'

'Can your daemon keep Jadin busy?'

Stone's eyes flashed red. 'We'll do our best. But if you put one crystal near me, I'm leaving you to deal with him.'

'That's fair. I've used small words with the elves, to make sure they understand you're not to be contained.' She studied Stone. 'The elves' fanaticism is directed at Jadin for now because of their losses, but I'd make a hasty and strategic retreat after the battle is done.'

'Noted. I won't hang around,' Stone promised.

'Don't.'

Stone took in Emory and I twined in each other's arms but he didn't say anything or so much as grimace. Maybe he really was over me. I was honest enough to admit to the tiniest twinge of regret – everyone likes to be wanted – though that thought didn't make me feel like I was a good person.

'Shirdal,' Emory called. 'You're on Amber. Keep her safe at all costs.'

Shirdal's lips pressed into a firm line. He cast a glance at me, but nevertheless he nodded. 'Yes, Prime.'

Now the witches, elves and vampyrs had arrived, we had time for a quick council of war. Hopefully Jadin wasn't expecting us to source reinforcements so quickly, but it was probably wishful thinking to hope that we still had an element of surprise.

Lord Volderiss looked as calm as ever. His dark hair was streaked with silver but it was an affectation. Vampyrs can choose to appear any age that they like, and Volderiss chose to look like a wise silver fox. Next to him was his secretary, Verona. Her ice-blonde hair was pulled into a long plait and her stunning blue eyes were sharp. She pursed her blood-red lips at me but said nothing. Today she was battle ready in black leather trousers, a black corset and a leather jacket.

Lord Volderiss looked at me. 'Is there any chance that I can persuade you to stay out of the coming conflict?'

I knew that his request was not out of concern for me, but for his son Nate. The master-slave bond between us was unusual, and no one was certain what would happen if one of us truly died. My flash in the pan death had lasted mere seconds – it had been enough to sever the bond with Emory but not Nate. What would happen to Nate if I permanently died and he was stuck bound to me? I guessed that it was good news for Nate that I had become an immortal dragon so neither of us would be dying of natural causes any time soon.

'No,' I answered. 'There is absolutely zero chance of me hiding in a tent while the rest of you try and fight the daemon.'

His lips tightened.

'Told you,' Nate smirked.

'I'll stay with the rear guard,' I compromised. 'Until I'm needed. I'll be ready to protect Amber.'

'How many men do you have?' Emory asked Lord Volderiss.

Volderiss folded his arms and leaned back in his chair. 'Fifty. That is by no means the extent of our power, but it should be sufficient for a skirmish like this.'

'And your men are fully aware that it is the Anti-Crea wizards that they are here for, not the dragons or the brethren?' Emory's eyes were hard.

Volderiss's eyes grew similarly flinty. 'They know what we're here for.'

That was all we needed; dragons and vampyrs get along like the Crips and the Bloods, and we didn't want this battle to descend into a feud. The vampyrs were here because of me and Nate, nothing more, nothing less.

'We'll need to get close enough to Leonard to place the crystals around him,' Caleb explained. 'I could do with a few vampyrs to run interference.'

'You have ten brethren, one griffin and a dark seraph,' Emory objected.

'All it takes is one of our elves to die and we're completely fucked,' Caleb said flatly.

'You can have five of my vampyrs,' Lord Volderiss offered. He turned to his secretary. 'Verona, select four others.'

'Yes, my lord.' She bowed and slid out of the room.

'Shall we, then?' I asked. 'There's no time like the present.'

'Are you in a hurry to die?' Lord Volderiss asked. He sounded genuinely interested.

'I'm a dragon shifter now,' I admitted. It was better that my allies learned that now than being shocked if I shifted on the battlefield.

Lord Volderiss raised an elegant eyebrow. 'And how did you accomplish that?' He answered his own question a beat later. 'Glimmer.' He grimaced. 'We should never have let you keep that damned thing.'

'I can't give it back to you. I've tried.'

'I'm aware of that. You seem to attract bonds like metal to a magnet,' he complained humorously.

'It's my winning personality.'

'No doubt.' Volderiss stood back from the table. 'The vampyrs and brethren are here to battle the wizards with their IR. We are to keep the elves safe so that they can contain Jadin. That's it. The best plans are the simplest ones.'

Through the flimsy tent material we heard the sound of a truck or something pulling up. 'Looks like the tank is here,' Emory said cheerfully. A tank? I wondered if he was kidding. 'It's go time. Stone, you distract Jadin while the elves contain him. Amber, keep out of the way until Jadin's contained then rune him to hell and back. Everyone else, keep the Anti-Crea busy. Let's move.'

I cleared my throat. 'Should we warn Lord Volderiss about the dark seraph?'

'Should you?' asked Lord Volderiss flatly.

'We have some airborne brethren,' Emory explained, without giving too much detail. 'Tell your men to ignore them, too.'

'More secrets, Elite?' Volderiss sneered.

Emory smiled, but there was nothing friendly about it. I stood up, drawing all eyes to me and breaking the tension that crackled between the two old enemies.

'Gato,' I called. 'Send me back to the Other. It's go time.'

Chapter 31

It turned out that Emory wasn't kidding about the tank. The truck-like sound was a black M1 Abrams armoured tank, complete with a huge cannon fastened on the top of it. Magic is all well and good, but nothing blasts a hole quite like a tank.

We followed it, letting it set our pace. I expected a tank to be slow and lumbering but it powered forward, sending up a spray of mud splatter. A team of brethren had been working on clearing the underbrush but they needn't have bothered; the tank was an all-terrain vehicle, all right. We trotted alongside it, making swift progress, eating the distance between us and the cabin in no time at all.

I was feeling edgy and nervous. I was a dragon shifter, and I had no idea what that meant for me in an aerial combat situation. When I'd flown with Elizabeth, I'd used my instincts to guide me; hopefully I'd be able to wing it this time as well.

I was jogging next to Emory and his fingers were laced casually through mine. If it hadn't been for the army of soldiers around us and the tank, it would have been quite romantic.

'Does Leonard know about the tank?' I asked, expecting Emory to say yes.

He flashed me a grin, 'Nope. This isn't the dragon's tank; it's my personal one. Leonard's never heard it mentioned.'

'And how does one go about acquiring a tank?' I asked curiously.

'Carefully,' Shirdal quipped.

Emory ignored him. 'From the US Army. I got an old, decommissioned one and fixed it up good as new.'

'That must have cost an arm and a leg,' I noted.

'And most of a torso.' Shirdal grinned.

I rolled my eyes at him, but I bore Mike's earlier comment in mind. Everyone deals with pre-battle jitters in a different way. I was dealing with them by being in denial about what was coming and Shirdal was dealing with them with jokes. My stomach was churning and I was feeling almost nauseous with worry and fear. When it started I'd be fine because adrenaline kicks in and does its thing. But beforehand ... the anxiety was crippling me.

I was relieved that Gato was pacing beside us, already shifted into battle cat form. His presence was solid and reassuring.

We reached the edge of the forest and advanced onto the exposed flatlands. The cabin looked like an old fort; its red-brick structure even had a protective wall running along the front of it. There was a high turret to keep watch from, similar to the one in which I'd been kept hostage.

No doubt alarms were blaring as our forces approached, but at least we didn't have to worry about any Common realmers stumbling across us. Anyone who was here was preparing to do battle. The only ones besides us were the Anti-Crea.

I knew our focus had to be Leonard and his daemon, but I wasn't letting Elliot Randall get away. He'd burned me. I wasn't his first victim – but I was going to be his last. Anxiety slipped away from me, replaced by grim determination.

I gave Emory's hand one last squeeze before releasing it. I wished we'd had time for another kiss, but I'd always wish for that. With my hands free, I took Glimmer from my belt. 'Shall we make you into a nice lightweight sword?' I suggested to the sentient blade. It trilled happily in my head.

Obligingly, Glimmer grew, though its weight remained light and manageable. I gave it an experimental swing and it made a pleasant swishing sound as it cut through the air. I probably wouldn't need it, but it was reassuring to have it in my hand.

Emory gave me a hard kiss. 'Be careful,' he murmured against my lips.

'And you. Let's kick some Anti-Crea butt.'

Emory shifted into his red dragon form and his golden wings beat the air as he flew skywards. A moment later Elizabeth launched her emerald-green body into the air next to him, golden wings effortlessly lifting her up high. They landed on the turret and started beating the walls with their spiked tails. The masonry shook but held against their onslaught.

The tank rolled forward and started its assault on the building. Its huge cannon rocketed back expelling a gargantuan shell casing after each shot, and soon the floor was littered with them. The brethren hustled up with more ammo and the tank continued firing until the front doors – and most of the front wall – started to crumble.

Now the party was getting started. Emory and Elizabeth flew down to the weakened walls and bricks rained down as they pulverised the walls. Wizards poured out of the building, obviously deciding that outside was now safer than inside. Everything is relative.

The brethren raised their guns and fired a volley at the wizards – but they were ready. The bullets struck a wall of solid air and slid to the ground uselessly, so we sent in the vampyrs. They ran so fast that you couldn't follow their movements but, as they launched themselves at the wizards, other vampyrs entered the fray on the side of the Anti-Crea.

I recognised one of them as the sneering vampyr from the bar in Liverpool; it felt like half a lifetime ago that I'd encountered him. At least he was putting his money where his mouth was.

The vampyrs were now fighting and the brethren were surging towards the wizards with guns and knives. The distraction of the vampyrs meant that a few of the wizards had lost their anti-bullet shields, but only a few of them. Then a few fire elementals came out to play on the side of the Anti-Crea. I *knew* Roscoe had been lying when he'd said he didn't have any rogues.

'Reynard!' I heard Tom shout. 'We need you!'

The sky above us darkened with hundreds of dark-winged seraph. They swooped towards the brethren as fire swept towards them. The flames hit the dark seraphs' black wings with no noticeable effect before they died away. Half of the dark seraph stayed to protect the brethren foot soldiers, while the other half took to the skies and flew towards the wizards. The wizards weren't prepared for attacks from above. The dark seraph shifted their hands into lethal claws and ripped into the enemy.

Your imagination is your limit with the IR, though I knew from experience that it was hard to come up with ideas when fear was crippling you. The wizards were Anti-Crea, but they weren't soldiers. They had far greater numbers than us, but we were trained and they were not.

I watched as Elizabeth abruptly shifted back to human form, clung onto the roof of the cabin and answered her phone. 'Now isn't the time for a chit-chat, Elizabeth!' I wanted to yell at her but I was too far away. Even with my new sharper-than-a-bat's hearing, I couldn't hear the conversation but I could see her swearing and waving her arms wildly at Emory. He swooped closer so she could tell him her news, then he let out a jet of flames. Not good news, then, whatever it was.

There was a loud roar and Leonard entered the fray, only it wasn't mild-mannered Leonard that rolled in but a red-eyed daemon dragon. His blue body climbed into the air and he roared a challenge at Emory.

Chapter 32

The battlefield was a chaotic maelstrom of fire and fury as the two armies clashed. Leonard's wizards took heart at the sight of his daemonic appearance and started their attack with renewed frenzy. Suddenly rocks were flying in the air and trees were being torn from the earth and flung at the soldiers.

The brethren weren't fazed by whirling rocks and timber. They stayed low as they fired their guns in rapid succession; the sharp cracks echoing through the air. They advanced grimly on the Anti-Crea; the deaths of Jackie and Dave were being avenged and no mercy was forthcoming.

Leonard screamed his fury as the brethren continued to gain ground. He accessed even more of his daemonic power and lightning bolts streaked across the sky, setting the ground ablaze. The bolts struck the brethren and the screaming started.

Emory dived down, jaws snapping at the wizards as his soldiers fought tooth and nail on the ground. He roared fire and the wizards cowered under a shield of ever-depleting air.

Leonard entered the fray once more. He sent a burst of fire towards the brethren, who were shielded by the feathers of their made-brethren counterparts. Where was Stone? He and Khalt were supposed to be dealing with Leonard, but they were nowhere to be seen.

Emory reached the same conclusion and wheeled around, clashing with Leonard mid-air. Their massive bodies collided with such force that it shook the very earth. Emory's sharp claws raked against Leonard scales while Leonard countered with a violent snap of his jaws at Emory's exposed neck. The two dragons spiralled and soared, biting and clawing, locked in a deadly aerial duel that made my heart hammer.

On the ground, Emory's brethren were moving forward and gaining ground. The wizards were distracted by the aerial combat, so now the brethren's guns and knives came into play. Their disciplined tactics and modern weaponry were proving a formidable force against magic itself, and they advanced with calculated precision, taking cover behind the tank and barricades and returning the wizards' magical fire with deadly accuracy.

Where the fuck was Stone? He should have been fighting Jadin. Had we been played? My stomach lurched at the thought, but I'd never sensed any duplicity from him or Khalt. Surely they were on our side?

One of the wizards ran out. 'My Lord,' he cried. 'Here!' He threw something up into the air that Leonard swooped and caught with his claws. I saw it glint in the sunlight – it was the Eye of Ebrel.

'What does it do?' I shouted at Elizabeth as she flew overhead.

'He can use it to open a gateway to the daemon dimension! It needs dragon blood to activate it,' she called back. Fuck. We didn't want that. And the problem was that Leonard had dragon's blood in spades.

The rogue fire elementals were throwing fireballs at the brethren whom the dark seraph were shielding. The fire wasn't the killing blow that the Anti-Crea needed it to be, but it slowed the brethren's advance and reduced their capacity for the deadly hand-to-hand combat at which they so excelled.

Emory dived at Leonard. This time Leonard reacted too slowly because he was gazing at the Eye. His lapse allowed Emory to snap his jaws around Leonard's wing and tear through its delicate membranes. Leonard cried out in pain and plummeted towards the ground. Screaming his fury, he landed awkwardly – but on his feet. Damn.

Suddenly I was enveloped in a rage so fierce that it took my breath away. The urge to destroy everyone around me swept over me and I wanted to lash out at my companions. I raised Glimmer towards Amber.

'What the heck? Jinx! Get a grip of yourself. The daemon is controlling you! Jinx!'

Amber's pleas had no impact on me but Glimmer's song did. It screamed loudly, cutting through the sudden fog in my head. I blinked my eyes and suddenly saw the brethren all around me. They were raising their weapons *at each other!* Emory was screaming at them, but they were ignoring him.

I lowered Glimmer, ripped down my mental shields and threw my consciousness around me. I pictured it snowing in my mind, pictured the soldiers lowering their weapons. I had no time for finesse; I *forced* calm on them all.

The guns were lowered slowly and I panted with relief. It was hard to maintain that calming effect on so many people but, with the daemon's hold on them broken, I let the calm go.

It was time to get my hands dirty.

'Gato, protect Amber,' I ordered. I felt far from relaxed, but I was calm and centred. I called up the mental waves in my head and shimmered and twisted into my silver dragon form. It was still so new, so novel to be a dragon that I wanted to marvel at my claws, my wings. But there was no time for such frivolities. Instead, I launched myself skywards and flew to where Leonard was resting, the jewel clutched in his claws. A moment later he shimmered into human form and then back into dragon form, a split-second shift, if that. Now he stood in dragon form again with all signs of his injuries gone. His wing had healed in his shift. Dammit!

He saw me coming and he looked furious. 'You don't deserve to fly,' he screamed at me and threw a lightning bolt. 'You're not a dragon!'

I felt the air crackle and I dived steeply to stop it hitting me. It struck the ground and exploded. Jeez. 'What's got your knickers in a twist, *NotLeo*?' I taunted. 'Give me the Eye and we can all go our separate ways.' Yeah, right. *Lie.*

Leonard snorted.

'JADIN!' Khalt roared, eyes red. Stone had finally entered the fray. I had no idea what had been keeping him.

'KHALT!' Jadin screamed back, his eyes bleeding red.

Khalt summoned his own lightning bolt and Jadin screamed as Khalt successfully struck his tail. His flesh singed and burned. I left the two daemons to it, because suddenly I had spotted someone else: Randall.

I flew to him and shifted back to human form. 'You're going to die,' I snarled at him and swung Glimmer in the air.

He laughed as Glimmer struck a solid wall of air. 'I've been using the IR longer than you've been breathing,' he said smugly. 'You're not going to kill me with that puny little knife.'

I felt Glimmer's annoyance at such a description. It shoved me aside, taking control of my limbs so it could hack at Randall. Again and again Glimmer rained blows down on him until he lost his cocky expression. His forehead was creased in concentration as he focused on holding me back.

'He's not dead you know,' I spat out, in an effort to distract him.

'What?'

'Your son, Evan. He lives and breathes. His neck has healed nicely. And now we're going to raise Harriet with him. Both of them will become creature-lovers,' I taunted.

Randall screamed at me and drew his own blade. It was mediocre in comparison to Glimmer but, mediocre or not, it still had a sharp pointy end. I'd wrestled control back from Glimmer to taunt Randall, but now I hastily tried to shove it back. I'd done my fair share of martial arts training but I had few knife-fighting skills. Randall gave me a hard shove and I stumbled backwards and tripped on a large rock behind me. As I fell, Glimmer went spinning out of my hand. Fuckity-fuck.

Randall didn't hesitate to press his advantage and flew towards me, blade swinging. My brain seemed to have stopped working and I couldn't gather the intention. The blade moved towards me as if in slow motion.

It never reached me – but Mike Carter did. He thrust himself in the way of the dagger and saved my life. Randall's blade sliced through Mike's jugular and his lifeblood started to pour out of him, thick and red. He fell to his knees in front of me before toppling, eyes glassy and empty.

'Mike! Oh my god, Mike!' I scrambled to my feet and hurried to his body. As I turned him over, his lifeless eyes stared back at me. They would haunt me for the rest of my life.

Rage consumed me. I picked up Glimmer and ran at Randall. I didn't need to give Glimmer control this time because my own rage was fully in control. I whaled on Randall and it was his turn to stumble back. I hit his blade with force and it spun from his hand.

I didn't give him time to regroup and gather his intention; I just shoved my sword into his chest with all of my might. It cut through bone, sinew and heart. I felt nothing but grim satisfaction as I pulled Glimmer free from Randall's body and he toppled forward, dead. Mike had been avenged.

Randall was dead, but at what cost? How many lay dead on the battleground? I surveyed the scene grimly. There were unmoving bodies as far as I could see. Too many. Far too many.

Chapter 33

Rage swept through me. This was Leonard's fault; this whole thing was his fault. People were dying – brethren, vampyr and wizard alike – all because Jadin wanted a jaunt in the Other realm and Leonard had happily hosted him. And for what? If I had to guess, then it would be that age-old temptress, power.

Leonard had infected an Elder, Darius; was that because he had his eye on becoming an Elder? Or maybe that was only a test run before he took a more serious swing at Emory, because it was definitely Emory who was in Leonard's crosshairs. It was Emory whom Leonard had booted out of office, Emory who had lost his Primeship. And my association with Emory had painted a target on my back, too.

Leonard and I had taken a dislike to each other, but I suspected it was more because he'd wanted to keep Emory too busy worrying about me to worry about himself. Leonard had sneaked up and betrayed him. That was enough for Leonard and Jadin to strike a deal – a deal made in hell. They both wanted us destroyed.

Well, enough was enough.

Still in human form, still with Mike's cooling blood covering my hands, I picked up Glimmer and ran across the battlefield. I found Caleb Smythe and his team hidden in the shadows, waiting for their time to strike. It was now; the daemon was going down *now.*

Stone and Leonard – or rather Khalt and Jadin – were locked in a deadly battle. They seemed evenly matched and were flinging everything they had at each other. Air whipped between them one moment, lightning bolts fired down the next, then they were throwing balls of fire. No matter what they did, neither of them managed to get the edge.

Now *I* was going to give Stone the edge. 'When he's still,' I ordered Caleb, pointing at Leonard, 'set the damned crystals and signal someone to fetch Amber.'

Caleb nodded and gestured for his team to spread out. His face was grimly determined; he owed the daemon for the deaths of his team, too. We were all on Team Reckoning.

I reached into myself, not for the rage that was burning in me but for the fear, the fear I had felt when I was held against my will. The fear I had felt as I was slowly burned. The fear that the bond between Emory and I was gone forever. The fear that we would never have a child together. The fear that the future I could give Emory without a child of our own would not be quite enough.

I wrenched the anguish and dread up from my soul and threw my terror at the daemon. Let *him* feel the paralysing fear that he had given me. As I tossed it out to him, I let it leave me. It was cathartic and freeing. Good decisions didn't come from fear.

Jadin froze, immobile, eyes wide in shock as my fear took hold of him.

'Stone!' I yelled. When he turned to me, his eyes flashed brown, I threw Glimmer to him. He caught it effortlessly and grew the blade into a sword. Damn it – it had taken me *months* to learn how to do that.

Stone flicked his lighter and summoned the resulting flame onto the blade. In a heartbeat, Glimmer burned white hot. Without a change in his expression, Stone be-headed Jadin while the daemon was standing frozen with fear. Stone had always been good at beheading. I expect it was the top line on his CV.

Stone's eyes flashed red. Khalt knelt swiftly and grabbed the Eye of Ebrel that was still clutched in Leonard's claws. He dunked the jewel in the blood that was still gushing from Leonard's neck and the Eye turned red as it soaked it up. There was a beat of total silence on the battleground and then the Eye flashed a pulse of white energy, making our bodies thrum. As the pulse sent me sprawling onto my ass for the second time that day, I looked up to see a blood-red portal appearing.

Khalt had opened a gate to the daemon dimension.

Betrayal rocketed through me. I scrambled to my feet and summoned a fireball, growing it in my hands.

Khalt looked at me sardonically. 'Ye of little faith,' he murmured, his red eyes amused. 'We need a way to get home. I don't want to be locked in by crystals.' He threw Glimmer to me. 'Thanks for the blade. We'll see you around.'

He strode into the portal with the Eye of Ebrel still pulsing in his fist. Once he was in his realm, he turned and watched us as the portal slowly closed. He gave me a mocking finger wave before he winked out of sight.

'Fuck,' Caleb swore loudly.

I wasn't sure how I felt about Khalt and Stone's exit. It was something to think about on another day. With the death of their leader, the enemy vampyrs phased away and the remaining Ante-Crea wizards held up their hands in surrender. The day was won, but at what cost?

For now, we had the dead to attend to.

Chapter 34

The battleground was chaotic. There were dead on both sides, but the Anti-Crea had come out of the affair significantly worse. Yes, there had been more of them, but with the brethren's guns, the tank, the dark seraph and a big dose of dragon fire, there were very few left alive. The survivors were rounded up and Amber set to work healing them. I had no idea what we would do with them. Perhaps Elvira would be getting another call soon.

The death toll was heavy on our side, too. Leonard had been liberal with his lightning bolts, and a number of brethren had been brained by rocks or flying trees. The vampyrs had mainly battled with each other, so it was hard for us to tell the number of casualties because the undead returned to dust once they were permanently dead. With all the air power swirling around, no doubt their ashes were thoroughly spread around by now.

Shirdal was grumpy. 'I didn't get to kill anyone. That's just not right. Protecting Amber should have put me in the thick of it but no – Reynard had to get all the glory. Did you see that the dark seraph turned their heads into actual wolves, like some sort of hybrid griffin cousin?' There was pride in his voice.

'Their heads turned into wolves?' I said incredulously.

'Complete with bloody maws. They ripped into the wizards. It was brilliant.' Shirdal sighed happily like an enamoured maiden.

That made me grin. 'I missed that. How did I miss that?'

'You were probably focused more on the dragons and daemons,' Shirdal offered.

'True,' I agreed.

'Did you get Randall?' he asked curiously.

Grief and regret body-slammed into me. 'Yes.'

Shirdal grinned. 'Good for you.'

'Not really. Mike Carter died.' I swallowed against the sudden rock in my throat. 'He died protecting me.'

'Oh, sweetheart.' Shirdal pulled me into a hug. 'He went out in a blaze of glory,' he murmured, his voice suspiciously thick. 'We'll write a song about him.'

My eyes burning, I nodded. A tear slid down my cheek. Shirdal released me and dashed it away. 'Let's get you home.'

Where was home now? The castle, or my little three-bedroom house in Bromborough? Shirdal read my thoughts. 'The castle, Prima. The castle is your home now.'

I guessed he was right. Also, Evan and Harriet were there and I had some horrible news to tell them. Vile as he was, Randall had been their father and now he was dead. It wasn't a cause for celebration.

Nate zoomed up to me. 'We're leaving. The other vampyrs are dead or gone, and it's hard for us with all of this blood in the air. We're going to leave before the urge to snack on one of the dead brethren overtakes our reason.'

'That wouldn't be well received,' I agreed.

'No doubt.' He studied me. 'Are you okay?'

'One of my friends died.'

'I'm sorry.' He looked at the grisly scene. 'I'm afraid you're not the only one who lost someone today.'

'No, you're right. How did you all fare?'

'We lost a few, mostly the more junior vampyrs. Father is on the warpath. At least five of the other side were part of the Red Guard and he's muttering about conspiracies.'

'How does your dad feel about Hes?'

'A vampyr that doesn't need blood to survive?' he asked drily. 'He can't decide if she's the future or an abomination.'

'Best keep an eye on her then,' I suggested.

'I'm on it. I'll keep her safe. For now, my protection is enough.'

'Until it isn't,' I warned.

He accepted the comment grimly. 'Indeed.' He kissed my cheek. 'Call me if you need me.'

'Always.'

Nate flashed me a brilliant smile that made my heart lift a little, then he stepped into the shadow of a tree and phased away.

'You look like poop,' Amber commented.

'Mike died.'

'Carter? Oh damn.' She paused. 'Does Summer know?'

I shook my head. 'Not yet. We'll do the death notifications once we're home.'

Amber grimaced. 'I'll come back with you in case she needs something to help soothe her.'

I smiled and pulled her into a hug. She stood stiffly, enduring it. 'You're the best,' I said.

'Don't spread it around. I have a reputation to protect.' Her voice was firm but I could tell she was faintly embarrassed at revealing some of her soft heart.

I mimed zipping my lips shut and she rolled her eyes at me. 'Have you healed everyone?' I asked, releasing her and changing the subject.

'Not everyone. I'm not a god.'

'Could have fooled me.' I nudged her.

'I healed everyone who would have died without inter-vention. The broken limbs and concussions will have to wait until we're back at the castle. Emory has summoned helicopters.'

Of course he had. 'Talking of Emory, if you'll excuse me I'm going to find him.' I left Amber with Shirdal still keeping a watchful eye on her.

Caleb and his elves had long since disappeared, taking their daemon-capturing crystals and staffs with them, and the vampyrs were melting away. Soon only the brethren and the dead were left.

Chapter 35

Emory was talking quietly with Tom. He had shucked off his customary suit jacket and his shirt sleeves were rolled up past his elbows, exposing the muscled forearms that I drooled over. He looked a little tired and there was a hint of stubble on his chin, but he was still alive, thank God.

And he was mine. I took a moment to be incredibly grateful for what we had. Throwing all my fear at Jadin like that had really lightened my soul. I had discarded my worries in a way I'd never been able to do before, and I felt at peace. If I'd died today, I would have only had one regret and that would have been not marrying Emory. I wanted – *needed* – us to spend our lives together, to have the hundreds of shared experiences that truly make a life together. Our future might not hold children, but it would hold *something,* something we could build and treasure.

Emory looked up and caught me staring at him, and his eyes softened with love. I could almost feel the rush of love from him that used to cascade down our bond. Our bond was silent but I knew that he loved me like I loved him, utterly and completely. 'Hello, Jessica Sharp,' he greeted me.

'Hi.' I moved closer but restrained myself from pulling him into a hug. If I had a hug, I'd want a kiss, and PDAs were a no-no.

Emory closed the distance until you couldn't have slipped a piece of paper between us. He looked into my eyes. 'Hi,' he repeated.

'Hi.'

He leaned down slowly, giving me plenty of time to pull away if I wanted to. But I didn't want to. His lips, firm and full, brushed against mine and his tongue demanded entry. I relented to his demands, sliding my eyes closed as I let myself just feel. When we pulled apart we were both breathing heavily.

'What happened to the no PDA rule?' I panted.

'It's a stupid fucking rule.'

'Still no to a *fucking* PDA,' I joked weakly.

He flashed me a grin. 'We'll see.'

I flushed. He could talk me into anything. He was a bad influence – but man, I loved it. 'Take me home?' I asked.

'Yes. Let's go. Chris is two minutes out. Tom, I'll leave you with the clean-up.'

'Yes, Prime. I'll alert Elvira, as we discussed.'

I looped my arm through Emory's as we walked away. 'We're clueing in the Connection?'

'We have to. There are too many dead to sweep under the carpet – they'd make the floor lumpy.'

'I guess it would be hard to hide hundreds of people suddenly disappearing.'

'Yes – and the families deserve closure,' Emory said sombrely. 'There are bodies to bury and Elvira can co-ordinate it. Let's go.'

'What was the deal with the Eye?'

'Elizabeth thinks that Leonard tampered with it somehow, and that's why it glowed red. It's all conjecture of course.'

'That sucks, but what I meant was, what about the Eye being stolen by Stone and Khalt?'

'Let's not borrow trouble right now, but maybe one day we'll take a jaunt into the Daemon realm and steal it back.'

I grinned. 'You know I love a heist.'

The familiar whir of the helicopter sounded overhead. Emory and I had a moment of privacy before we'd be surrounded again, so I took the opportunity to tell him about the crazy thought in my head. 'I think we should get married,' I blurted out.

He froze mid-step and looked at me, a grin tugging at his lips. 'We *are* already engaged, right? I distinctly remember proposing.'

I grinned back at him, parroting the words I'd said to him what felt like an age ago. 'I didn't say we should get *engaged*. I said, we should get *married*. Let's just do it.'

'Vegas or Gretna Green?' he asked with a smirk.

'The castle. Home. I don't want to go another day not being married to you. I don't care about the day, the dress, the cake. I want you. I want to be married to you. Can we do that, please?'

'To be clear, you want to get married *today*?'

'Yes.' I nodded firmly. 'Today. We could have died, both of us. Life is too short.'

'I'm not sure the seer will be available at such short notice.'

'Screw the seer – anyway, she was weird. Let's just have Reynard marry us. I don't need a big ceremony with a bunch of people there in fancy clothes, I just need you.'

Emory smiled and his expression lightened. 'Back at you. Just give me a second.' He trotted back to Tom and gave him some super-secret instructions. Tom beamed at me and gave me two thumbs up.

It had been one hell of a day, filled with stress and death and misery. Now it was time to turn it around and end it with some much-needed life-affirming happiness. I was going to have my wedding day. And if anyone tried to arrest me this time, I was going to set them on fire.

Chapter 36

The whirring wasn't the sound of one inbound helicopter but a whole fleet of them. They landed on the battle-field and medical personnel started rushing out to help the wounded. Amber took charge, imperiously ordering people around and pointing to the injured men in the correct order of triage.

They had it under control, so Emory and I went to Chris's helicopter to head for home. Gato, Shirdal and Reynard joined us. I politely ignored the way the two men quickly checked each other over for injuries.

'You're all right?' Shirdal murmured to Reynard. His whisper was quiet but my super-hearing picked it up easily. Emory flicked me a warning look and I rolled my eyes. Of course I wasn't going to mention it. I'd give them the illusion of privacy, if nothing else.

'I'm okay,' Reynard admitted, also keeping his voice low.

'Nice trick with the wolf head,' Shirdal gestured to his face.

Reynard smiled, blue eyes warm. 'Thanks.'

'Did your wolf come back to you?' Shirdal asked curiously.

Reynard's smile wilted off his face. 'No,' he said shortly. There was a world of pain and loss in that one word.

'I'm so sorry.' Shirdal touched his arm lightly.

'Don't be. Maybe later you can help me forget.'

'I can do that,' Shirdal promised. The two men separated, both still in their winged forms, ready to escort our helicopter. I suppressed a squeal of excitement. Maybe Emory and I wouldn't be the only ones getting our happy on.

We climbed into the helicopter. Gato turned three times and laid down on the floor. We did up our safety harnesses and put on our headsets. I toggled mine, 'Chris?'

'Yes, Prima?'

'Do you remember how I once asked you to fly me to my wedding?' I asked him.

'Yes?'

'This is it. Emory and I are getting married today, come rain, shine or snow. So make the flight memorable,' I instructed.

'Yes, ma'am!' I heard the grin in his voice and we took off, leaving the battle behind us in more ways than one.

Chris took me at my word and flew us the scenic route home, showing us rivers and mountains, the beach and the sea. He dipped low, skimming the land, then rose as we passed Llanddwyn Island. I saw the phoenix; the sun was setting and she was coming into her own power. She must have been at her biggest size because, even with so much distance between us, I could see her watching us with her beady eyes as she threw back her head and breathed a fireball into the air. It could have been a greeting or a threat, but I chose to believe it was the former.

The sun was glinting off the stunning landscape all around us, casting an orange glow as it made its way to bed. Burnt orange mixed with light lilac, giving the sky a pinkish-red hue unlike anything I'd seen before. It was a unique sunset for our wedding night.

Chris had taken us the long route so we had plenty of time to talk. As Gato rested his heavy head on my knee, I missed Indy's exuberant presence. A battle wasn't the place for a pup any more than it was for a child, but I missed our bitey little lady. She had wormed her destructive way into my heart.

Finally we turned towards the castle and I saw that some of Elizabeth and Tom's secret instructions had borne fruit.

Someone had erected a wooden gazebo in the courtyard and laid out chairs. Twinkling fairy lights wound around the gazebo, giving it a soft glow as evening drew in. The aisle was marked by torches of burning oil thrust into the earth. It was rustic and beautiful in its simplicity.

Chris set us down on the helipad atop one of the castle towers and Emory helped me out. 'Thank you, Chris. That was a perfect flight,' I called.

He climbed out and saluted me. 'I'm honoured to serve you, Prima.' As he bowed low I felt faintly awkward but I ignored it because it was my issue, not his.

'Thank you.' I didn't even bitch about his salute; we all needed our crutches to get through today.

Shirdal and Reynard landed next to the helicopter and Shirdal shimmered into human form. 'Thank you, both of you,' Emory said. 'And Reynard, please extend my thanks to the dark seraph. They did me proud today.'

Reynard puffed out his chest. 'We are honoured to serve you, Lord Prime Elite.'

'Prime Elite is probably enough,' I suggested and grinned, trying to lighten the mood. 'How much did it kill you not to swear just then?'

'So bloody much,' Reynard growled.

'We have something to ask you Reynard,' I said. 'We would be honoured if you would officiate at our wedding – tonight.'

Reynard stilled. 'It would be my honour,' he said finally, his voice choked with emotion. 'I promise not to swear during the fucking ceremony.'

I laughed. 'Don't worry about it. Just be you and it'll be perfect.'

Reynard went down on one knee. 'As you will it, Prima.'

'Erm, thank you. Yes.'

Emory flashed me a grin at my dorkiness, took my arm and led me into the castle. We left Shirdal and Reynard to have a moment alone.

The corridors and rooms were eerily empty of brethren who were still heading back from the cabin. No doubt our soldiers would be joining us soon.

'We need to do some death notifications,' I said regretfully. Man, I didn't want to do those. I had found my parents' bodies when I was eighteen and I'd never had a formal death notification, but I still remembered the cop who'd tried to comfort me. He had offered empty platitudes which had enraged me, even though I knew I was being unfair.

'Tom has already passed the list of the dead to Veronica and she's been doing them. They should be finished by now.' That made sense: Veronica headed and ran the brethren and they were at the heart of everything she did. If it were me, I'd want to receive heavy news from her.

'Evan, Harriet?' I asked.

'She's spoken to them too,' Emory confirmed.

'We should still speak to them. And I'd like to speak to Robbie, Mike's brother, and to Summer.'

Emory drew us through the castle into his main office. As always, Summer sat at her desk, guarding the entry to his space like the dragon she really should have been. She looked up as we walked in and gave us a watery smile. Her eyes were puffy and her nose was red; she'd been crying her eyes out. 'I'm so sorry, Summer.' I started forward. She stood up from her desk and let me pull her into my arms.

She nodded, and then she started to cry again in earnest. Emory joined us and rubbed her back as she wept. He never shied away from displays of emotion, treating them with the respect that they deserved. As her tears slowed, he handed her some tissues. 'Sorry,' she muttered hopelessly.

'Don't be,' Emory said firmly. 'We've lost a lot of good men and women today.'

'Mike would be so proud to have served you, Prima. To have saved your life,' Summer said to me.

I nodded and my own eyes filled. 'I know,' I managed. 'I would be dead without him. Every moment I have from here on is because he gave it to me. I will never stop being grateful to him.'

Summer nodded and dabbed at her eyes. She gave me a brave smile. 'I managed to dig out your spare wedding dress.'

'You don't think it's disrespectful, do you? Getting married today?' I asked, panicking suddenly. I didn't want to upset anyone else today.

'Not at all! I think we need something to celebrate, something to lighten the darkness. Mike would have danced his ass off.'

'He had some terrible dance moves,' said a voice from behind us. I knew before I turned around that it was Robbie Carter. He even *sounded* like Mike.

'Robbie,' I greeted him. 'I'm so sorry.'

He stepped forward and knelt before me. 'It is my honour to serve you. I call thee dragon-kin, and I will protect all that is thee and thine with all that I am. So mote it be.'

'So mote it be,' I responded, because I had learnt that was always the thing to say after someone else moted you. I reached forward, took his hand and pulled him up. 'Thank you. I am honoured by your service as I was honoured and blessed by Mike's.'

'It is me that is honoured. How may I serve you, Prima?'

'I'm so sorry about Mike. You should be with your family now. You don't need to stay on duty.'

He shook his head. 'I'd rather keep busy, if I may,' he admitted, his voice tight. 'Please, command me.'

We all deal with grief in different ways, so I nodded. 'Can you find the younglings, Evan and Harriet? If they would talk with me, I'd like to see them. If they would prefer to be left in peace to grieve, then that is okay too.'

Robbie saluted briskly, turned on his heel and marched out.

'I need to keep busy too,' Summer said. 'I sorted out the chairs and the gazebo. The flowers were a bit of a disaster, but some of the brethren are collecting wild flowers for you. What else can I do?'

'Can you speak to Mrs Jones? We'll need food for anyone that attends,' Emory suggested. 'I would also like it to be known that attendance at our wedding is not required. Anyone is welcome, but no-one's attendance is requested. If they would rather grieve...'

'No,' Summer said firmly. 'Most of us want an affirmation, a celebration of life. After all we've been through with the Anti-Crea during the last few months, this is something we *need*. They're not going to stop us living our lives, and we'll honour our dead by doing just that.'

Chapter 37

After our discussion with Summer, Emory and I went into his office where Indy was waiting impatiently. I looked around in surprise. 'Who's a good girl? I can't see anything broken!' I gave her a full body rub. 'Who's a clever girl? Well done, Indy.'

Gato gave me a superior look, like he didn't need the praise because he was a good boy *all* the time. I grinned at him. 'You're a good boy, too. The best boy.'

There was a timid knock at the door and Emory opened it. It was Evan and Harriet. Robbie gave us a nod but stayed out of the room, guarding the door.

The children had been crying. 'I'm so sorry,' I offered brokenly. Randall had been a foul man but he was their father. Their red-rimmed eyes told the tale of their grief without them saying a word.

'Not sad tears,' Evan admitted. 'Relieved ones. I always feared that someone would make me go back to them – him and Jonathan.'

'Daddy Dearest wasn't the nicest man,' Harriet agreed. 'You might have noticed that.'

'Yes, but that doesn't mean you can't feel sad for your loss,' I argued.

'He wasn't even my real father,' Evan said with a shrug.

'He raised you like his own for a number of years, though. You're allowed to mourn that loss,' I said firmly.

'Yeah, he raised me like his own until I manifested as a dragon – then he beat me half to death and killed our mum for cheating on him. I mourned the loss of the father image I had in my head long ago. That man didn't really exist.'

I winced. 'I'm sorry. That's awful.'

'That was Dad in a nutshell – awful.' Harriet shrugged. 'What will happen to me?' she asked in a small voice. 'Where will I go?'

'If you want to, you can stay here with Danny and Sophie, like Evan.'

'Will I be your ward too?' she asked Emory.

'If you'd like to be,' he offered.

She nodded. 'Yes, otherwise Evan will lord it over me.'

'I will not!' Evan protested. 'I'm just glad you're alive and finally safe, with me.'

'Yeah. Me too.' Harriet looked at Emory and me. 'So you're really getting married today?'

'Yeah, we really are,' I said.

'Nice. We'll leave you to get ready then, because right now you look like shit.'

'Harriet!' Evan's voice was scandalised, but then he grinned at me. 'She's rude, but not wrong. A shower would help.'

'I'll shower,' I said drily.

'Hey, can we play with Indy and Gato? We can keep them out of your hair,' Evan offered.

I turned to the two dogs. Indy wagged enthusiastically and Gato gave a couple of swishes of his tail. 'Go play,' I murmured, giving them both pats. 'Be good.' I turned to Evan, 'Make sure you give them something to eat before you play with them.'

The kids scooted off, leaving Emory and I alone. I stepped closer to him. 'So apparently I stink.'

Emory laughed. 'I expect we're both a bit ripe. I don't care. Do you?'

'No, not really.' We hugged, stinky smell and all.

'I should get ready,' I said. 'What time shall we get married? We could do something symbolic like doing it at the stroke of midnight or something.' We checked the time: it was 8.30pm.

Emory yawned. 'I'm not going to make it to midnight. It's been a long-ass day.'

'Hey! You better get some energy. It's supposed to be a long-ass night too!' I winked.

He grinned. 'I'll grab an energy drink.'

'Whatever you need … old man.'

'I'm going to get you for that later.' His eyes glinted.

'Promises, promises.' I gave him a lingering kiss. 'We'd better split up. It's bad luck to see the bride on her wedding day.'

'If we're being technical, it's probably bad luck to marry after a bloodbath,' Emory responded drily.

'Pfft. As long as the tank didn't break a mirror, we're good. Last time, Lucy broke a mirror.'

'Ah. That'll be why you got kidnapped then,' he said sarcastically.

'Exactly. So no breaking mirrors and we'll be fine.'

'How long do you need to get ready?'

An hour at least to shower, dry my hair and do my face. 'An hour and a half?' I suggested, giving myself some time to panic about my eye makeup.

'Okay. We'll aim for a 10pm wedding. Good?'

'Good,' I confirmed.

I needed to get my skates on!

Chapter 38

I stepped out of the shower and nearly screeched when I walked out into a bedroom full of people. 'Fucking hell!'

'Hi, Jinx,' Amber said, amused.

Summer waved. 'We popped a bottle of champagne. You want a glass?'

What good was dragon hearing if it was drowned out by a shower? I nodded – yes; I absolutely wanted a glass of fizz. Hes, Audrey, Amber and Summer were lounging in my room, hair and makeup already done, looking beautiful and wedding-ready.

'How come you've all got ready so quickly?' I complained.

'Not all of us were swanning about in a helicopter for an hour!' Amber bitched. 'This perfection takes time.'

I grinned. She looked perfect in a soft-blue dress that was stunning with her pale skin and auburn hair. I tried to suppress a shard of disappointment that Lucy wasn't with us. She had her own thing to do, her own emergency to handle, but damn – I wished she was here to see me get married.

Summer handed me a glass of champagne and I let the bubbles fizz on my tongue. I was getting married. To Emory. And this time, nothing was going to stop me.

There was a knock on the door. Summer opened it. 'It's Elizabeth and Veronica,' she called. 'Can they come in?'

I nodded. 'The more the merrier.' Veronica had always been on Team Jinx and I had warmed to Elizabeth after the whole 'getting kidnapped together' thing. A spot of torture is good for bonding, though it's not a method I'd recommend; clothes shopping and bingo seem safer bets.

Hes put on some music — the Dixie Cups' 'Chapel of Love'. As it blared out, I had a sudden flashback to my almost-wedding and I prayed with all my might that this one would end on a happier note. Then I pulled on my underwear, slipped on a dressing gown, hung the wet towel in the bathroom and moseyed back into my bedroom to do my makeup.

'Sit down,' Amber ordered, pointing to a chair. 'You're terrible at makeup.' *True.* Ouch. 'Summer, you sort her hair. I'll do her face.'

'I'm on it.' Summer picked up a hairbrush with a gleam in her eye.

Elizabeth and Veronica were both wearing ball gowns. They looked overdressed to me, but it was a timely reminder that dragon weddings and matings were a big deal.

I expected my nerves to start fluttering but they remained still. I was just so damned excited to finally marry Emory. And there was the hope, a tiny one, that our fractured bond would somehow be restored by our formal vows.

Summer dried my hair, while Amber put some sort of pore-smoothing gunk on my face. I let them fuss over me without complaint. We needed these moments together.

Audrey and Elizabeth were reminiscing about Audrey and Cuthbert's wedding, laughing over the drunken antics of a brethren member, long dead but remembered fondly. It was nice to hear their laughter. Summer put my hair into heated rollers and I sat there with a toasty warm head as Amber studiously worked on me. As she carefully applied my makeup, I couldn't help but admire her. By her own admission she was over forty, but she didn't look a day over twenty-eight. Not only did she radiate youthful energy but she also had a cool aplomb that I could only dream of acquiring.

When she'd finished, she rooted in her trusty black tote and pulled out a jar of shimmering purple gloop. 'When witches get married, their family draw protective runes onto their skin. Will you allow me to paint some for you?'

Tears welled and I blinked rapidly to stop them falling. 'Thank you. Yes, I'd be honoured, Amber.'

She nodded briskly, extended my arm then painted runes onto my hand. The purple liquid shimmered as she swept it on. Hes discreetly took a few photographs, and I beamed at her.

Summer unrolled my hair and eyed me clinically. 'I was going to do an updo, but it looks perfect down. What do you think?' she asked the room at large.

'Down,' Audrey agreed.

'Down,' Elizabeth voted.

'Who am I to argue?' I smiled. 'Down it is. Can you hairspray it to death? My hair is unruly.'

'I will,' Summer promised, and spritzed me liberally.

Amber continued painting, biting her lip in concentration. The delicate runes were beautiful and they reminded me of Indian wedding henna tattoos. 'There,' she said finally, smiling in satisfaction. 'Now you're blessed by the goddess, by the earth and the sun. So mote it be.'

'So mote it be,' everyone in the room chorused.

'Give them a minute to dry, then they'll stay visible for the next twenty-four hours.'

'Will they rub off after that?'

'No, they'll still be there but they'll have soaked into your skin. They're with you for life.'

I was touched. 'Thank you, Amber.'

She checked the time. 'We've got to go in fifteen minutes. Let's get you into your dress and do the finishing touches.'

'I'm not done yet?'

'Not quite. I have one final gift for you,' Amber said.

Summer pulled a dress bag down from the curtain rail and I unzipped it. It was the same dress I had worn to my first – interrupted – wedding day. 'It's the same!' I squealed in delight.

'Emory had two identical dresses made at the same time. That man loves a contingency plan.' Summer rolled her eyes.

'It's not paranoia if they really *are* out to get you,' I interjected.

'No one is going to get you today,' Elizabeth said firmly. 'I'll roast anyone who approaches you into shish-kebab.'

'You say the nicest things,' I laughed. Summer held my gorgeous wedding dress and I slid into it, then she zipped me up while Hes started patiently hooking the buttons.

There was a knock on the door. This time it was Robbie carrying a cardboard box with a large bouquet, a smaller bouquet and a wreath of flowers resting inside it. 'Perfect,'

Summer called. 'Thanks, Robbie.' She placed the wreath on my head and secured it with loops of hair and bobby pins.

Audrey clapped her hands. 'Beautiful. Just perfect.' As she touched up my lips, Hes passed me brand-new Converse trainers. I slipped them on with a grin.

I peered into the box of flowers. The bouquets were made up of wild blossoms that the brethren had picked for me from the surrounding area. The thought of those beautiful people going to such an effort was enough for a rock to take up residence in my throat. I picked up the smaller bridesmaid's bouquet – and gave a start as I saw Sally the Salamander resting in it.

'Don't eat the flowers!' I ordered her quickly. She gave me a flat look and swallowed the last bit of flower in her mouth. Laughing helplessly, I plucked her a flower from my much larger, bouquet. No one would notice. 'There you go, you can have that one, too.' I stroked her little back as she ate and she made happy chittering noises. She felt a little cold so I conjured a small flame into the palm of my hand and held it out for her to hop onto if she wanted.

Sally gave a happy noise, jumped into my hand and settled into the flames. She purred. When she turned and looked at me, her eyes flashed silver. She ran up my arm and settled against my neck under my curtain of hair.

'She bonded to you,' Elizabeth said joyously.

I resisted the urge to do a face palm. I really did collect bonds like metal to magnets. Elizabeth's triumph was so complete that I turned to her. 'Another part of the Revival Prophecy?' I asked in a resigned tone.

She grinned. 'Yes!'

I bit my lip. 'We've lost the Eye of Ebrel – Khalt has it in the daemon realm. Does that mean dragon kind is doomed?'

Elizabeth shook her head. 'I don't believe so, because it isn't referenced again in the prophecy. I believe its role has been fulfilled.'

I nodded. 'Good.' Doom and destruction had been averted. Then I put aside all thoughts of the prophecy; this wedding was for Emory and me and no one else. The Revival Prophecy could wait its turn.

I picked up the smaller bouquet of flowers. 'Amber,' I said awkwardly, holding it out. 'Would you?'

She nodded briskly. 'Of course, I'd love to.' She took the flowers. Despite her brusque tone, her eyes were glittering with unshed tears.

I looked in the mirror and I smiled at my reflection. I looked like me, me on a good day.

It was going to be a good day.

Chapter 39

Déjà vu. I was making my way to my wedding – take two. Once again, a harpist was playing Pachelbel's Canon, but this time I didn't have Lucy or Manners by my side and I quietly regretted that. Instead I had Gato trotting alongside me and Amber acting as my bridesmaid. Everyone else had gone ahead to take their seats.

Amber and I stood in the hallway before we walked out. 'As promised,' she murmured. 'One last gift.' She pulled out a metal amulet but she didn't pass it to me; instead she looped it around Gato's head. 'Lucy and I worked together on this. It wasn't ready last time, but I finished it earlier today. It's kismet.' She smiled at me. 'Touch the amulet and you'll be able to speak to your father.'

Tears welled, hot and sudden. 'My god, really?'

'Really. I'm not sure how long the magic will last for, so use it sparingly. The more you use it, the quicker it will run out. This is only the prototype. I'll keep on refining it.'

'It's amazing. Thank you.' I hugged her as hard as I could before releasing her and stepping up to Gato. 'Dad?' I reached out and touched the amulet around Gato's neck.

'Hello, Jessica.' His voice was warm and exactly like I remembered it.

'Dad!'

'Your mother and I are so proud of you. We love you so much. I'm sorry she's not here to see you today, but I've no doubt that she's watching us both from some-where on high.' His voice broke a little and he cleared his throat. **'I'm honoured to walk you down the aisle, even if it is on four legs.'** He sounded amused. **'Come on, Jess, we mustn't keep Emory waiting. You've both waited long enough.'**

'We have,' I agreed. I kissed Gato on his giant head. 'Thank you,' I said to Amber. 'It is *everything* to hear his voice one more time.'

Amber kissed me softly on my cheek. 'You're welcome. Congratulations on your impending nuptials. They're go-ing to be perfect.' She smiled, and it was with the most warmth I'd ever seen from her. Then she opened the heavy doors and revealed the wedding party waiting for us out-side.

As we'd discussed, she swept down the aisle in front of me, chin raised at her imperious best – but now I knew the warm heart that she carefully concealed beneath her brusque attitude.

It really was a perfect wedding setting. Night had fallen and the fairy lights glittered. We were at the castle, the dragons' symbolic stronghold. Emory could have ordered the wedding to take place in the hall, as was originally planned, but he knew how much I wanted to be outside, so here we were in the courtyard. The strains of the soothing music washed over us. I smiled as I followed Amber down the aisle, with my dad at my side.

I spotted Jack Fairglass and Catriona, Hes and Nate. Even Lord Volderiss was in attendance. I spotted the herd master and Alfie. The courtyard was crammed with brethren that wanted to celebrate with their Prime and Prima. To one side, Bastion and Shirdal stood together, a sea of dark seraph around them.

This wedding was far bigger than our little affair at Ness Gardens, but no less special. I beamed at them all. They'd risked it all to battle for us and I could see bandages littering the members of our wedding party, but it didn't matter a jot.

And there was my Emory at the end of the aisle – and this time he was out and out grinning at me. I beamed back. Screw the ceremonial marching. I ran the last few steps to him and he caught me with a laugh and swung me around. He gave me a long kiss and the crowd tittered and whooped.

'Go Jess!' I heard a tinny voice call. Huh?

Emory caught my quizzical look and tugged me over to a small table a few feet away on which a laptop was resting. I had assumed it was for music, but then I'd seen the live harpist. The laptop wasn't playing a soundtrack, it was showing a video call.

Lucy gave a happy scream as I came closer. 'You look amazing! I love those flowers in your hair!'

Tears welled in my eyes for what felt like the sixty-billionth time that day. 'You're here!'

'Of course I am. Did you think that I'd miss it?' She was dressed in a pink silky number and she even had a fuchsia headpiece. Greg was sitting next to her in a three-piece suit.

'Thank you both so much for coming,' I said.

'Thank goodness for video calls! We didn't have time to drive all the way to you, and Emory was selfishly using all of his helicopters – so here we are. Virtually attending.'

'Thank you so much for virtually attending,' I gushed. 'And thank you for Gato's amulet.'

'Oh! Amber got it to work? Amazing! We've been working on it for weeks. Now I'm going to shush and cry a lot because Reynard is super-nervous and he's been rehearsing over and over again. Let's put him out of his misery.'

I blew her a kiss and went back to the top of the aisle where Emory was waiting for me with a visibly sweating Reynard, who was dressed in suit trousers and shiny leather shoes. His chest was out, muscled and proud, and his black wings stretched behind him. I flashed my biggest smile. 'Thanks for doing this.'

'It is my honour,' he murmured. In a much louder voice he called, 'Dearly beloved, we are gathered here today to celebrate the ... union of Jessica Sharp and Emory Elite.' As Reynard spoke, I noted he stumbled occasionally where he studiously omitted his swears.

'Reynard,' I whispered to him during a moment when he paused. 'Just fucking swear, okay?'

Emory laughed aloud. 'Yeah, Reynard. Just fucking do it.'

'Thank fuck for that,' Reynard breathed, making us both laugh. 'It's killing me.'

When we got to the part where he asked for objections. Reynard paused dramatically 'If any person here present knows of any lawful motherfucking impediment to this marriage, they should declare it now.'

Emory and I turned to our assembled guests and waited. Suddenly, there was a commotion at the back of the gathering; Elvira, in a Connection inspector's uniform, was trying to approach. Robbie had headed her off and placed a hand on his gun. 'I'm not here to arrest her, you idiot,' she hissed into the silence. 'I'm here to watch my friend get married.'

'You're in uniform,' Robbie growled.

'I didn't have time to change. I barely made it as it is.' She grimaced. 'I'm sorry. I should have changed clothes but it's been a helluva day and I didn't want to miss some goddamn happiness.'

'It's fine,' I called loudly. 'Please let Elvira in, Robbie.'

'Yeah, Robbie.' She tossed her long ponytail out of the way and marched down the aisle. Giggling, Hes reached out and pulled her into one of the front rows. Hes moved onto Nate's lap, freeing a place up for her to sit down. Elvira cleared her throat. 'Do go on.'

'Thanks,' Reynard said flatly, making us all laugh. 'Well that's it; the time for objections has passed. It is time to get this sodding show on the road. It's vows time! You guys want to do your own thing, right?'

'Right,' I confirmed. 'And then the traditional Celtic vows.'

'Rings!' Reynard called.

Gato trotted over with a black velvet pouch in his mouth. 'Thank you,' Emory murmured. He pulled out the two wedding bands and passed the little velvet bag to

Tom for safe keeping, then he handed me his wedding band.

Emory smiled at me. 'Jessica Sharp. Some know you as Jinx, but you are far from a jinx to me. You are a blessing, the light of my life, and my one true love. My mate. You make me smile and laugh more than I ever thought possible, and you love and accept every facet of me. I am honoured to have you stand by me, now and for always. I call upon these persons here present to witness that I, Emory Elite, do take thee, Jessica Sharp, to be my lawful wedded wife. I promise to care for you, to give you my love and friendship, and to respect and cherish you through the rest of our lives together.'

I waited for the cheers and whoops to die out before I started my vows. 'Emory Elite. Some know you as Prime Elite, but you are more than a title to me. You are the other half of me, the yin to my yang. You are always supportive; you have an overwhelming belief in me and my abilities. With you by my side, I know I will always be the best version of myself. I am so grateful that you are my mate and I will stand by you, now and for always. I call upon these persons here present to witness that I, Jessica Sharp, do take thee, Emory Elite, to be my lawfully wedded husband. I promise to care for you, to give you my love and friendship, and to respect and cherish you throughout the rest of our lives together.'

Then we spoke the Celtic vows together, chanting in unison: 'You cannot possess me, for I belong to myself, but while we both wish it, I give you that which is mine to give. You cannot command me, for I am a free person, but I shall serve you in those ways you require. The honeycomb will taste sweeter coming from my hand. I pledge to you that yours will be the name I cry aloud in the night, and the eyes into which I smile in the morning. I pledge to you the first bite from my meat, and the first drink from my cup. I pledge to you my living and dying, equally in your care, and tell no strangers our grievances. This is my wedding vow to you. This is a marriage of equals.'

We fell silent and Reynard gave a loud sniff. 'Fucking beautiful. Now face each other and repeat after me. With this ring, I thee wed.'

Emory smiled. 'With this ring, I thee wed.' He slipped the ring onto my finger, and then passed me his hand so I could do the same.

'With this ring, I thee wed,' I said clearly.

'You may kiss the bride!' Reynard pronounced.

Emory smiled at me and the moment was ours. God, but I loved this man so much. He leaned forward achingly slowly before he finally kissed me. It was no chaste kiss. He slipped me the tongue, making me giggle as we snogged shamelessly in front of the guests. No PDAs my ass.

Our gathered crowd exploded once more into cheers and whoops, and music started playing. The moment was perfect, but it was made even more so by the sudden, overwhelming love that rushed through me. The love wasn't my own but Emory's. Our bond was back. I grinned triumphantly and felt his lips curl up against mine in answer. We were Mr and Mrs Elite.

Watch out Other Realm, here we come.

What's Next

Well, what did you think of *Revival of the Court?* I hope you enjoyed it. I felt incredibly emotional writing this one. My mum made it to my wedding day, but died entirely too soon afterwards. A lot of the wedding stuff was based around my own day. I even watched The Notebook with my bestie the night before! So if it was *too much wedding* for you, please forgive me, it was so nice to indulge in those memories. If you want me to write more Jinx and Emory, then please review and let me know. This could be the end of their path, or just the beginning. I listen to my readers, so please do get in touch!

If you haven't read Lucy's trilogy yet then dive in with *Protection of the Pack.* Charles De Lint reviewed The Other Wolf trilogy in his "Books to Look For" section of Fantasy and Science Fiction Magazine. He said that he "didn't warm to Lucy immediately" but he went on to say that "one of the things I ended up liking most about the series was her character growth. It's much better when they grow and change because of their experiences, and let me tell you, Lucy gets a lot of intense experiences over the course of this series." So if you're looking for a character that has a wonderful growth arc, do give Lucy a try. She'll surprise you.

If you've already read my entire backlist, DO NOT PANIC! I've got you covered. Next on my writing roster is a trilogy for the one and only Amber DeLea. *Hex of the Witch,* book one of The Other Witch series is coming out 30th September 2023. You can pre-order it here. Amber and Bastion are going to have to work together and they are NOT happy about it.

I am also writing a prequel story for Amber, that will be available for FREE to my newsletter subscribers in due course. In the meantime, if you would like two other free books, then subscribe to my newsletter here.

Reviews

As always, I appreciate reviews SO much. I really do read them all. One of them recently said they hate the use of the word "whilst" in my writing as it seems old fashioned.

I have used "while" this time, just for you dear reviewer. So please do review, I promise I listen to them. The really nice ones make me beam for hours.

Please review on Amazon, Bookbub, and/or Goodreads! I'd also appreciate a mention on genre appropriate Facebook groups if you can.

Reviews and positive buzz from readers makes a huge amount of difference to us little Indie Authors and I really can't thank you enough for taking the time to review for me, wherever you can.

Patreon

If you'd like to support me *even more* then you can join me on Patreon! I have a wide array of memberships, ranging from £1 per month – £300 per month. No one has taken me up on the biggest tier yet but a girl can dream!

I give my patrons advance access to a bunch of stuff including advance chapters, cover reveals, art and behind the scenes glimpses into what goes on into making my books a reality. I would love it if you could join me there!

About the Author

About Heather

Heather is an urban fantasy writer and mum. She was born and raised near Windsor, which gave her the misguided impression that she was close to royalty in some way. She is not, though she once got a letter from Queen Elizabeth II's lady-in-waiting.

Heather went to university in Liverpool, where she took up skydiving and met her future husband. When she's not running around after her children, she's plotting her next book and daydreaming about vampires, dragons and kick-ass heroines.

Heather is a book lover who grew up reading Brian Jacques and Anne McCaffrey. She loves to travel and once spent a month in Thailand. She vows to return.

Want to learn more about Heather? Subscribe to her newsletter for behind-the-scenes scoops, free bonus material and a cheeky peek into her world. Her subscribers will always get the heads up about the best deals on her books.

Subscribe to her Newsletter at her website www.heatherg harris.com/subscribe. As a welcome gift, you also get two free novellas for subscribing!

Too impatient to wait for Heather's next book? Join her (very small!) army of supportive patrons at Patreon.

Contact Info: www.heathergharris.com

Email: HeatherGHarrisAuthor@gmail.com

Social Media

Heather can also be found on a host of social medias including Facebook, Goodreads, Bookbub, Instagram and Tiktok.

Reviews

Reviews are the lifeblood of an indie author. Every single one means so much to me. Please take a moment to review my work if you can! Heather is not too proud to beg!

Glossary - The Jinx Files

Jinx's Other Log – An aide memoire

Amber - A feisty red-headed witch. Business-like, money minded, she lost her partner Jake who was coaxed to death by Bastion (see below). She's one of the contenders to become the next Coven leader.

Bastion – paramount griffin assassin. Laconic and deadly. He can coax (make someone take a course of action that they're already considering). He thinks of me like an niece, and although he kills people, I still think he's a good man under his kill count. Has a daughter, Charlize.

Chris – Emory's brethren pilot. Always on standby with a helicopter.

Emory – yum yum dragon shifter king. King of a bunch of creatures. So far I've ascertained that he's the Elite of the following creatures: centaurs, dryads, gnomes, mer, gargoyles, griffins, satyr.

Elvira – Inspector Elvira Garcia. She used to be kind of betrothed to Stone, and she loved him. She's prickly but I think she's warming to me. I think she's an honest person, underneath the prickles.

Elizabeth Manners – Greg Manners' mum, member of Emory's dragon circle.

Fabian – member of Emory's dragon circle. Saw him once at Ronan's ball raising money for making more Boost. Query his motives for being there.

Gato – my Great Dane turned out to be a fricking hell hound. He can grow huge with massive spikes and he can play with time like it's his favourite ball. He can send me between the realms for a magical re-charge. He also houses my father's soul. He used to have Mum too but she died closing the daemon portal.

Glimmer – A sentient magical blade, created by Leo Harfen, the elf. It can take magic from someone Other, and be used to make someone Common become magical. Or, make someone magical have an even bigger skillset.

The transference of power always changes the magical gift somehow, in unknown ways.

Greg Manners - brethren soldier. I used to turn his hair pink to get a rise out of him but lately the only one getting a rise out of him is Lucy. He's her second in command and all round enforcer of all things Lucy, so nowadays I don't pink his hair.

Hes – my once-Common assistant. I rescued her from Mrs H's clutches, but Glimmer made her magical, she's a vampyr that doesn't need blood.

Lucy – my bestie! I turned her into a werewolf using Glimmer. Now she's accidentally a werewolf alpha, with her kick-ass wolf Esme.

Nate – Nathaniel Volderiss is the son and heir of Lord Volderiss. He also has a master/slave bond with me. We can sense each other and he has to obey me. I need to be so careful in how I phrase things so I don't accidentally force him into an action he doesn't want. He used to date Hes but when she betrayed his trust he dumped her to the kerb.

Reynard – He was once a squat, grey-skinned little gargoyle but the Other Realm waved a wand and now he's something else. Something new. The Other realm doesn't like new. Watch this space.

Roscoe – Head fire elemental, used to run Rosie's Hall where I got introduced to the Other Realm. Partner to **Maxwell Alessandro** (see Lucy's files).

Shirdal – head honcho of the griffins. He appears to have a drinking problem but everything is deceptive when it comes to this man. Always dressed in rumpled, mismatched clothing I once saw him kill thirty men without breaking a sweat, yet I trust him …

Stone – Inspector Zachary Stone, he died in a hellish fiery portal, closing the daemon portal to the daemon realm. He was raised Anti-Crea but despite his father's best efforts, he ended up being a good man.

Tom Smith – Emory's right hand man (brethren). He's loyal, taciturn and loves to hide in bushes.

Printed in Great Britain
by Amazon